Go Lightly

Go Lightly

a novel

Brydie
Lee-Kennedy

HARPER PERENNIAL

NEW YORK • LONDON • TORONTO • SYDNEY • NEW DELHI • AUCKLAND

HARPER ● PERENNIAL

Originally published in Great Britain in 2024 by Bloomsbury Publishing.

Mr Norris Changes Trains by Christopher Isherwood © Christopher Isherwood, used with kind permission of Penguin Random House UK.
"Sadie (The Cleaning Lady)," performed by John Farnham, written by Ray Gilmore, Johnny Madara, Dave White, extract on page 12.
"Crazy," performed by Gnarls Barkley, written by Brian Burton, Thomas Callaway, Gian Franco Reverberi, extract on page 124.
"White Wine in the Sun," performed and written by Tim Minchin, extract on page 330.

HarperCollins books may be purchased for educational, business, or sales promotional use. For information, please email the Special Markets Department at SPsales@harpercollins.com.

FIRST U.S. EDITION

Library of Congress Cataloging-in-Publication Data

Names: Lee-Kennedy, Brydie, author.
Title: Go lightly : a novel / Brydie Lee-Kennedy.
Description: First US edition. | New York, NY : HarperPerennial, [2024] |
 Originally published as Go Lightly in Great Britain in 2024 by
 Bloomsbury Publishing
Identifiers: LCCN 2023023713 | ISBN 9780063338029 (trade paperback) | ISBN
 9780063338036 (ebook)
Subjects: LCGFT: Romance fiction. | Queer fiction. | Novels.
Classification: LCC PR9619.4.L45 G6 2024 | DDC 823/.92--dc23/eng/20230523
LC record available at https://lccn.loc.gov/2023023713

ISBN 978-0-06-333802-9 (pbk.)

24 25 26 27 28 LBC 5 4 3 2 1

For Heather (and her tool box)

'The other day I made an epigram. I said, Anni's beauty is only sin-deep. I hope that is original? Is it? Please laugh.'

One

It started at dawn the way long days do when they run straight on from very long nights. Ada was on a streak of long nights and her days were relatively brief, starting in the afternoon and vanishing by lunch which was, in fact, dinner, but meals didn't matter because she was twenty-six. Regimented mealtimes are for toddlers and families and the very, very old and to try to force an 8 p.m. curfew on the appetite of a twenty-six-year-old is to misunderstand the beast.

So the days were short but this dawn was in August, in Edinburgh, where the nights are lit like afternoons. When Ada first moved to London, it was summer and she was amazed by the flexible, bright evenings, eating dinner outside during European hours. She didn't know then that the stretching light was to compensate for the months she'd be plunged into darkness. She called her parents in Sydney the following January and told them seriously that she was concerned the winter was permanent.

'We're eighteen days into this year and the sun hasn't come out yet,' and when they countered gently that that's simply how seasons work, spring will come, it'll come, she nodded like she believed them but actually she wasn't sure. She'd never lived through winter like this. Sydney winter was London

1

spring, composed of brisk baby days. Spring did come wetly in eventually but by then Ada knew not to trust it.

Next summer she spent desperately, suspiciously, outside, waiting for the drop.

And this was the summer after that.

It started at dawn and Ada was perched on the corner of a sofa at the party after the party after the closing night gig of the Edinburgh Fringe. Ada was at the end of a season of a particularly worthy play about London knife crime, written by a drama school student who grew up in the Cotswolds. It was a bad play, Ada knew, but the director came from money of some kind and was willing to blow that money on Equity rates. Ada hadn't auditioned but had been recommended by her friend Ben, who was already in the cast because he'd gone to the director's drama school and that was how Fringe theatre worked. Without those connections to fall back on, Ada relied on referrals. So she gave it her all in her three scenes playing the teacher everyone trusted, doling out advice to teenagers played by people her age. And then at night she did whatever she wanted.

She was talking to a friend of a friend – the kind of person who's always at the parties after the parties but never at the parties themselves – though she realised this friend of a friend hadn't been at any parties all month, not with her anyway, so maybe this was special. They were sharing a bottle of supermarket-branded bourbon, one of a selection Ada usually kept in her room but, as the month had dragged on and her pounds had drained out, moved into her handbag.

People found it charming, her carrying around a bottle of cheap bourbon, and she was aware that if she were a man or old or if she laughed a little less confidently or if she didn't sleep with so many people, then? It would be worrying, this bourbon-bottle-in-the-bag situation. But she didn't plan to stop laughing or fucking any time soon and age was a threat that was hard to take seriously at 5 a.m. It was particularly hard to take seriously as Sadie, the friend of a friend (of many friends actually, none of them close) shifted closer to her and nudged her so she toppled from the arm of the couch onto her lap.

'That's better,' Ada said and touched Sadie's face and Sadie shrugged and looked away. Sadie was wearing a plain white singlet and dark skinny jeans, an outfit that would barely contain Ada's body but sat neatly over Sadie's. Ada wanted to ask her about her name because Sadie was Australian and no Australians were called Sadie. There was this famous song from the seventies about a cleaning lady called Sadie and since then everyone avoided the name so she said, 'Sadie, what's with——?' but Sadie was already talking to the person on the other side of her.

The party had divided into a grown-ups and kids table vibe, with Ada's friends firmly at the kids table, which was covered in baggies and squashed-up cigarette papers with gum inside. Sadie was talking to Confirmed Adults, the actors who got reviewed by *The Times* and the comedians who were regulars on *Mock the Week* and didn't cheat on their wives. Ada knew that Sadie was a playwright – because every Australian at the Fringe was vaguely aware of every other – and the people in this circle wanted to talk to her so she was probably pretty good. But when Ada leaned in to join the conversation Sadie made space for her, slightly squeezing out the older woman with the RADA accent who had opinions on Sadie's career and no opinions at all on Ada's.

Sadie liked her enough, Ada decided, for this morning only and the morning would end soon. Chatting about a song would waste their time so she tapped Sadie's arm and, when that didn't work, pulled on her ear so she had her attention. Ada said, 'Can I take you home now?' and Sadie said, 'You don't want to stay longer?' and Ada said, 'It's morning' and Sadie said, 'OK. I'll get our coats.'

It was weird to hear an Australian say, 'I'll get our coats,' Ada thought but didn't say because she didn't want their only connection to be their foreignness. Watching TV as a child lying backwards on her parents' couch under a spinning fan and the mom on screen is saying, 'Get your coat, we're leaving!' or the nanny whispers, 'Children, get your coats,' or the man leans in to the woman and says, 'Should I get our coats?' No one ever told Ada to get her coat in her whole sunny childhood because she simply didn't own one and the ritual collection of coats as a means of exit was a northern hemisphere fantasy. Now Ada had three coats, none of them good.

Sadie was getting one of those bad coats when Bernie touched Ada's arm. Bernie was probably thirty-five in human years but had an eternal carnie spirit, always at a festival, the host of the party though this wasn't his flat. He had also hosted the mixed bill show that Ada had performed on that night, where she sang a passable version of 'Nothing' from *A Chorus Line* for drink tickets, a holdover from her musical theatre phase. Bernie liked her in the neutral sort of way men in their thirties liked her, because she was rude to them and conciliatory (and discreet) to any age-appropriate wives or girlfriends who would show up along the way.

'You're not leaving!' Bernie said and then without pause, 'Something for the road?' and he opened the bathroom door and Ada followed him in. She said, 'You should be leaving too, old man,' and he laughed – thirty-five-year-old men loved to be called old though it had less of a hit rate when they were forty-five – and he said, 'Ah, you're probably right. But tomorrow we go back to real life!' as he racked up four thick lines. Ada bent over the unsteady board he was holding – did he take this from the kitchen or did whoever owned the flat keep chopping boards in the loo? – and inhaled once, twice, then paused to watch Bernie take one of his own.

Sadie knocked on the door and asked if she was ready to go. Ada offered Sadie the final line – 'Hey!' said Bernie and Ada laughed and said 'No more for you, pops' – and Sadie leaned over and inhaled. After she stood up, she took Ada's hand and the board hit the floor and they sprinted through the flat, opening the heavy door with three locks, and down the stone stairwell into the grey entranceway with bikes and fliers with bike tracks on them all over the floor.

They made their way out onto the doorstep and Ada turned to Sadie and pinned her lightly, watching her face in the pink and grey. They shivered and Ada was briefly annoyed because yes it's dawn but shouldn't it be warmer than this? Then she kissed Sadie and tasted coke in her mouth. She pulled away and said, 'I had to make sure we had chemistry before you came home with me, wouldn't that be embarrassing?' and Sadie smiled and closed her eyes and said, 'Yeah we'd never have recovered.' Ada wanted her to open her eyes so she dragged her off the wall by the wrist. They passed crowds of university students, spending their holidays doing experimental dance pieces for audiences of eight and fucking for the first time and that was Ada recently but she felt contempt anyway.

Why would you be twenty-one when you could be twenty-six? Why would you be thirty-one? Ada's contempt was usually gentle, sometimes closer to pity, but not now in the early hours as she pulled a woman steadily closer to her room. She had never wanted to be any age other than this one and she was going to be this age for as long as she was allowed.

They entered the building with Ada's flat in it and it looked exactly the same as the building they'd just left. Every building in Edinburgh looked exactly the same to Ada, except the castle and the various Fringe venues that looked like they were also castles but were in fact part of the university. Ada had spent all night in a science building recently, watching immersive theatre about ancient Greece and being distracted by the Bunsen burners in storage cupboards behind her head. The actors were probably pretty good but then Ada thought everything was good at 1 a.m. and better at 2 and the guy playing Helios was hot which was probably the point. She wondered if he was in on the joke.

All four of Ada's flatmates were asleep. She whispered to Sadie that she was living with some actors from her show who were 'too serious about their craft to party' and Sadie said, 'Orson Welles would be horrified,' and Ada said, 'Very current reference.' Sadie said, 'Sorry, I've been staying with my producer who is literally fifty,' and Ada put her finger to her lips. They crept through the creaking living room with leather chairs that were somehow too hot to sit in even here and they went into her room.

This room, like all the rooms in the flat, usually housed a university student, and when Ada had arrived at the start of the month it was empty but for a bed and a desk and a melted stub of a candle stuck to the mantlepiece. Students fled Edinburgh in August to go back to their families and the friends from home whose news they were mostly indifferent to, and Ada felt contempt for that too. August was the only time she wanted to be in Edinburgh, when people like her climbed into the nooks left behind by the students, smeared make-up on their sheets and covered their old musty buildings with posters. She was aware that this wasn't how she was supposed to feel – it was disrespectful to the locals and to history, probably, to care so little about the city that was home for one twelfth of her year – but she found the place frictionless without the Fringe. She'd been a plus-one to a wedding in Edinburgh in February and it was so quiet and cold and no one in the streets smiled at her when she passed them and she wondered what the point was. There was a beach just outside town that no one even used and that was all she needed to know about that.

Ada and Sadie undressed by the window, each removing their own clothes, Ada staring hard at Sadie and Sadie with her eyes closed, again, closed to Ada, smiling. Ada didn't like that at all and she said, 'Open your eyes, my god,' and Sadie did, looking surprised, then kissed Ada with her teeth a little bared and pushed her over to the bed. Sadie came and kneeled over her. Ada knew that Sadie thought she had to take over now – hard-edged women like Sadie expected certain things of girls like Ada and those things were 'very little' – and Ada loved to surprise them. Because Ada was exactly herself when she was naked with someone. Some people are more themselves, some people retreat but Ada was exactly the same and it unsettled her partners.

Ada pulled Sadie down and climbed on top of her and Sadie raised an eyebrow then closed her eyes again and said 'All right, Ada,' and just saying her name almost made up for the closed eyes. Ada bent to her neck and grazed it with her teeth while running her nails down the space between Sadie's breasts. Sadie's skin was dark and Ada wondered briefly why her nipples hadn't been visible through her white top. She felt Sadie ease towards her and smiled then sat up. And saw blood. Blood smeared on Sadie's cheek and neck and on the blue and brown striped sheets that had come with the flat – 'I'm like a boy of fourteen again,' she'd said to her flatmate Ben the first time she put those sheets on and he said, 'What do you mean?' and she hadn't bothered explaining. She touched her nose and when she pulled her hand away, blood, right from the source.

She sat back on Sadie and said, 'Sadie, I need to tell you something,' because she was still lying there with her eyes closed and that would normally have upset Ada but it was pretty funny under the circumstances. Sadie smiled and said, 'Tell me anything,' and Ada started to laugh, right from her belly, which made her rock forward on Sadie in a way that they both liked until Sadie finally, *finally* looked at her and saw her covered in blood, her long dark hair dragging in it, and Sadie drew her legs in and backed up the bed. Ada kept laughing but gestured to her nose and said, 'It's this, it's just this,' and Sadie gradually understood and she laughed too, though she looked uneasy, possibly revolted, and Ada thought, *Good.*

Ada stood up eventually, grabbed her make-up wipes from the desk and threw them at Sadie. 'Clean yourself up girl, you're a mess.'

Sadie laughed again, a little more assuredly this time as Ada tipped her head back to stop the bleeding. It stuck in her throat, mingling with the leftover chemical taste and she felt powerful. Once it stopped running, she opened a water bottle over her head and it drained off her onto the floorboards and she was vaguely aware that she needed to move out of this room in twelve hours but instead of drying the floor, she dabbed herself with a towel, turning it streaky and pink. She turned back to Sadie, who was watching her, and who said in a flat voice, 'The black-widow look is good on you,' so Ada dropped the towel and crawled towards her, climbed up the bed and wrapped her many legs around this woman who could take or leave her an hour ago. She licked her fingers and Sadie shuddered but she just used them to scrub the blood from Sadie's left ear.

'This is our Paris, you know,' she said conversationally as Sadie tightened her grip on her hips.

'What does that mean?'

'You know, the line, "We'll always have Paris"? Well we'll always have … this.'

Sadie shook her head and said, 'You're disgusting,' and later Ada sang 'Incy Wincy Spider' as she moved down Sadie's body and it should have been embarrassing but it wasn't at all.

And then they lay apart, Sadie on her side facing Ada who stared at the high, sculpted ceiling, the bare bulb hanging from a wire that would swing threateningly if this were a horror movie but was now obedient and still. Ada wondered if that made this a romance instead of a horror movie or maybe it was a horror movie and she was the murderer. After all, she'd covered them both in blood. But it was a peculiar sort of feminism that meant that a woman who looked like her would never be the killer. She wasn't an icy Gillian Flynn blonde or a dark-eyed femme fatale. Women who kill weren't round-cheeked and hard around the calves but soft at the biceps. They didn't freckle as easily as they smiled.

Ada thought of her face as one that no one could hold in their head for long. Sometimes she caught herself in a bus window and saw herself drained of expression and she was anonymous. She knew that guardedness and reserve are attractive qualities in a woman, she was attracted to them herself, but other women's physical features contained more value on their own than hers. Ada let every thought she had play across her face and that was both her instinct and also by design. If she couldn't draw people to her using an air of mystery she'd do it by being so open they thought she must be lying.

Ada rolled towards Sadie who turned quickly onto her back so they weren't facing each other. This annoyed Ada and so she said, 'That's annoying, why are you always turning away from me?' and Sadie said, 'Sorry, sorry, I'm just really high,' and she did sound sorry but she didn't sound that high. Ada lay her palm flat on Sadie's ribs and felt a whole world moving underneath and said, 'You don't seem high. You're so calm. You seem exactly the same as you did at the party,' and she knew there was doubt coating her words and she hoped that Sadie would turn to her and deny it, say everything had changed, she'd never been so dragged out by a woman, she couldn't look at her because she was afraid of what she'd feel! But instead, Sadie sighed and closed her eyes and said, 'Sorry I'm not manic enough or whatever.' Ada felt like she was being separated from her friends in class for talking too much.

Ada said, 'You did, like, one line though,' and even as she said it she wanted to leave it alone. Sadie laughed and started rubbing her feet together and said, 'I don't do coke much, you know how expensive it is back home.' Ada reached out and rubbed her hand over the side of Sadie's fuzzy, growing-out undercut and said, 'Well yeah, but that's the thing about coke, you don't buy it, it's just always around. Hey, did you hear that Bernie's girlfriend is pregnant? He asked me if I think he'll be a good dad.'

Sadie shifted her head slightly, enough for Ada to know to withdraw, and said, 'Men don't offer me coke, Ada. So unless they offer it to a woman who offers it to me...'

Ada laughed. 'Wow, I never knew femmeness was so key to drug muling, do gender studies professors know about this?' But Sadie was quiet so she couldn't tell if she found it funny. Ada felt tired of performing for her but that didn't mean she was ready to stop. She considered telling her that, actually, she did think Bernie might be a good dad, that she'd told him he should call the baby Ada and he'd smiled affectionately and kissed her head. But she didn't think Sadie liked Bernie much.

Sadie got up to use the bathroom, getting fully dressed to do so, making Ada anxious she wouldn't come back. But she did and as she undressed again – grateful, Ada felt so grateful – she looked at the little bowl on Ada's desk.

'Blackberries?' she asked and Ada sat up in bed.

'They call them brambles here and you can forage them, like just take them from the bushes. I got these near Arthur's Seat, the big … rock thing.'

Sadie said, 'Yes, I'm aware of the big rock thing, I've done the dawn climb a few times,' and Ada said, 'You went UP it? OK, Tank Girl. Well, I brought them back to ripen so I could make a crumble but I guess I'm out of time.' Sadie picked up a little handful and brought them to bed, held out her palm and Ada ate some, directly off it, and her throat tingled as they slipped down. Sadie dropped the rest into her own mouth, swallowed and said, 'Yeah, they're not ripe at all.' And she lay down and closed her eyes.

They were silent again, for longer this time, long enough for the light through the window to warm up and one of Ada's flatmates to turn on the shower in the next room. Sadie slept and Ada drifted but she didn't want to lose time so she kept pressing her palms over her eyes to see the fireworks, or that might have been a dream. Another flatmate turned the coffee maker on and the noise was enough to pull Sadie a little way back to her so Ada took her chance and climbed up onto her knees. She leaned over and put her face as close as she could to Sadie's until Sadie said, 'What?' and Ada said, 'If you're way older than you look, you have to tell me.'

Sadie opened her eyes and she was dead on with Ada but blurred at the edges.

'Why,' asked Sadie, 'would I be older than I look?'

Ada started to sing, into Sadie's face, louder than she needed, 'Oh scrub your floors, do your chores, dear old Sadie,' and Sadie pushed her away. Ada was off balance and fell onto her back, the mattress creaking beneath her and Sadie sat up and shook it off.

'I should never hook up with other Australians.'

Ada laughed and said, 'So either your parents are massive Johnny Farnham fans or you were born before that song came out so you're like sixty. Nice tits for an old cleaning lady, I have to say.'

Sadie glanced over at Ada and said flatly, 'There's still blood on your throat,' and Ada started to sing again.

'Sadie, the cleaning lady, will clean the blood off me … uh … Sadie,' and Sadie climbed on top of her and clamped her hand over her mouth. She was still looking slightly over Ada's head, smiling at whatever phantom floated there and without lowering her eyes to Ada's she said, 'I think I'm sobered up now.'

Ada lay perfectly still because she knew if she moved it would be obvious how desperate she was for this morning to continue. Once Sadie was out in the world she'd be gone, this would be gone; this room wouldn't be hers by 4 p.m. and nothing that had happened here made her believe that there'd be another room for them. Their Paris. Had she said that out loud?

Sadie slowly removed her hand from Ada's mouth and said, 'I think I know what your problem is,' and Ada said, 'Is it that I know the words to a John Farnham song? Sorry for being a patriot, Sadie—' and Sadie finally lowered her eyes and said, 'No, your problem is that I was too jittery last night to fuck you. So I think I'll do that now,' and Ada was nervous, which was new, or old, a memory of what she used to feel like before sex and she started to sing again but she couldn't get the words out because Sadie opened her up and their morning held on.

Two

30/08/2017

Stuart Parkes 10:23

Hey, sorry I know it's weird to message someone I don't know on Facebook but I saw you at the gig last night and your song really blew me away! I've been going to stand-up and cabaret shows every night all month and it was all really samey but you were so good and you said you don't even usually sing. That might have been a lie now I think about it. Anyway I hope you had a good festival, I'll definitely come see you perform again if I can. I wish I'd seen the play you did.

Stuart Parkes 12:03

I just realised I sound like a weird fan creep in my message. I was in Edinburgh doing a play with some uni mates, not just watching shows. I hope that makes it better! It shouldn't though, our play was shit.

Stuart Parkes   **12:21**

OK if I were you I would ignore the previous messages because they literally don't say anything or ask you anything ha fuck. OK you can ignore this one too but I'm really hungover and I'm leaving the city tomorrow and you probably are too so this might be my last chance to do this. Are you going back to Australia? That's your accent, right? I was pretty drunk during your set so if you're a Kiwi don't be mad. I live in Liverpool but if you heard me speak you'd know that. Fuuuuck ok so I know this is fucking weird but I would really like to buy you a drink or sit next to you while we drink drinks we've bought ourselves? I swear I don't just go to shows and then stalk hot singers (actors?) afterwards. Are you a comedian? Your act was kind of cabaret I guess. See I don't know so you know I haven't been googling you or whatever. I looked you up on Facebook and we have 8 mutual friends weirdly so ask them if I'm a psycho before replying. I mean don't ask Lee lol but any of the others. So would you like to go for a drink?

Stuart Parkes   **12:23**

I haven't done anything to Lee he's just a prick, you can ask him if you want, I was joking

Stuart Parkes   **12:31**

I don't know if this helps but I really liked your set but I'm mainly asking you out because I think you're hot? In case you're worried I only want you for your mind haha ah this is getting worse for me isn't it.

Stuart Parkes 12:44

I'M NOT AN ACTOR. Sorry I just realised I said I was in a play and you might think I'm an actor. I wouldn't respond to an actor either, disgusting people, can't be trusted. Unless you are an actor? Oh shit. I was just in a play so I could hang out with my uni mates for the summer, we all graduated this year so sort of a last fling thing. Some of them actually are actors so I guess we can't be friends any more now they're doing it in the big world haaaaaaa. I'm unemployed actually, is that hot. I was a student and then I did this play all summer and I guess today is my first day of being unemployed, don't get too turned on. I want to draw things for money but I accidentally did an English degree. I also smoke, that's another thing.

Stuart Parkes 14:50

Lol this was stupid and I'm very embarrassed now. You can't dump me, I'm dumping you!!! Sorry for being a fucking idiot, I really do think you're talented. I also promise I don't usually send so many messages in a row. It's been a long month. But let's pretend this never happened and you can keep being cool and I can cut myself off from the internet forever.

Stuart Parkes 15:36

OK, last one genuinely. When you were performing last night I thought of this song, I guess because it's Australian like you (I checked with Lee, he's suspicious now) and it's just really restless and pretty. I can't explain it better than that but I woke up with it in my head and then I sent you all this bullshit. I don't do this, I promise, I'm fucking mortified. Anyway the song is called 'Even Though I'm a Woman'. I did my gap year in Australia, I heard it then I guess. PLEASE IGNORE ALL THESE MESSAGES but it's a banger.

Ada Highfield   **16:50**

I love that song.

Stuart Parkes   **16:51**

Wait who are you?

Stuart Parkes   **16:52**

So drink?

Ada Highfield   **16:55**

I'm on the train back to London mate. These all went into my 'other' folder with the other freaks' messages. I just saw them now.

Stuart Parkes   **16:56**

Fuck.

Ada Highfield   **17:01**

What are you complaining about, at least I'm reading your messages now. Have a nice last night in the Burgh as no one calls it. I'll be on here tomorrow and we can talk more. Or if you want to waste your last night with your friends in a beautiful city, we can keep chatting now.

Stuart Parkes 17:02

I love wasting time, did you not see that I spent the summer doing THEATRE

Ada Highfield 17:18

OK freak, waste my time

Three

Ada leaned back in her train seat and put her phone face down on the plastic fold-down table in front of her. She looked out the window and tapped her fingers against it, trying to keep rhythm with the fat raindrops hitting the glass. It would start soon, she knew, the bad grey bit of the year, and she needed to find a way to enjoy this time. She stopped tapping and pulled out a bag of Percy Pigs, grabbed three and crammed them into her mouth. She chewed briefly then took them all back out again and turned the pink mess over in her hands, rolling it into a gummy ball then popping it back in. Her appetite was reckless but not careless, these ticks of teenage diets past creeping in when she was tired. The morning was already dripping away, sliding off the windows and under the train.

Mel sat back down in the seat next to Ada and reached over, shoved her hand into the Percy Pigs bag Ada was still holding and pulled out a fistful. She dumped them on her lap, picked one up and nibbled at its ear.

'The toilet was bad. Do not use the toilet. Why does Branson think I want someone talking to me while I'm pissing?'

Ada smiled. 'Maybe he's got a piss fetish?' and Mel said, 'That makes sense, he's very rich.' Ada leaned against Mel's shoulder and felt grateful that everything seemed the same.

Mel and Ada had been living together in London for over two years but had been living separately up in Edinburgh, and Ada realised now that she'd been afraid it would take them time to get their rhythm back. Intimacy was important to Ada and she'd never managed to maintain it over distance. She worried that without her immediate presence, all her short-comings became more obvious, her flakiness and irritability looming in a person's memory without the counterbalance of her body. She didn't photograph well, needed to be seen in motion, and she wondered if she was an experience more than a girl. She was aware that a lot of her value was in how she made other people feel about themselves, and when she wasn't working with that skill she flickered out.

Ada glanced sideways and saw herself reflected in the window, blank, and forced her face to listen. She thought about a habit she'd had when she was small. She would climb onto the sink in her family bathroom and kneel on the porcelain with her face as close to the mirror as she could get. Knees wet and a little bit soapy. And she would think about a feeling she'd had or even one she'd just heard about and she'd make the face for that feeling. She'd keep going over and over until the face in the mirror matched the one in her head and then, next time she spoke to her family or a friend, she'd try it out.

Her mother would say, 'This week has been a thousand days long and it's only Tuesday,' and Ada would think 'sympathy' and her features would shift and her mum would look at her and smile. 'You're a sensitive little bug, aren't you?' Or Harvey at school would yank her ponytail towards his table and she'd feel angry but her brain would say 'superior' and she'd turn towards him and say, 'Can I help you?' and next time Harvey spoke to her it was while running down the hall with the book that she'd intentionally dropped, to see if he'd pick it up.

When Ada was sixteen she was reading the weekend paper, her feet up on her dad's lap, ignoring her sister slamming a distant door. The front-page profile was about female psychopaths, how they presented differently from men because women are socialised to please. And one of them, this CEO of a pharmaceutical company, she said, 'From a young age I knew I didn't feel things like other people. But I knew no one would like me if I was too weird. So I became very good at pretending. I used to look in the mirror and make my face look like other people's faces so no one would suspect me.' Ada hadn't thought about her mirror thing for years and it hit her suddenly that this wasn't something other kids did. Unless those kids were psychos apparently.

For weeks, Ada carried round the fear that she was going to turn out to be a murderer. She checked her reactions constantly — like was it OK to be so angry when her sister ruined another dinner by storming out over some bullshit fight with their mum? Why were her crushes more like obsessions and why did they rarely last longer than a week? And then she was watching the news and they were talking about the war — they were often talking about the war when she was sixteen, though not as much as they had when she was thirteen — and a reporter was interviewing an activist and the activist was saying that journalists always reported the deaths of allied soldiers: 'But it's not just soldiers who are dying. The US army and their allies are killing innocent Iraqis every day. The numbers are staggering but even if they weren't, one child dead is one child too many.' And Ada felt her chest pull in on itself and she started to cry because it was true, of course. One child dead is one child too many. But a psychopath wouldn't know that. And so she let that theory of herself go.

Ada tried to tell a boyfriend about her psychopath phase

once. She was twenty and she loved him and they'd been together for two years so had talked about most of their stuff and one day she said, 'You know I went through this phase where I thought I was a psychopath, like, clinically,' and he laughed and said, 'You? Come on. If anything you have too many emotions, not no emotions. You have an exhausting number of emotions.' And Ada dropped it and made a note to start telling him less internal shit. Eventually they broke up and if she'd been charting the decline of their relationship objectively, that psychopath conversation would've been an inflection point. But she barely remembered it after much worse stuff got said. Later she would accuse him of psychopathy, the very thing she'd feared in herself, and he had said, 'It's not psycho to want you to shut the fuck up sometimes,' and it was the hottest she'd found him in months. When he finally left her she wept at his feet and now five years later she couldn't tell you a single identifying thing about his face.

Ada's current theory of herself was that she had done the mirror thing as a child not because she didn't have the same feelings as other people but because she did, and she needed that to be obvious. She felt things so sharply they'd cut her open if she didn't let them out, and her face, her round soft canvas, was the release. As she got older, she realised that people's motivations generally ran counter to hers – they wanted to be known less, not more – but by then she'd also realised the power that came with her openness. Everyone felt they were intimate with her and they felt it so quickly. She would never be alone if she kept everyone's secrets but her own. She would also never become the CEO of a pharmaceutical company and that was probably for the best.

'How's Gabby?' Ada had hoped that when Mel came back from the bathroom she'd want more details of her morning with Sadie. Ada had told the story like a comedy, pitching the line about Paris as though it was something hilarious that her too high brain had vomited up. But as she'd told it, she felt her story lacked something. She wasn't getting across just how good it had felt to draw Sadie to her, how goofy she'd felt singing to her when what she wanted to do was fall in love.

She knew she wouldn't see Sadie again even though Sadie had mentioned spending a few months in London. Ada had sent her a message earlier thanking her for the orgasms, which was only polite in her opinion, and Sadie had just written back with a laughing face emoji. Because she was a joke to her. Not in a cruel way, people like jokes. But there wasn't any magic in them. So Ada wanted to tell Mel how she'd allowed herself to collapse on this person because it would never amount to anything and how the longing for Sadie, the idea of her if not the reality, was going to feel so good, sustain her so much over the grim months ahead, but she hadn't had a chance before Mel went to pee and now she was asking about her sister.

Ada yawned. 'No idea, I haven't checked in on her personal pregnancy diary this week.'

Mel leaned over and said, 'Go on then, fire it up, let's see how the Madonna is faring.'

Ada opened Instagram and saw Gabby's most recent post straight away. Mel's obsession with her sister had fooled the algorithm into thinking *Ada* was obsessed with her sister so now Gabby was inescapable. She clicked over to her profile and opened the Stories section and chucked the phone to Mel. 'Go nuts, stalker.' She leaned back in her chair and closed her eyes as Mel chatted.

'She's at this giant supermarket … OK this is actually pretty funny! She's looking for big pads … That's weird she isn't getting her period while she's – Oh wait, OK they're big pads for after the baby comes. Why do you need pads after the baby ... never mind, I don't want to know. OK so she's looking for the pads and they keep them in the PICNIC aisle! I guess because they're all freaky Christians in the south and they don't want to talk about vagina blood? Anyway—' and at the same time Ada and Mel said, 'hashtag Florida Baby,' and Ada opened her eyes.

'You know, you could just follow her yourself and then I could occasionally, oh I don't know, use my own phone.' She looked over at Mel who was now scrolling down Gabby's feed, checking all the recent bump photos.

'I don't use Instagram,' she said, without looking up, and Ada was warmed by Mel's lack of self-awareness.

Mel loved everything she pretended to disdain whereas Ada just loved everything, and she knew Mel appreciated the cover that provided her. A month after Ada moved in with Mel she'd been watching Bring It On on her laptop and Mel had asked her what the hell it was and had gradually sat down to watch with her and mocked every second. But then at the end she said it was pretty interesting how the Clovers won. 'Kind of progressive for the time, right?' She still joked about the 'terrible' TV shows she'd started watching since Ada moved in, and their artsy friends smiled at Ada indulgently like she was a very stupid puppy who was teaching Mel how to love. The artsy friends had of course all seen Bring It On years ago and that was the difference between them and Mel. Some people would be put off by Mel's snobbery but Ada knew that Mel grew up with three older brothers and her elegant parents and no one else close. Her highbrow taste wasn't her fault.

Mel handed her phone back to her and said, 'This one's actually pretty cute,' and Ada looked at the post that was open.

It was two pictures of Gabby in a bikini (in her kitchen? Why was she wearing a bikini in her kitchen? Why was Gothy Gabby wearing a bikini at all?), the first featuring Gabby's partner, Hank, kissing her naked belly and the second featuring him pointing at the big lipstick mark he'd left behind around her belly button, the same colour smeared across his face. She stared hard at Hank, trying, as she always did, to figure out if he was hot. She settled, as she always did, on him looking American. It was the teeth of it all, probably. And the clear eyes of a one-beer-with-the-football guy. Enough of this. A message from Stuart flashed up on the screen and she opened it then closed it without replying.

Mel leaned over to try to see the phone and said, 'Wait, what was that? Who's messaging you? Are you hooking up with someone?'

Ada pulled the thread up and handed it to Mel to scroll. 'No, just some guy who found me on Facebook. I think he's like … a fan.'

Mel scanned the messages then gave back the phone. 'He seems kind of crazy, why did you respond?' and Ada said, 'You went to the toilet! I was bored!' and that was all the answer Mel needed as Ada put the phone away.

She wasn't playing the 'who'll message next' game with him, though she was sure he'd think she was, that everyone did at the start of something. She didn't though, didn't believe in making people wait for her if she wanted them, nor of holding on to them when she was ready to move on. She prided herself on emphatic come-ons and respectful break-ups because what she wanted more than anything was reciprocal honesty. Mel told her all the time that people didn't obfuscate on purpose. They just didn't know how they felt as clearly as she did. But Ada could never quite believe that.

Feelings announced themselves in her experience and it was a choice not to hear them. But while it frustrated her, she also knew that if everyone started feeling things fully and openly she would no longer seem special. She sometimes thought she'd do better in LA than London but everyone there seemed sort of like her but thinner and that would be an exhausting tide to rise above.

One day she was walking past Mel's room and Mel was playing an old record because Mel had a record player because of course she did. And a song that she'd never heard before pushed through the door and she started to cry, immediately, and she threw the door open and startled Mel, who said, 'What's wrong?'

And Ada gestured hopelessly at the record and finally squeaked out, 'Song ... is so sad,' and she fell into Mel's arms.

Mel said, 'I'm sorry, I didn't know Pink Floyd was a thing for you,' and Ada said, 'Is that who this is?' and Mel held her out and stared at her. She couldn't believe that a song Ada had never heard before would tear at her like this. Surely it reminded her of a long-lost love or maybe a troubling childhood memory? A scene from a favourite film? But it was just a sad song. It made Ada sad. Since then Mel would call Ada her crazy diamond and Ada would shrug and say, 'It's a really good song!' and they'd drink their wine and laugh. It was one of their bits and they both loved it.

Ada was falling asleep now. She eased off her sneakers and tucked her feet under her, leaning her head on the gently vibrating window. She was nearly gone when she decided to be kind. She pulled her phone back out, responding to Stuart, 'I'm passing out, not ignoring you I swear,' then closed her eyes and let go.

Four

02/09/2017

Stuart Parkes   21:18
I do plan to get a job

Stuart Parkes   21:19
For rent and cigarettes and other essentials

Stuart Parkes   21:20

But I can't work at the cinema because I worked there when I was a teenager and my old manager is still there and it's fucking depressing

Ada Highfield   21:24
How bourgeois of you

Stuart Parkes   21:25
Yeah I'm middle class don't tell anyone

Ada Highfield   21:27

I swear if one more british person tells me what 'class' they are when I have never ever asked them I will fully spit

Stuart Parkes   21:28

I'm annoying you aren't I

Ada Highfield   21:31

No tell me again about how your grandad owned a farm or something so now you can't work retail

Stuart Parkes   21:32

Is it fun pretending not to understand stuff that you definitely do understand

Ada Highfield   21:33

Yeah it's pretty fun

Ada Highfield   21:34

And I'm pretty drunk

Stuart Parkes   21:35

On a school night?

Ada Highfield   **21:37**

Bro it's Saturday. I think. Anyway you're not the only one without a job

Ada Highfield   **21:38**

But I'm unemployed in a chic mysterious kind of way

Stuart Parkes   **21:39**

Who are you drinking with?

Ada Highfield   **21:42**

Mel (flatmate), overground was down so she had to bus home and needed something very alcoholic at the end

Stuart Parkes   **21:43**

What are you drinking?

Ada Highfield   **21:45**

That's a very personal question

Stuart Parkes   **21:46**

OK then what are you wearing

Stuart Parkes   21:47

That was a joke

Stuart Parkes   21:50

I was joking I swear

Stuart Parkes   21:52

You have no body to me, I'm not interested in your clothes or anything else

Stuart Parkes   21:54

Man I'm a dickhead

Ada Highfield   21:59

That was fun

Stuart Parkes   22:00

??????

Ada Highfield   22:02

Watching you spiral

Stuart Parkes   22:03

Ah so actually you're the dickhead

Ada Highfield 22:05

I can be nice too

Stuart Parkes 22:06

I don't believe it

Ada Highfield 22:08

Ask me again what I'm wearing

Stuart Parkes 22:09

Why?

Ada Highfield 22:16

Because I might tell you this time

Five

Days passed back in London as Ada and Mel found their rhythm together again. Ada woke up to Mel's alarm through her wall and made her tea in her underwear. She left it outside Mel's door and went back to bed, knowing Mel didn't like to talk in the morning. She would hear Mel shower, dress, leave for work, and then sometimes she'd fall back asleep and sometimes she wouldn't. Around midday, she would go walking, down to the canals, listening to podcasts about everything that was wrong with America except when she couldn't bear that and then she listened to Australian indie bands from when she was fifteen. She walked and drank coffee in parks and sometimes took her book to a pub in the afternoon and tried not to think about money. More accurately, money didn't occur to her in these moments because while her credit card worked, she didn't need any.

Every so often over the last year Mel had tried to have The Money Talk with Ada, explaining that credit cards are only a good idea if you know how to pay them off which seemed backwards to Ada. Surely people who can pay them off don't need them in the first place? And of course, if she got desperate she could pay them off, because she knew her parents wouldn't let her suffer. She never asked them, though, in case she was wrong, and anyway, Gabby had always been enough for them to handle.

But she listened politely to Mel's advice while pouring them both triples of gin and then she'd explain that she had a plan. 'I'm going to marry rich!' and Mel would laugh and roll her eyes and Ada would say, 'I'm not joking. And if I get really desperate, I'll just live with you in your increasingly fancy flats,' and then they'd lie back on Mel's bed and talk about the best book they were assigned at school and who got their period first in their grade and whether New Year's Eve was fun still.

They hadn't had one of their money chats since they'd got home from Edinburgh and Ada figured that was at least partly because she'd been cooking them dinner every night. She loved cooking but when she was doing a play or had more money to go out she tended to live off 2 a.m. falafel and heavy dark wine. But she wasn't performing at the moment, apart from the cabaret open mic that she hosted for £40 and a burger every Tuesday night. She was a chatty but not particularly experienced host and she had only been given the gig because quiet Steven, who played the piano there every week and was, as far as Ada could tell, entirely asexual, hated to talk so he asked his loudest friend to split the job with him.

Steven hadn't done the Fringe this year, so at Ada's first week back at the show, he fell upon her gratefully when she arrived and said, 'You can never leave the city again,' and she said, 'I couldn't afford to anyway.' Ada had arrived at the pub at seven for sound check and her weekly veggie burger. The bar itself was full, as it always was, of Camden goths and men in suits who had mistakenly picked this place for a Tinder date and were now having to yell over the music. The theatre upstairs was a sanctuary that didn't fit with the atmosphere of the bar at all but the patrons of each cheerfully tolerated each other and they had enough different kinds of beer on tap to accommodate them all.

Steven went upstairs to plug things in – Ada refused to find out what and Steven indulged her ignorance, indulged her everything – so Ada climbed onto a bar stool and waited for the manager, Clem, to notice her. Clem was an expansively tattooed lesbian in her forties who made it clear the first time she met Ada that she no longer found girls like her cute. After they had agreed to this premise, Ada was free to flirt wildly with her, enjoying the stonewalling she got in response. Clem rode a motorbike, a real, actual, leather-and-screams motorbike, and Ada said to her, 'Before I met you, I thought Dykes on Bikes was just a Mardi Gras float.' And Clem had gruffly said, 'You're on thin ice, girl,' and Ada had said, 'I hear that a lot.'

Tonight, Clem leaned over and ruffled Ada's hair in her usual aggressive show of platonic disdain and asked how the month had gone. Ada overplayed the victories and under-played the lack of reviews and Clem said, 'And you're broke now, right? You all come back broke from that thing.' Ada conceded that yes, she was broke, and Clem asked whether she'd be interested in picking up some shifts at the bar. Ada looked at the vinyl-clad clientele and said, 'I'm not sure I fit the vibe,' and Clem said fair enough. Then Ada sighed dramat-ically and said, 'Can I come back to you if I get desperate?' and Clem said, 'Wow, I'm flattered, sure, I'll be waiting by the phone.' But later when Steven called Ada to the stage – 'Introducing Camden's own Sally Bowles, returned from the bitter north to the uh … bitter south, Ada Highfield!' – and there was applause and the lights hit her eyes, Ada knew she wouldn't take a job at the bar. Making money was something to do in private, not right downstairs from her job.

When Ada moved to London, she had hoped the plays would be plentiful but quickly learned that actors here often gigged to get by. Gigs didn't come to her the way they did to other performers and she knew it was because she wasn't the best of her type available. There were comedians with better punchlines and cabaret artists with deeper pain and maybe if she picked a genre she'd be more popular, more successful, but also maybe not. Ada figured that by refusing to be clearly categorised she seemed artistic and romantic when really she just didn't know any other way of being. When people asked what she did she said she was a 'performer' but then under-cut the horror they felt by saying, 'but honestly I'm a better receptionist than anything else,' and they'd laugh and think her self-deprecating but unfortunately it was probably true. She hadn't called her temp agency to tell them she was back in London. Maybe she wouldn't have to this time.

Ada was doing a lazy set to open the show that night, aware that the crowd was full of regulars who were already as warm to her as a London crowd could be. There were people there who would sometimes smile at her in the street and she'd smile back, maybe wave, assuming she knew them and only the next night when they reappeared in an audience would she realise ah, no, she didn't, but they knew a kind of her. So she had done a few minutes of chatter up top about surviving the Fringe that Steven riffed underneath and then, spurred on by the Sally Bowles remark, she'd winkingly dedicated her next number to the people who got her through the month. And she launched into 'Mein Herr'.

Ada had sung this so many times since her first misguided attempt at a school talent show at fifteen that her mind drifted as her voice rolled up and down. She turned her head slightly and a light caught her eye, bringing her back into herself as she realised she was about to hit the German verse. This was terrible timing as she would have been fine rushing through it on autopilot but her rearrival in the moment tripped her up and she was sure she messed up a couple of lines. But there was no recognition of that from the crowd so she finished with a hard stamp of her foot and introduced the first act over applause, then headed to the side of the stage to watch and drift off again.

The worst part about temping was definitely how easy she found it. Ada would show up at a new office knowing nothing about their business and within hours she would be conversant in, say, how Brexit was going to affect their sales in the Irish market and she'd ask smart questions about it when taking the boss his tea. And then she would gossip with the other receptionists or, the holy grail, the office manager, so by the end of the week they'd declare her a very naughty girl and make sure she was invited to the pub at 5 p.m. By week two she would always have a crush on someone in the office, pickings often being slim but never invisible, and she would fill the empty minutes fantasising about them or, if they seemed amenable, openly flirting.

She had a 'good phone manner' and she had been told by her temp agency that Australians were very in demand for reception jobs. Apparently British people brought a lot of classist preconceptions to every call and would change their view of the person on the other end based on what the person's voice told them. As an Australian, she was a blank slate and what was unspoken was that it was Australians in particular who got away with this chameleon behaviour because the British assumed they were white. And in this case they were right.

Ada had a little section of her wardrobe devoted to fitted

black and grey dresses and one purple pencil skirt for when she was feeling comfortable and she wore them with shiny lip gloss and one swipe of mascara and she knew she had reached the balance of professionalism and sex appeal that meant she intimidated no one but was admired by some. She had never excelled at maths but she could take good notes, manage an Excel spreadsheet and sometimes after months of being around other actors, of trying and striving every day to entertain, she welcomed the relief of tidy lists and a well-kept calendar. She preferred it to bar work and it paid better and yet she was vaguely embarrassed when she told other actors that this was her lean-times job. Bar work was much more the done thing so she avoided talking about her quiet, cheerful days in temperature-controlled comfort.

Mel knew though, how at peace Ada often felt when the money was coming in and she was setting an alarm at 7:45 and choosing a Pret salad for lunch every day. One salad, one bread roll, one elderflower soda. Mel had suggested gently a couple of times that maybe Ada could look into production work, put those spreadsheet skills to creative use. But Ada knew the second her efficient office cosplay collided with her ambition then both sides would fail to please her. She didn't compartmentalise her lovers from her friends but she would never invite a temp colleague to drinks at the Soho Theatre bar and those lines were drawn very clearly in her mind. Mel never pushed it, like she never pushed the money stuff generally. She thought she wanted Ada stable and provided for but if that happened then who would Mel look after? So temping was off the table for now and Ada wondered exactly which bill she would struggle to pay this time that would lead her back there.

So, after the pub it was Tesco for ingredients and then she'd be cooking, playing *Reply All* through the Bluetooth speaker in the kitchen when Mel got home. It was Thursday and they'd been back for just over a week when Mel dropped her heels in the hall and jumped on the kitchen bench as usual. Mel's oldest brother owned the flat but they called it 'their' flat because he lived in Belgium now and had let them paint their bedrooms in the spring. Brendan had been the sole recipient of an inheritance from their grandfather for bullshit patriarchy reasons and he'd bought this generic east London new-build with the money when he was twenty-nine, then immediately taken a transfer to Brussels. Mel said she figured he felt guilty and that's why their rent was so low, though not, Ada observed, 'guilty enough to split the money in the first place.' Mel thought that over and said, 'Well, if he'd split it, none of us could have bought flats. At least now there's one,' and Ada said, 'You're either a really good person or a fucking idiot,' and Mel said, 'I'm both.'

Ada was frying some black beans for tacos and Mel performatively coughed at the spices filling the air. Ada turned and said, 'I'm sorry, my little English rose, I hope this cayenne pepper doesn't literally murder you,' and Mel said, 'I remember a time before you moved in when I thought my palate was normal.' Ada turned back to the stove and said, 'No, you're my sweet baby girl,' and then Mel said, 'OK, OK. So, give me the Stuart update.' Ada smiled because this was all she wanted to do but she said, 'Are you sure you don't want to talk about work?' and Mel said, 'I never do,' which was true actually and Ada found it pretty weird.

Mel worked in radio, making fancy documentary shows about suffragettes and wind power and the rental market in Berlin, and it seemed like a cool job. She'd taken leave in August to produce a Very Important Theatre Piece in

Edinburgh and it had done OK but privately Ada wondered why you'd bother with the non-legit shit when you could work in the arts in a real, salaried way. She always said she couldn't wait to sell out and Mel would tell her she didn't know what she was saying but she was pretty sure she'd choose slightly less creative freedom and slightly more ability to pay for her own dinner in Islington. But no one was offering her a job with sell-out kind of money, so it was easy to believe that.

Ada began her daily Stuart debrief. Between the tea every morning and the canal walks and the pub and Tesco and cooking there was Stuart. He had already messaged her when she woke up – he'd sent a link to the Wikipedia article for Girls Aloud and she wasn't sure why until she realised at some point the day before she'd complained that British reality shows didn't make any sense to her because she didn't know who the celebrity contestants were. While she'd wandered towards Victoria Park, she tried to convince him to let her call him Stu and he'd refused and she'd said he shouldn't have a nicknameable name if he didn't like nicknames. The afternoon passed with her suggesting new names for him before he finally agreed to let her use Stu so she deliberately typed 'Stew' in every message from then on until he threatened to log off. But he didn't.

He also didn't show her any of his art even though she asked at least five times a day. He told her to just imagine he was really talented and she said she never assumed men were talented and he said, 'Harsh but fair,' and then they discussed whether Nicholas Cage was the best or worst actor of all time. Stuart said worst and Ada said he needed to watch *Moonstruck* and he said he was making a list of all the things she told him to watch and read and she liked that.

She had told him that, in her experience, seeing a person do something they're really passionate about is either extremely hot or cringey in the extreme and he had said that hadn't made him more inclined to show her his art. So she googled him and eventually found a picture of teenage-him next to a sculpture of a bird. He had won a local Liverpool competition and when she sent him the link he told her she was a weird old perve looking up pictures of high schoolers and then she asked him what the bird symbolised and he said honestly it had just been a bird.

Ada told Mel about all of this and continued as she stirred. 'He seems kind of young but he's out of university and he did a gap year so he has to be like … twenty-two, right? Are twenty-two-year-olds fun when you're not twenty-two any more? Wait, were they fun when we *were* twenty-two?' Mel shrugged and opened the alcoholic ginger beer Ada had taken out for her. Ada knew Mel liked to drink that first before moving on to wine and when they headed to one of their rooms to watch TV there would be gin and neither of them would ever, ever suggest they shouldn't do that every night.

'I was dating ancient dudes when I was twenty-two so I dunno, let's call this an experiment. But he's pretty cute. I was going through all his Facebook photos again but there's only like two from this year because who is still uploading photos to Facebook regularly, you know? And his Instagram is private which is rude, honestly. But yeah, I was scrolling and once I hit his high school graduation I knew I'd gone too far so I liked it to freak him out and now he's calling me Mrs Robinson.'

Mel raised an eyebrow and said, 'You're like three years older than him,' and Ada said, 'Maybe four? I dunno. I refused

to tell him how old I am so now he thinks I'm like forty probably, which is pretty funny.'

Mel said, 'And he's still interested in this evasive forty-year-
old who creeps on his Facebook?'

'Yeah, I mean he's extremely Male Feminist. Dating an older
woman is praxis.'

Mel jumped off the bench, shaking the spice rack off the
wall behind her as every flimsy bit of new-build wood in the
kitchen rocked. Mel's body fascinated Ada. She had the kind
of build that would lead a man to rugby, average height but
broad all over, with tiny breasts and thighs like bronze. Once
at a crowded pub Ada felt herself get lifted off the ground
from behind and placed to one side and felt a rush of lust
towards the abstract sensation of strong, hard hands. A second
later she turned and saw it was Mel, who needed to pass her
to get to the loo and the moment snapped, but she wondered
sometimes what Mel could do with those hands if she wasn't
afraid of herself. She wore pencil skirts and kept her hair long
but when they'd painted their rooms she put on an old pair of
dark green coveralls and looked so correct that Ada privately
cursed Mel's austere, pale parents for their lack of imagination. Mel even built Ada's bed frame with its ornately carved
head but she didn't like to talk about it, though Ada did, to
everyone who she slept with in it. The next morning over tea
they'd watch her professional flatmate scrub a spot off her
dark blazer and apply a nude lip and wonder if Ada was lying.

'You kind of like this guy huh?' Mel was replacing the
spices one by one and when she ran a hand through her hair
a streak of something powdery appeared and Ada's heart filled
just a little bit more.

'I think so but let's be honest, I'm also totally bored. Like he's unemployed and I'm whatever you call unemployment when you're not being honest with yourself—'

'—the gigs will come, they always do—'

'—so we have a lot of time to talk. He's keeping me occupied and maybe I'm in love with him on Messenger but I might not be in person, you know?'

Mel was reading the back of a jar of paprika. 'This expired before we moved in.'

Six

Stuart Parkes   20:03

I told my brother about you

Ada Highfield   20:03

You told him that you have an imaginary friend who's a pervy old lady? Is he worried about you

Stuart Parkes   20:04

He was but I told him that you're hot and also that you seem to like me and now he's less worried about me. He's kind of worried about you but that's because he doesn't think any normal person would like me

Ada Highfield   20:05

This is probably the bit where I say I'm not normal but I am. I'm just like the other girls.

Stuart Parkes 20:05

Just like the other 40-year-old girls.

Stuart Parkes 20:06

Sorry that I said you seem like you like me. That was arrogant lol

Ada Highfield 20:08

I think I like you a lot actually. Maybe not as much as you like me but then you've seen me in real life. Maybe we could even that score somehow. I can get on a train to Liverpool and climb a tree outside your house and watch you through a window. Maybe I'm doing that now.

Stuart Parkes 20:08

I live on the ground floor at the back so if you're doing that then you're looking at my housemate Tom

Ada Highfield 20:09

Shit really? Is he single?

Stuart Parkes 20:10

It's nice to think of you looking at me. Really nice.

Stuart Parkes   **20:11**

Would you consider looking at me at the same time as I looked at you? A compromise? You could still get the train here just like knock on my door when you do.

Sadie Ali   **20:11**

Hey sorry if this is weird and you can totally say no if you want but I'm kind of in a bind. I've been staying with a friend in south London and I can't any more long story

Ada Highfield   **20:11**

Fuck are you OK?

Sadie Ali   **20:13**

Would it be weird if I came and stayed on your couch for a night until I find somewhere else

Stuart Parkes   **20:14**

Or I could come to you? I don't really like London but it's never had an Ada in it before

Ada Highfield   **20:14**

Oh my god of course, I'll just tell my flatmate. We have a fold-out you can use and a shitload of wine

Stuart Parkes   **20:21**

I'm guessing that's a no on the visit, sorry that was a weird thing to suggest. I'm broke anyway haha

Ada Highfield   **20:23**

You OK?

Stuart Parkes   **20:27**

Have you seen *Annie Hall*? My housemate's watching it and I fucking love that movie but like I feel like we're not supposed to watch it any more right? Should I say something? He might not know

Sadie Ali   **20:32**

Sorry, yes. I know this is sudden. Can you send me your address? I really appreciate this.

Ada Highfield   **20:33**

It's 8/53 Parlour Rd, E5 7UB. The postcode is the most important bit here

Sadie Ali   **20:36**

Awesome Google Maps says an hour 20 on tube and bus. Big city. Heading now

Ada Highfield   **20:37**

Yeah sorry I'm way east. My flatmate Mel and I are going to set up the living room for you now and there will be wine and chocolate waiting for you.

Sadie Ali   **20:37**

Legend thanks

Stuart Parkes   **20:37**

I'm going to say something

Seven

Sadie moved in gradually and all at once. That first night Ada and Mel made a show of setting up the living room. They laid clean sheets and towels next to the sofa, pushed their coffee table aside to make room for the fold-out. Mel asked Ada if Sadie would use it, weren't she and Ada kind of a thing? And Ada said, 'Nah it was just a one-off. She's going back to Australia in October, it's not like we could date.' And Mel said, 'Maybe she thinks you're going back too?' and Ada said no, she didn't think so, and anyway Sadie lived in Perth which was 'basically another country from Sydney. Like literally three time zones away.' Mel said, 'OK but do you want it to be something? Even like a short-term thing?' and Ada said, 'God I don't know, I bled on her, like this is weird territory.' And Mel said, 'She clearly didn't mind ... Hey, it'll be OK either way.'

When Sadie arrived dragging her bag behind her, the three of them sat together on the floor, awkwardly at first. But after a bottle of red and some free-poured bourbons – as always, Mel made a point of saying that bourbon is for children, Ada really needed to learn to like Scottish whisky, but then drank it anyway – it was easy. Sadie told them that she had gone to stay with a former lover who she'd thought might be a new lover again but the other girl, she didn't use her name, the other girl was in a long-distance relationship with someone in America now and only wanted Sadie as a friend.

'When we hooked up last year, we didn't even talk about a relationship. London to Perth ... it just didn't even come up. I thought it wasn't on the table but now she's doing it with someone else,' and Mel nodded sympathetically and said, 'I bet it's just because America is in the northern hemisphere, so it's closer and easier, you know?' and this made no sense to Ada who could tell Mel was drunk but Sadie smiled at her. 'That's probably it.'

After five nights in the spare room (a spare room? In Camberwell? Ada noted it and decided the other girl was probably rich and therefore easy to hate), the proximity became too awkward and Sadie messaged Ada.

'I'm sorry, I have other friends in London, it's just ... you'd said ... you know, you'd said we could hang out,' and Ada said, 'Oh don't be stupid, I mean I'm so glad you messaged, you know, we're friends!' and no one mentioned the fact that they'd only met that one time.

After an hour, Mel realised she'd seen the play Sadie wrote for the festival, the one with all the posters that had got funding from the Australian Arts Council, and she was overwhelmed. 'It was ... I mean, it shook me to my *core*. I can't relate to the immigrant experience of course, I'm so embarrassingly white, but I felt like that mother was my mother. I hope that's not insensitive, ugh. I'm not expressing myself right. I loved it. You got reviewed by the *Guardian*, didn't you?' and Ada interrupted, 'I didn't see it, sorry,' and Sadie said, 'That's OK,' and Mel started asking her about the process of touring with actors of such different ages. Ada watched Sadie rubbing the back of her neck and trying not to enjoy the attention and she wondered what it would be like to be wanted by Sadie and not to want her back. This girl in Camberwell was as unknowable to Ada as an ancestor.

Watching Mel and Sadie stirred uncommon anxiety in Ada. Mel was polite to everyone Ada brought home and usually even laughed at their jokes if she had the time. But this admiration was new and Ada wasn't sure she wanted Mel thinking so highly of someone who had shared her bed. Mel thought Ada was too good for her partners but maybe not this partner and Ada felt a dangerous urge to tap dance for the grown-ups' approval. As Mel said 'dramaturgy' to Sadie, Ada felt the situation ricochet out of her control but then Sadie turned towards her and said, 'Well, Ada's an actor, I'm sure she knows all about this.' Ada said, 'I'm untrained—' and Mel jumped in protectively to say, 'Only by rigid standards, she's actually so good,' and Sadie said, 'Training often undoes natural talent, I find,' and Ada felt all cuddled up.

When Mel mentioned a show they'd seen together at the Almeida a few months back, Sadie turned to Ada and asked what she thought of the direction and Ada remembered it was a cool director, one of the young hot ones, and so she almost deflected. But instead she said what she actually thought, which was that the actors seemed like they weren't having a good time, like they were being moved around the stage rather than acting. And Sadie laughed and said, 'Right? God he's so full of shit,' and Mel said, 'See, she's so smart about this stuff, I can never tell what's directing and what's just bad acting,' and the conversation moved on but Ada felt a part of it now.

After eleven, Mel took herself to bed, apologising for keeping normal-people hours and Sadie said, 'Staying up past eleven is rockstar hours in your thirties, don't worry,' and Ada knew a little more about her. After Mel had gone, taking their taco plates with her, Ada resettled her legs so that they were a fraction closer to Sadie and when Sadie looked down at them she felt her stomach burn. Silence, and then, 'Do you need help setting up the couch? Sorry we don't have a spare room, that's kind of a luxury in London,' and Sadie smiled and said, 'It's a luxury anywhere.' This embarrassed Ada, whose socialism was still emerging and mostly Twitter-based. Sadie stood up and looked at the sofa and Ada said to her back, 'It's pretty straightforward and comfy. Or ... you can also sleep in my bed ... with me, I mean. As friends or, I mean, in whatever way you wanted. But no pressure either way. Obviously!' The silence stretched and Ada pushed her shoulders back and wondered why she was pretending to be skittish. 'I would like you to, to be clear. But if you say no, I won't bring it up again.'

Sadie didn't turn around and Ada poured herself another glass of wine and drank it to stop her mouth from moving. Sadie said quietly, 'I would like to share your bed,' and Ada burned just a little bit more. Sadie finally turned back to her and leaned down to help her off the floor. She pulled her to standing and kept her hand on Ada's wrist. 'I'm sorry I didn't really respond to your messages after Edinburgh. I thought I was moving in with Bill and that she and I would start some-thing so I didn't want to give you the wrong idea and then when that didn't happen ... like I guess I still thought it might for a couple of days. And then I needed a couple more days to just feel like total shit and then—' Ada interrupted, '—and then you messaged me. That's OK, I love picking off women at their lowest. You're like a wounded gazelle,' and Sadie squeezed her wrist, hard, and said matter-of-factly, 'I actually feel OK right now.' And she led Ada to her own room and just like that they lived together.

The sun hitting Ada's face early let her know that she hadn't closed the curtains before they got into bed, and she glanced at Sadie then put her head under her pillow to drift away. She knew Sadie would be there when she woke up again. She had nowhere else to go.

When Mel's alarm woke her through the wall, Ada eased out of bed, leaving Sadie lying completely still, unbothered by the sound. Ada raced to the kitchen to plug in her phone – she'd moved all her chargers to the kitchen as a way of forcing herself out of bed in the morning, which she called a lifehack and Mel called a sign of a very sick person. As she boiled the kettle for Mel's tea, she watched her phone come to life and saw Stuart's name cascade down its screen. She hadn't forgotten him. When Mel and Sadie were talking about whether opera could be redeemed as an art form, she'd wanted desperately to take out her phone and ask him what he thought because asking what he thought had become a habit of hers. But she'd looked down and seen that it had died and she didn't want him enough to leave the circle.

Now she scrolled his messages, the last one sent at 1:43 a.m., saying he assumed she was asleep and hoped she was OK. They had said good night to each other every night for a week and Ada knew she didn't owe him this but she also knew if he had failed to do so she would have spent the night in Mel's room asking her what it could mean. She didn't think he had a Mel, though he lived with four other men. Ada had fed his fascination with her and then, without meaning to, withdrawn and she knew he wouldn't believe it was accidental.

The kettle boiled and she sent Stuart a quick message saying her phone had died and she'd had a friend over and she was sorry, so sorry, and he replied immediately saying of course it was fine, he wasn't upset about it, but she looked at the clock and saw that less than six hours had passed since his last message. She felt a thrill which she pushed aside to apologise again. She left her phone charging and carried Mel's tea up to her door then climbed back into bed where Sadie was naked, awake and checking her own phone.

'Anything from Bill?' Ada asked and Sadie said, 'Yeah,' and then put the phone down and smiled right at Ada, who took this as an invitation to cuddle but, it turned out, it wasn't.

Ada was unmoored, as a rule, a floating vessel who bumped up against others and then drifted steadily on and as she lay on the bed that no longer felt like hers she considered that Sadie might be the same. She felt a sudden urgent need to pin her down, physically, and question her for hours and she wondered if that meant that she was obsessed or just insecure. Sadie was allowed to not want her, she conceded, but was she allowed to not want her when she was sitting up on her pillows, rubbing her eyes? Ada said she was going to shower and Sadie nodded and then Ada left her there, comfortable in their space, the space that now contained them both.

Ada grabbed her phone from the kitchen and took it into their pale grey bathroom that never quite dried. She turned on the shower and then sat in the bath letting the water run over her feet, her arm hanging out of the tub as she read through Stuart's texts again. His most recent message was an attempt at normalcy as he asked her whether she'd finished her *New Girl* rewatch. His favourite character was Winston and he included a gif of him in the message and that was just a little too pathetic for Ada's tastes. She told him she still had a few episodes to go and asked what his plans were that day and he was job hunting again and it was the same really as the conversation they had yesterday morning except that the cracks in her life she'd been filling with him were shrinking.

Ada put her phone on the side of the bath and lay down, bending her knees slightly so her back could press full length against the base of the tub. She shifted her thighs so they covered the drain and let the shower run up her body and slowly fill the space around her until the water covered her ears and she could listen to the thundering. When it started to spill onto her mouth she sat up, letting everything rush away from her and down the drain. She considered shaving her legs but Sadie didn't, so. Her hair was wet and matted but not clean so she spun around in the tub and washed it, still seated, putting her head in and out of the stream of water and gasping when it hit her face at the wrong angle. When the water started to cool, she stood up and rinsed for a moment before climbing out and standing dripping on the floor.

Ada usually dried herself by laying flat out and naked on her towel on her bed but she sensed Sadie might consider that a waste of time which, of course, it was, which, of course, was why she did it. She had time to fill and she worried that her normal empty day would look like idleness to Sadie. Stuart liked her flexibility and her refusal to, as he put it, 'chain yourself to work culture which is so toxic' and he never asked how she could afford to do it. The answer really was that she couldn't, but only Mel knew that and Mel wasn't inclined to judge her for it. Ada was good at evading judgement by being exactly the version of herself most permissible to her company at any time. She was never someone else but there were enough hers to carry her through most interactions. But Sadie was living in her room now and it was hard to know what to be all day. What would be the least exhausting Ada for them both.

Sadie knocked on the bathroom door. 'Ada, will you be out soon? I have a lunch meeting in Soho,' and Ada felt desperately relieved that they wouldn't be forced to bump up against each other for the entire day because she had no idea if they'd have anything to say to each other over a sober afternoon. She opened the bathroom door and stood naked before Sadie, who smiled at her then leaned over and cupped her breast affectionately. Ada didn't know how to take this lightness in Sadie which seemed to appear only when she was nude, a state which usually made people nervous or overly appreciative or deliberately cold. She leaned in to kiss Sadie who lightly responded then stepped back and around her and turned on the taps.

'There's not like a tonne of hot water left, sorry,' she said and Sadie said, 'That's OK, it's in my best interests that you stay nice and soft,' but she didn't turn around so Ada wasn't sure if she was smiling while she said it. Ada lingered long enough for Sadie to start undressing then let herself out and headed to her room. To their room, really.

Sadie had hung her shirts up in the corner of one of Ada's three exposed clothes racks filled with vintage polyester dresses and her terrible coats. The sharpness of Sadie's crisp linen sent shame pinging through her. Only five shirts hanging and then three angular, folded pairs of pants still in her luggage. The bag stacked neatly in a corner with a pair of boots, a pair of Nikes and a pair of grey Birkenstocks lined up next to it. Ada's shoes were shoved under the bed so she covered herself in dust every time she collected a pair but she wore her ratty raspberry Converse most days because they paired or clashed perfectly with every dress she owned. Too many dresses, obviously, she could see that now.

Ada inspected the shirts more closely and realised Sadie had freed up the hangers for them by double-hanging five of Ada's dresses. Ada imagined Sadie lifting each gaudy piece off and replacing it with her own clean lines and she had to lie down. She glanced across the bed to Sadie's side – which meant Ada had a side too, she never usually had a side, she had a bed – and saw that Sadie was reading *Dune*. Ada's ex-boyfriend had made her watch that old movie and she'd hated it and when Sadie entered the room wrapped in her towel she told her that.

Sadie started getting dressed and said, 'You should try the book – it's basically exactly the same but you might find you get more from it than you did the movie,' and Ada said, 'OK, I guess we can both read it, I'll try not to lose your place!' and Sadie laughed and said, 'I meant you could read it after me but OK, let's call it a Bedroom Book Club,' and Ada was a little embarrassed but she didn't think Sadie would want her to be. Ada said, 'I'm actually trying to finish this book of acting theory which will take me like a year so I'll wait,' but Sadie didn't look at where she gestured.

Sadie was dressed and she scooped her yesterday clothes off the floor and looked around the room. Ada pointed to the boxy window seat that had clearly been created by a frantic architect urged by their boss to add some storage to the flats in their building. It was covered in her laundry and she said, 'Just put it there, I don't have a basket.' Sadie didn't say anything but did as she was told.

She looked around the room and said, 'Where … please tell me if the answer is nowhere but where would be best for me to work while I'm here?' Ada said probably the kitchen bench, that's what she and Mel used, and then she asked what Sadie was working on.

'Nothing original, just I had some interest from West End people. But it's … you know, it's a one-act so I'd need to extend it if I wanted it to tour.' Ada said, 'Well, let me know if you need fresh eyes on it or anything,' and Sadie said, 'God, yeah, only if that wouldn't be boring for you?' Ada thought it might be kind of boring but there was nothing boring about Sadie wanting her opinion so she said, 'No, I'd love to help.'

She picked up her bag and said, 'Speaking of, I'm meeting the programming guy at the Tristan Bates today,' and Ada said, 'Great theatre.'

'I'll be back—'

'—for dinner? I mean, I'm cooking for me and Mel tonight so—'

'—yeah I should be home, back here I mean, by six but you don't have to cook for me—'

'—I'm already doing it so yeah.'

And Sadie said, 'OK, thanks, that'd be nice' and there was a moment where she could have kissed Ada on the cheek before she left for the day but she didn't.

And then a week passed the same way except on the third day Sadie came home with a leopard-print laundry basket which wasn't quite Ada's style but felt like an effort nonetheless.

Eight

12/09/2017

Stuart Parkes   10:44

Yesssssssssss! It's a good day baby. Pop a bottle for me

Ada Highfield   10:44

Can the bottle be milk, I'm making coffee

Ada Highfield   10:45

Wait did you get the cafe job???

Stuart Parkes   10:47

Yeah! I'm psyched, one more day of job applications would
have drained my tiny soul of all remaining fluid

Stuart Parkes   10:48

And there are much better ways to be drained of fluid (plays a
sad trombone sound)

Ada Highfield   10:50

I'm so happy for you and also that's so gross! When do you start?

Stuart Parkes   **10:53**

I start on Monday and I get paid weekly so in like 2 weeks I'll be RICH apart from my crushing debt haha and you know what that means

Ada Highfield   **11:01**

I'm about to receive many fine jewels? Which I can then sell to pay off my own crushing debt?

Stuart Parkes   **11:02**

If by fine jewels you mean my … hmm no wait that's too crude, reel it in Stuart. Anyway I thought I was your sugar baby, why else would I date an older woman

Stuart Parkes   **11:04**

It means I can afford a train ticket to London soon! But it's minimum wage so I probably can't afford anywhere to stay, any ideas on that front

Stuart Parkes   **11:07**

Hmm was that not clear enough, I'm asking if I can stay in your flat, in your bed or I guess your housemate's if she's hotter than you

Stuart Parkes   **11:17**

Ahhhhhh ok maybe not, please pretend I didn't say anything, let's talk about how cute I'm going to look wearing a little apron

Ada Highfield   **11:19**

You're going to look so cute. But hey, so I do want us to do the in-person thing but it's a little complicated having you come stay with me

Stuart Parkes   11:19

OK ...

Ada Highfield   11:23

So I know we should have talked about this sooner but we didn't and honestly I sort of keep expecting us to stop doing whatever this is because like ... it's so weird? But it also makes me happy talking to you and trust me I really have been thinking about doing other stuff with you too.

Ada Highfield   11:28

You know how I told you a friend was staying with us? That's true and she really is just a friend. But she's staying in my room, with me. In my bed specifically, it's not a bunks situation. I had bunks when I was a kid though, the GOAT bed structure imo.

Ada Highfield   11:30

Anyway I know it's kind of a weird set-up but I guess I have like a casual live-in lover who is mostly a friend. Very chill normal arrangement. But it doesn't stop me seeing anyone else. Just maybe stops me seeing them in my home.

Ada Highfield   11:41

Surprise I'm bi lol

Stuart Parkes   11:44

Does she know about me?

Ada Highfield   **11:45**

No but that doesn't mean anything. I wouldn't know what to tell her really.

Ada Highfield   **12:04**

I've ruined your big cafe announcement, I'm never getting that sweet staff discount now am I

Ada Highfield   **15:02**

What's happening friend

Stuart Parkes   **15:51**

I'm thinking

Ada Highfield   **16:32**

OK lil buddy, I can wait

Nine

Mel and Ada were climbing the stairs to a divided Kentish Town terrace and Ada's sweaty wedge heels slipped slightly on the stone. Mel steadied her.

'So what is like ... the purpose of this party? They're moving out so it's a house ... cooling? Does that mean we can trash the place?'

Mel looked at her quickly to make sure she was joking and said, 'They don't want to take all their alcohol with them to the next place so it's a drink-up-the-booze party mainly.'

Ada pretended to be amazed. 'Wow, imagine booze lasting long enough in the house that you need help drinking it. How the other half lives, I guess.'

Mel shifted away from her and said, 'Look, you didn't have to come. You don't have to hang out with my friends at all.' Mel pressed the buzzer and then Ada took her hand.

'Not hang out with my dear wife's friends? What would the boys at the office think about that,' and Mel laughed but Ada could tell she was anxious. Ada asked, 'Why are they doing this on a Thursday?' and Mel said, 'Probably to keep it low-key. And it's Wednesday,' and Ada had more questions but kept them to herself.

Mel had invited Sadie to come with them tonight but Sadie had said she needed to work. They'd left her sitting at the kitchen bench with her iPad open to a script and her notebook next to her and the kettle boiling. Ada had been annoyed at Mel for inviting her then annoyed at Sadie for declining, for working into the night when she could have been out with them.

They were buzzed in and as Ada opened the door she asked, 'And Paul's wife is called …' and Mel said, 'My god Ada, you've only met her fifty times, it's Claire,' and Ada said, 'Of course, I'm sorry.' When they were let into the flat, Ada headed straight to Claire in the kitchen to hug her and thank her for the invitation. She turned and gave Mel a thumbs up but Mel just shook her head and looked away. The couple's extensive liquor cabinet had been laid out on the kitchen bench and for the next two hours Ada declared herself the bartender and mixed drinks for everyone at the party according to their vibe – that's what she said: she didn't take orders, she just 'read vibes,' and everyone seemed to like that except Mel who she didn't see the whole time.

Ada was sitting up on the bench drinking a peppermint schnapps and vodka when a tall, impossibly fair man – his hair, his face, his eyes, all milky – entered and leaned over her.

'I hear you're the drinks witch,' and the word 'witch' combined with the Eton tone made her clench her fists.

She didn't move but politely said, 'You're going to need to take like three steps back,' and he laughed and straightened up and walked backwards.

'One … two … and three. So what do you have for me?'

Ada scanned the depleted supply next to her and said, 'I think I'll make you … the Posh Cunt.'

He smiled at her and steadied himself against the fridge. 'What's in that then?'

Ada picked up port, sloe gin and ginger ale and mixed them roughly together. He reached out to take the cup but she pulled it back.

'Not ... quite done.' She stuck her index finger in her mouth and swirled it around then took it out and stuck it into his cup. Then she handed it to him and without breaking eye contact he drank it in one go.

'Ah, the taste of home.'

Ada jumped off the bench and found Mel sitting in the living room with their bags, talking to a man with plain clothes and trendy glasses. Mel said, 'Ada, this is Will! He works with me and Paul. Ada's my housemate, she was a friend of a friend and then,' and Mel told their story to Will while Ada waited for a break.

When it eventually came, she knelt down to get her bag from beside the couch and said, 'I'm so sorry to be rude and Will, please don't take this personally, you seem lovely and I honestly love your glasses so much but I'm experiencing a small heartbreak at the moment and I have to go home and lie in the dark sadly.'

Will said, 'That doesn't sound like a small heartbreak,' and Mel said, 'He still hasn't messaged huh,' and Ada pulled her phone out of her bra and said, 'No, I've been checking every five minutes because I'm a total psycho, it's been like thirty hours or something.' Will nodded and didn't say that thirty hours wasn't that long and Ada filed it away in the 'pro' column. Mel tried to leave with her but Ada said to stay and she clattered down the stairs, into the night, onto the Overground, all the way home. Sadie was sleeping and she didn't stir even when Ada put her hand in her hair.

Ada woke up the next day to Sadie lazily stroking her back and she wriggled her hips backwards until they were wedged tightly together. They were both naked, they were always naked in bed, and Sadie propped herself up slightly and ran her hand down Ada's side before reaching over and down and then up up up. Her other hand held the back of Ada's neck, steadying herself and trapping Ada and Ada felt she'd be trapped by her forever, she'd feel the weight of Sadie on her forever, she'd never turn around, never look into her face, just feel her pinning and pushing.

Ada felt coveted and stolen and when Sadie eventually flipped her over she felt a rush of thrilling shame. They hadn't spoken yet this morning and they hadn't seen each other last night and they were strangers sharing a bed and Sadie looked flushed and kind of furious. She held up a hand as if to say 'stay' and Ada nodded and Sadie lay that hand on Ada's forehead as she lowered herself onto her face. Ada lost herself and Stuart was lost to her too and later when Sadie was dressing – she wasn't going anywhere today, a quiet day in, but she put on jeans just the same – Ada started to cry.

Sadie sat next to her and took her hand and Ada said, 'I'm not crying for bad reasons, I just feel … I think I'm overwhelmed,' and Sadie said, 'It's OK, I hope I didn't—' and Ada said, 'No, god, no, I didn't want it to ever end, I don't want you to think—' and Sadie said, 'I can go out if you need some space?' But Ada pulled back her hand and wiped her eyes because she had somewhere to be today and going out while Sadie stayed in felt like a victory. She was meeting her friend Ben in Tooting because he'd gone flat broke at the Fringe this year and had moved back in with his parents until, as he put it, 'Someone starts paying me to be stunning.' They were meeting up to smoke weed and lie in his local park but she said to Sadie, 'We're actually going to discuss a project for us to do together. He's an actor … maybe something for the Fringe next year?' and Sadie said, 'That sounds great, I know you've been looking for a project,' and Ada wasn't sure what that meant exactly but she agreed.

She pulled on a bra and a blue velvet baby-doll dress because lying in a park getting high felt like the nineties to her and then she dug through her underwear drawer. She paused then walked to Sadie's bag, opened it and pulled out a plain black pair of briefs. She pulled them on, turned to look at Sadie who smiled and said, 'Have fun,' and then picked up her book.

Later, on the tube, Ada shifted in her seat and felt the tag of Sadie's underwear rub against her lower back and felt nauseous so she turned up the podcast about Trump's border policy playing in her ears to drown out any other sensation. Her carriage had filled gradually before emptying at Leicester Square, families with northern accents and young people with accents like hers pouring out for their Day In Town. Ada cultivated her messy, bored look so as to differentiate herself from the tourist hordes, wondering if her skin gave away a childhood spent in the sun rather than under London skies. Still, it didn't matter when she'd got here. This was her city. Not Sadie's. Sadie was her guest.

As the tube paused at Leicester Square, the wifi kicked in and Ada's phone vibrated in her hand. In the drop of time between then and the moment she looked at her screen all of her possible futures with Stuart flooded her system. His hands, his mouth moving in front of her, his mouth moving on her, a fight, a recovery, a hangover, him learning to braid her hair – but it was an email from her mother, who already knew how to braid her hair.

•••

Hi Baby,

I have such exciting news! Your sister called last night and she's changed her mind. She wants all of us there to meet her little bubba as soon as possible! Your father and I are over the moon, waiting until Chrissie would have been torture. Now the flights are obviously very expensive on such short notice and your sister was so apologetic about that and then the craziest thing happened. Her lovely man Hank jumped on the call and said he was paying for all our tickets! I told him absolutely not, we wouldn't stand for it and we bargained him down to splitting the cost, but your sister said of course that we couldn't expect you to buy yours so Hank said he'd do it and you're not to argue. He seems so happy to do it! I can't wait to meet him in person, such a lovely man, such a change for your sister! Anyway, we're arriving 20 September, two days before the little one is due, so try to come in at the same time? How long do you think you can get off work? Anyway, I'll pop Hank's email at the bottom here, do get in touch as soon as you get this. What a wonderful surprise for us all! Florida!

Love you, Baby,

Mama x

•••

'Your sister said of course that we couldn't expect you to buy yours.' Ada rolled this one around. Two years ago there was no question that Gabby would have meant this in its cruellest possible form. A reminder of Ada's shiftlessness, as

Gabby saw it. Pointing to the money Ada never seemed to have. Gabby hated her job as a ... what, consultant? Whatever that was. But at least she had a job. That's what she'd meant. That's what Ada felt she'd meant.

But Gabby didn't have a job now. She'd met her partner on a work trip to Chicago and after a week together they went back to their respective lives in Melbourne and New York. When that became unbearable, she'd quit her job and flown to stay with him and before she could find something new she'd got pregnant. They quickly moved to Florida, where Hank was from, into a house that was mysteriously available to them (a family home? Was Hank rich-rich or just consultant rich?).

So maybe that was her job now, growing a kid and living in Florida, but if it was, she could hardly shame Ada for a lack of drive, could she? Maybe the meaning had shifted along with her Instagram filters. 'Your sister said of course that we couldn't expect you to buy yours.' Because it would be rude, at the last minute, to expect her younger sister to drop everything, all her many projects, her hectic life, to fly out to meet a baby. It would only be a reasonable thing to ask if the flight was a gift. Maybe that's what she meant. Mel, Ada was sure, would say that that's what she meant.

Ada copied Hank's email address and pasted it into a new draft and then stopped. She and Gabby hadn't spoken in months, since the last family Skype in which they both dutifully answered their parents' questions and then waved and said 'Love you' before hanging up. Ada tried to remember the last time she and her sister were alone together and found she couldn't grab hold of a specific memory. Gabby had moved to Melbourne when she was twenty-one and Ada was eighteen and then there had been Christmases with the cousins and their dad's sixtieth. One funeral, an aunt, and Gabby left for her flight before the wake.

Ada remembered the fighting, though. Would Gabby want her there for this?

The tube stopped at Tooting Broadway and Ada locked her phone and stepped off. She rose out of the underground, thinking of Stuart because she'd left space in her thoughts again and he slipped back in. She wondered at his withholding from her, after the effort he'd put in for her attention. With anyone else she'd consider this a game, but she knew, really, that she'd hurt him.

The endless words of the past couple of weeks had made them intimate but there was so much he didn't know about her. He knew she was precise with punctuation but not that she dotted her letter i's with circles when she wrote the old-fashioned way. He knew the bands she had loved most in high school but not what it looked like when she danced. He knew her face but he didn't know the patch of eczema that flared up on her neck in winter because it wasn't there in Edinburgh and it wasn't there in her profile picture and when she messaged him that picture was all he saw. He knew her and he didn't and she wanted him to want more because she wanted more but mostly because she wanted more wanting.

Ada stood outside the station, pressed against a wall to avoid the frenetic tide and waited for Google Maps to load. As she did a message popped up from Ben. He hoped she got this before she got on the train but he had an audition, last-minute thing, so sorry, if she was on the train they probably passed each other in a tunnel, it's in Soho, could they reschedule? She replied they could but she was busy all next week, maybe the week after? She waited a few minutes but evidently Ben was travelling or in his audition. She briefly considered admitting that she could do any day next week, any day at all, but a pretence at working seemed smarter. She closed the app then opened it again and typed, 'Kick that audition in the dick hunny, I know you will xxxxx' and no one in the world could say she didn't mean it.

Ada opened her messages from Stuart. Scrolled to a random point and stopped.

•••

09/09/2017

Stuart Parkes   23:14

7? No offence to your parents but you should have known how to tie your shoes before you hit 7. Actually full offence to your parents.

Ada Highfield   23:15

Wow that is not the way to get on the Christmas card list

Ada Highfield   23:15

Anyway I always wore velcro and Mary Janes

Stuart Parkes   23:16

Like … weed shoes

Ada Highfield   **23:17**

No like little shiny shoes with buckles, please be less of a boy

Stuart Parkes   **23:18**

OK I just googled them and they're very cute, your parents are forgiven

Stuart Parkes   **23:18**

Hmm apparently they make these shoes in adult sizes too

Ada Highfield   **23:19**

Yeah I have a pair, mainly for temping but they're under my bed

Stuart Parkes   **23:20**

Maybe you could teach me how to buckle them and I can teach you to tie your laces

Ada Highfield   **23:21**

I can tie them now jeeeeez like 90% of the time I can tie them just fine

Ada Highfield   **23:21**

But you can tie them up for me if you like

Stuart Parkes 23:22

You're pretty cute you know

Ada Highfield 23:23

Wow who knew Mary Janes would do it for you

Stuart Parkes 23:23

I think you could have guessed

•••

Ada exited the app, opened her email and started writing to Hank, swiping through the barriers at the tube station without looking up. Northern line, screeching and hot. Victoria line, sleek and empty in the middle of a work day. Overground, open and easy, like home. She got out at her station and crossed the street to sit in the park, pulling the book of theory out of her bag and failing to open it. The sky was grey and she needed the jacket that she'd left on her chair so she went home.

When she let herself in, she heard Sadie and Mel singing in the kitchen. It was *The Last Five Years*, the wedding song, and Mel was doing a perfect Jamie while Sadie flatly tripped over Cathy's lines, giggling through her vocal tumbles. Ada eased off her shoes and left them in the hall, coming in to see that Sadie was assembling a vegetarian lasagne. Leeks, pumpkin. Spinach in the ricotta. She was tearing thyme then rolling it into the cheese, her hands reckless and smeared. She turned and smiled. Mel reached over to kiss Ada on the cheek and Ada climbed next to her on the bench and leaned heavily.

'How was your friend?' asked Sadie, her fingers covered in green and white.

'He cancelled,' said Ada, suddenly too tired to lie. 'He cancelled because everyone in London is very very busy except for me.' She started to cry and Mel instinctively pulled her in, rubbed her hair and her face while Sadie watched, holding her hands up as if to say, 'I'd hold you too but I don't want to get you dirty' even though Ada felt that wasn't true. Mel was saying the things she said when Ada cried and Ada wiped her face and said, 'Also, I'm going to Florida to meet Gabby's baby. In two weeks. Hank is paying,' and Mel was saying that sounded wonderful and Ada hopped down and said, 'I'm turning off my brain now.' She lay on her side on their sofa watching *Friends* and after a few minutes Mel came in with tea and lifted Ada's legs to sit under them.

Ada cried off and on over the next three hours, through *Friends* – the Brad Pitt episode was on, he was actually under-rated as a comedian, she said to Mel – then more *Friends* on the +2 hours channel until eventually they hit the same episode. But by then the lasagne was ready and Sadie pulled their little dining table out from the wall, set it beautifully with all matching plates (which took time to find in their flat), poured out a Sancerre and asked how she was.

'I feel OK now,' Ada said, and she did apart from the violence of Stuart's absence on her phone. She imagined sending him something perfect, or something naked, or writing a poem that was bad on purpose to make him laugh. She imagined telling him she'd sent Sadie away but then she looked at Sadie tossing a green salad with radishes she'd pickled the week before and couldn't imagine actually doing it. 'Hey, have you heard from your ex?' she asked and Sadie didn't look up from the salad but said, 'Yeah, I think she wants us to be friends but I'm not sure my ego is ready for that yet,' which surprised Ada because she had been sure that Sadie was fine.

That night when Ada came in from brushing her teeth, she found Sadie moisturising her legs. 'I didn't know you liked musicals. You and Mel were singing?' and Sadie laughed and said, 'Who doesn't like *The Last Five Years*?' and Ada said, 'I would have guessed you didn't like it.' She stripped off and lay on her side with her back to Sadie and after a moment Sadie said, 'I think … you think I'm not very fun.' Ada rolled to face her and said, 'You're fun, you're just not like … goofy. Jason Robert Brown musicals are goofy.' Sadie smiled and put her hand on Ada's face. 'Do you want me to sing "The Schmuel Song"?' and Ada felt drunk and sad and closed her eyes and that's how they fell asleep.

Ada woke up in the dark and felt a rushing in her gut. She sat up and tried to ease out of bed but she didn't move quickly enough and a smudge of dark blood dragged across her sheet. She grabbed a still-damp towel from the floor and waddled to the bathroom with it tucked up between her legs. She got to the toilet and sat down, moaning as her body released and clenched and released again. After a few minutes she sat up, pulled her head out of her hands and staggered to the cabinet. She grabbed a tampon and two ibuprofen, swallowed the tablets quickly and started to clean herself up.

When she returned to their room she pulled on underwear and a pad from her bedside table and then she stood, sweating, holding her stomach and staring at the dark mark on her sheet, so close to Sadie's sleeping form. A growl emerged from somewhere in her chest and she fell against the bed, waiting for the wave to pass. Sadie opened her eyes and Ada whispered, 'I'm sorry' and gestured at the blood. Sadie sat up and crawled over to her, right over the bloody patch and lay her hand on Ada's forehead.

'Nothing to apologise for. Have you taken painkillers?' and Ada nodded, too dragged into herself suddenly to feel embarrassed.

Some blurry time passed as Sadie helped her pull on a slip dress that covered her just enough and walked her to the living room. Sadie lay her on the couch and pulled a blanket over her and then distantly the sound of the washing machine. Her body pulsed and clenched, pulsed again, and she was hot all over and then the painkillers finally offered peace and she slept. When she woke up Sadie was reading on the floor by the couch and Ada had no new messages.

Ten

From: Hank Mathers
To: Ada Highfield

Dear Ada,

Just wanted to confirm that I've got you on a flight leaving Gatwick on 23 September. I've attached the ticket and all the information to this email. Your sister and I are looking forward to your arrival. My parents are going to bunk in with my brother so their house will be free for you and your parents to use. It's right on a lake so don't forget your bug spray! I can't wait to meet you in person and to have our whole big family together for this joyous arrival. Please email me with any questions and let me know if there's anything I can do to make your stay easier. We appreciate you taking time out of your life for us on such short notice.

All the best,

Your new big brother Hank

Eleven

Ada finished reading the email aloud and waited for Sadie's response. She had spent the day on the couch with a hot water bottle under her back and Sadie had been soft with her. Plain buttered toast and a run to the shop for marshmallows and bocconcini balls and patiently looking up from her book whenever Ada saw something funny on Twitter or needed her water bottle refilled or groaned and shifted positions or read emails from her sister's partner aloud. Sadie had rolled up her yoga mat against the wall and was using it for cushioning and she smiled at Ada now and raised her hands palms up in a gesture of surrender.

'I don't know what you want me to say but he sounds ... nice. I mean like I'm not personally a fan of the "I'm your brother because I married your sister" thing but he's American. They're weird like that.' Ada was interested because she also thought Americans were weird like that but she didn't know how to explain what 'that' was so she said, 'Weird like how?'

'Like ... the way they always act like they're being friendly, and maybe they are, but it's friendly in a ... learned way? He "appreciates you taking time." OK doesn't that sound like something he read on LinkedIn? But he also probably does appreciate it, he just doesn't know how to say it in an original way. It's like how The West Wing made everyone in America think they had to be inspirational to their colleagues or whatever, or to a reality show judge, and they're all using that kind of stirring language, and like some of them got really, really good at it, Obama mainly, so we hear that cadence of voice and we expect to feel inspired. And you read this email from this guy and you expect to feel welcomed because he's using like ... welcoming language. But you have no idea how he actually feels ... but I'm sure he is excited to meet you, god I don't want to make it sound like he hates you or anything. Sorry, this is my shit. Playwright brain.'

Ada loved Sadie just then, she loved her. 'You talk shit about people in the most academic way,' she said and under those words were, 'I love you I love you,' and Sadie smiled and said, 'I wouldn't say I'm talking shit, I'm sure Hank is great,' and under those words were, 'I know I know,' and Ada tried a different way in.

'I just think he sees me as her fuck-up little sister who ran away to be famous and hasn't made it. Last time we Skyped Gabby asked if I had any auditions coming up and I said I'm not just an auditioning actor any more, I'm mainly doing cabaret now, and she was like, "Oh, so how do you get those roles?" And I had to explain that like ... I make the art now, I don't just wait for someone to choose me for their art, and even as the words came out I was like ... wow I sound fucking cooked.' Sadie put her head to the side and looked like she might laugh but she didn't and Ada said, 'I do have some self-awareness even though you think I don't. I know how I sound when I talk about this stuff but it's what I do so ... so I have to talk about it.'

And then Sadie launched a direct attack by saying, 'Well, what are you working on right now?' and Ada knew it was deliberate and said, 'You shouldn't be so rude to me when I have period pain, whatever happened to women supporting women,' and they both laughed. Sadie said, 'OK, I respect the confidence,' and Ada said, 'Most people don't. Like all the memes tell you to have the confidence of a mediocre white man and then I do and everyone *hates* it.' Sadie got up to make tea and get Ada some more painkillers, and as the water started to bubble in the next room Ada held her swollen tummy and thought of Stuart.

They had messaged each other for thirteen days and now he had cut her off for three and those numbers shouldn't have hurt the way they did. She longed for him in a way she found grotesque and she blamed herself and she blamed her generation. In decades past he would have loved her from the audience and then never been able to find her again. Maybe they would one day have attended the same party and his throat would seize up when he saw her – that's her, that's the girl from Edinburgh – and he would spend all night figuring out how to talk to her. She would glow and he would shield himself, circling her, finding a safe way to get close. And she could dazzle him at this party, and when he confessed he'd seen her perform, she'd be self-deprecating but in a way that showed she loved herself enough to drag out his inadequacy. Maybe he'd get her number that night or maybe he'd keep going to parties, hoping she'd be there, lusting alone while she thrived invisibly.

But instead, he could message her, just like that, and when she felt normal, shining for no one, alone at home picking at the dead skin on her heel, he could send a perfect little joke and he had her interest. The imbalance of it all. What right did he have to admire her and then withdraw? People thought Ada was flighty and unreliable but she said what she meant, and she could have lied to Stuart but wouldn't that have been worse? Why didn't he see that she could have told him something so much worse?

Ada opened up Tinder and closed it and opened it again, and the first photo was a man with a 'summers in the south of France' tan and she shut it again. She could hear Mel and Sadie discussing her in the kitchen, Sadie asking if the cramps were always this bad and Mel saying it depended on the month. Ada felt like a sick child listening to the hushed grown-ups wondering if she was well enough to go to school.

Ada tried Instagram and saw Gabby and Hank in a restaurant together, the ocean visible behind them. Hank was leaning forward to blow out a candle surrounded by a tray of prawns and the caption read, 'Happy birthday to my spunky Yank (don't tell him what that means, it's better he doesn't know). Bump and I will try to make 36 your best year yet. Love you darling one, thank you for saving my life.' And Ada realised Hank had booked her a plane ticket and written her a lovely email on his own birthday and no one had told her, especially not Gabby. Ada liked the photo so Gabby would know she knew. What a nice thing he did. What a very nice man he was.

Ada scrolled back further, past the thousands of Hank photos, the millions upon billions of images of the growing bump. She reached Australia, the time before Gabby moved, then further back again to the time before Gabby knew Hank existed. There was a photo of Gabby out with work friends and then her toasting their parents by the Christmas tree, the first year Ada wasn't there. She wondered who took the photo and remembered her dad saying they had invited a lot of people over for that particular Christmas lunch 'to distract us from missing our baby'. Her mother said, 'And even ten extra people weren't as loud as you,' and Ada said, 'Hey!' and they'd all laughed on the family Skype, even Gabby, from memory.

But Ada wasn't mentioned in the caption of the photo by the Christmas tree. It just said 'Tis the season!', which was a phrase Ada was pretty sure Gabby had never said out loud because when Ada used to decorate the whole house on the first of December, blasting Mariah Carey, Gabby had hidden in her room and refused to join in. But suddenly 'tis', suddenly 'the season'? OK, Gabby.

It had stung then (no 'toasts to absent sisters'? No 'it's a little different this year'?) and Ada had complained about it to Mel at the time. Mel pointed out that Ada had never mentioned her sister in her Instagram captions which seemed like a deliberately obtuse thing to say, but it was Christmas morning and they were staying with Mel's silent parents and it had put both of them in a weird mood so she had dropped it. That night, after a long, sober lunch and then an enforced 'Christmas walk' through some frosty, muddy woods, Ada and Mel had got into bed together and drunk terrible 'festive' gin right from the bottle while watching The Muppet Christmas Carol and even then Ada stewed over the caption.

Sadie came back in with peppermint tea and Ada lifted her feet slightly. Sadie looked down and said, 'Oh no, don't make yourself uncomfortable.' She put the tea next to Ada and took her place back on the floor and Ada thought about saying that it would have actually been very comfortable to lay her legs on Sadie, but then a wave of nausea came. She closed her eyes and let the smell of peppermint ease her through it and then opened them, ready to be cheerful.

Sadie was watching her. 'You should talk to a doctor; these seem like really bad cramps.'

Ada said, 'What's a doctor going to do? I am simply paying my feminine penance. Original sin!' and Sadie said, 'Yes, I know all about that, I went to Catholic school,' and Ada said, 'Your family is Catholic?' and Sadie said no. And they passed the time talking about their convent schools. Ada said she always played Mary in the liturgical plays and Sadie said, 'That figures, it's always the prettiest white girl, which isn't strictly historically accurate.' And Sadie told Ada that the Catholic school thing was another failed parental attempt at assimilation but that, 'as it turns out, it was a great place to be gay'. Ada tossed over whether it was nice that Sadie had called her pretty or bad that she had kind of implied she was racist.

Mel joined them and said she couldn't relate to all the Catholicism chat. 'But while we're talking about guilt, how does everyone feel about breaking the household meat rule and getting fried chicken?' and Ada said, 'Yes, my uterus needs this,' and Sadie laughed and said, 'Go on then.' It felt like family, almost, right down to Sadie asking Ada if she should be mixing her ibuprofen with quite so much wine and Ada explaining that she felt it made both drugs more effective, actually. Ada had vaguely thought Sadie had somewhere to be that night but no one mentioned it. They let Ada choose the movie so she went with Obvious Child, cute enough for her to cope with in her current state but with enough feminist politics that she wouldn't hear about it from Mel.

After the movie, Mel tidied up and Sadie disappeared upstairs, then called Ada's name. Ada dragged herself up and saw that Sadie had run a bath and left a tumbler of bourbon on the side. She looked embarrassed, maybe. Whatever it was, it wasn't familiar, and she said, 'Sorry if … it just occurred to me that it might be nice for the pain.' Ada said, 'Wow Sadie, this is so romantic,' and it was so quiet then that she said, 'I'm joking. I am currently dropping clots from my body, sorry I'm just saying shit, it's not romantic,' and Sadie laughed and it was almost OK again. Ada undressed and Sadie let herself out but said to call if she needed anything. Ada set a podcast going about Dolly Parton's place in the American canon and eased into the water, feeling the pressure on her torso ease enough to breathe in the steam.

She stayed in the water until her drink was done and the edge of a chill was setting in around her body, then dried herself and did her teeth. She came to bed to see Sadie still up and reading and she said 'thank you' and Sadie said, 'Did it help?' and she really seemed to hope it did.

'Yeah, I feel pretty good now. Could be the drugs of course,' and Sadie said 'good' and looked back down at her book. Ada reached into a drawer and pulled out her M & S pyjama shorts and a grey T-shirt she had stolen from a one-night stand, big and well worn. She realised it would be her first time sleeping next to Sadie with clothes on and thought maybe that was nice actually.

But when she got into bed and Sadie kept reading and didn't look over at all, she wondered if maybe it wasn't that nice. She wondered if this was Sadie's way, if this was the most she ever had to offer, but then she remembered that Sadie slept in that other girl's spare room for a week, just waiting for the girl to love her, and she figured it probably wasn't. Ada had been in one relationship, only one, that felt balanced, like both of them wanted and felt wanted, and that had been with the guy who thought she had too many emotions. She hadn't minded him thinking that because she liked that he saw her as passionate. But in the end, she frustrated him and he bored her and they held on out of equilibrium. Ada knew she would never do that again and being the wanter wasn't so bad when your object sometimes ran you a bath.

Ada closed her eyes and dreamed of Gabby. They were swimming but the water was hot and rough, knocking them around and into each other and away again. Gabby seemed grateful to Ada for something, she kept trying to thank her, but every time it seemed like the words might come out, she would be dragged away and under by the boiling tide. Ada felt a tugging underneath her and looked down to see she was pregnant and she knew she was carrying the baby for Gabby because Gabby had needed a break, why wouldn't anyone give her a break?

But Ada didn't want to do this for Gabby. Why should she? If she was going to carry this for her then this was her baby and Gabby and Hank could go get their own! Gabby had drifted a long way out now and was floating on the steaming sea, free of her burden and Ada started to swim to shore. If she could get out of the water and find Mel they could keep this baby. She'd be gone before Gabby even noticed she was missing. But the shore stayed the same distance away no matter how hard she swam and while Gabby floated out out out, Ada felt herself dragging under.

Later when Ada kicked herself awake, stomach hot, sweat cold, she wondered what life Gabby felt Hank had saved and then she was gone.

Twelve

16/09/2017

Ada Highfield   **20:48**

I think you're not talking to me which is fine but I was reading the *Guardian* (an actual newspaper, we get it every weekend, Mel is 60 years old cosplaying as 30) and I saw that there's an exhibition at the Tate in Liverpool of queer British art. No pressure or anything but it's closing soon and I thought it would be cool to see. So … I dunno! Maybe I come to Liverpool! Know anyone fun there?

Ada Highfield   **21:01**

Just realised it's Saturday so you've probably had a busy day at the cafe. Jobs are useful for keeping track of the days, I guess, maybe I should look into getting one some day. Anyway I hope you're well. Drawn anything good lately?

Ada Highfield   **21:13**

OK freak I'm a little high and I need to say that I think you're being mean. And kind of immature but that's no sin. I liked talking to you. I miss that. You now haven't spoken to me for like a third of the time you did speak to me. Does that make sense

Ada Highfield   21:14

Maybe a quarter of the time. Fuck I can't even do maths not high what am I saying.

Ada Highfield   21:16

I guess I'll never see the home of the Beatles, what a loss, I love that one song they have about a car

Stuart Parkes   21:31

You're a loose cannon you know

Ada Highfield   21:32

Is that hot

Stuart Parkes   21:33

Unfortunately for me, yeah, I think it is

Ada Highfield   21:35

I'm really sorry I didn't tell you about Sadie but I didn't know what either of you were to me. I still don't but I know I want to come to Liverpool and find out.

Stuart Parkes   21:37

Is she still at your place?

Ada Highfield   21:37

Yeah she is but

Ada Highfield   21:40

Ugh I wish I knew how to explain to you that you shouldn't be threatened by her. She's a friend, we barely know each other but she needed somewhere to stay and we started sleeping together. We did that before you ever messaged me. Like she's cool, I like her. But she lives in Australia, she'll be gone soon. And me and you live here.

Stuart Parkes   21:42

Has it occurred to you to stop having sex with your houseguest who you barely know

Ada Highfield   21:44

Not really, no. For you? I don't know you either. But I want to. I'm saying let me.

Ada Highfield   21:51

I wish this was the 20s and then your letters would take like a month to get to me and it would be fine. Fuck I might be too high for this

Stuart Parkes   22:05

OK come to Liverpool. Stay with me. I'm off work next weekend, it's week on week off with weekends

Ada Highfield   22:06

SOLD YES

Ada Highfield   22:07

Shit wait no

Stuart Parkes   22:07

. . .

Ada Highfield   22:09

Funny story I'm going to Florida next weekend

Stuart Parkes   22:10

To see your sister?

Ada Highfield   22:12

No I felt a sudden urge to go to meet Mickey Mouse. Yeah my sister and the baby. I fly out Saturday, I'm going for two weeks so fuck

Ada Highfield   22:13

Fuck when can I come to Liverpool?

Stuart Parkes   22:15

You couldn't make this easy could you

Ada Highfield   22:17

I have my usual gig on Tuesday night and I'm MCing a burlesque thing for charity on Wednesday

Stuart Parkes   22:17

Thursday then

Ada Highfield   22:19

For only one night? Won't you have to work?

Stuart Parkes   22:22

Feels sort of now or never, doesn't it?

Stuart Parkes   22:25

I'll swap shifts. Otherwise I think maybe this is it, not trying to be a dickhead but what do you want from me here, Ada

Ada Highfield   22:28

OK freak, I'll do it. I'm out of my mind right now so I can't figure out the train website but I'll book first thing in the morning. I promise

Stuart Parkes 22:29

You will

Ada Highfield 22:31

I will. I have to go to bed. I'm so glad you're talking to me again.

Stuart Parkes 22:33

I don't want to think about you going to bed. Good night.

Stuart Parkes 22:40

Book in the morning

•••

17/09/2017

Stuart Parkes 07:13

Booked yet?

Thirteen

Sadie had given Ada her entire day. The previous Saturday, they'd had morning sex and then Sadie had gone to meet an old university friend for lunch and she'd gone to the theatre that night and Ada and Mel had friends over to watch the football. Mel was a United fan and Ada joked that she was a Posh Spice fan, which was close enough. Ada had texted Stuart the whole time. He supported Liverpool which she said was boring – 'oh you support the team in your home city, very original' – because she knew it would drive him nuts.

Sadie had come home and said hi to their friends and ended up settling in to talk football, about which she knew a surprising amount. When Ada mentioned this, she raised an eyebrow and said, 'It's only white Australians who don't know about soccer,' and their friends had laughed and got more drinks. Sadie started bragging about the Australian women's team to friendly boos and Ada turned back to her phone.

But this Saturday was theirs. Ada had mentioned during her couch day that she had forgotten to make plans and Mel was going to see her parents. And Sadie said she didn't have any meetings or any tickets. She'd thought maybe she could check out a local gallery but Ada said, 'On a Saturday?' and Sadie said good point. So when they woke up they both knew the other had nowhere to be. It made Ada nervous and she loved being nervous.

Ada scrolled in bed while Sadie read, soft touches when one needed to change position, no kisses but a lazy scratch of Ada's back, a hand moving on its own. Sadie asked Ada if Instagram stressed her out, but in a pretty non-judgey way. Ada explained that she mostly followed friends back home – whose lives were so different to hers that it was like watching a reality show – and plus-size influencers – who took photos in their underwear and wrote long captions that she didn't read. Sadie said, 'But you're not plus-sized,' and Ada said, 'I'm subverting the consumer gaze,' and Sadie said, 'OK if you say so,' and Ada said, 'I'm kidding, I just like hot people. I also follow zoos all over the world. Look at this, a snow leopard litter was just born in upstate New York,' and Sadie actually did put her book down to look. When Sadie went to the bathroom to shower, Ada considered messaging Stuart and then lectured herself on dignity for a while. She also realised she didn't exactly want to message him right at that moment and that made her proud.

Sadie offered to get breakfast but Ada had taken painkillers and wanted to show her, suddenly, the life she had made for herself. They dressed together, Sadie passing Ada her light denim jacket without being asked, then holding out her shirt from the day before for Ada to sniff and pass judgement on (it smelled fine, she put it back on) and they left. They picked up coffee and cardamom-spiced pastries because London bakers had just discovered cardamon. Ada said this was her regular cafe and Sadie said they didn't seem to know her and Ada said, 'Because it's London, Sadie,' but actually they did know her, she was pretty sure. She usually flirted with the hot person who made the coffee but they were super busy and anyway Ada wasn't quite sure that flirting in front of Sadie was appropriate today.

The streets were busy so they detoured down the River Lea, weaving through groups of women with prams and dodging the Saturday Cyclist, determined to tire out his calves and avoid going home to his children. When Ada said this to Sadie, a line she had prepared in advance, Sadie laughed properly then said 'fuck those guys' and Ada felt like she could fly. She told Sadie about the friend of hers who had tried to walk home along this path drunk and had mistaken a houseboat for a bridge – at least that's what he thought had happened because he remembered thinking, 'this bridge is moving,' and then the next thing he knew he was in the water. Sadie was a great audience this morning, laughing and saying, 'No, oh god this water is disgusting though!' at all the right moments.

They stayed by the water, talking, not touching, walking in comfort with each other, reaching Hackney Wick and finding a brewery to pee in that they agreed was too loud to drink in. Sadie marvelled at the architecture, so industrial, like Berlin, she said, and they passed what looked like an old school bus. It was open at the back selling pizza by the slice, pretending at being New York. Ada almost walked past but Sadie bought them each a slice, plain, margherita, and Ada realised they were on a fast-food bender together, the fried chicken and sugary pastries and pizza. When Sadie took a huge bite and grease smeared on her chin, Ada thought it might be sexy to lick the spot but she didn't want to ruin the mood by trying. Another detour down the canal, looking for a crossing, and then into Victoria Park, finding a dappled patch, not for reasons of romance but because Ada wanted to lie in the sun and Sadie asked for shade.

Ada knew Sadie had brought a book but she didn't take it out and Ada didn't take out her phone except once to send a selfie to Mel. They talked about their families and Sadie said her brother was ten years older than her and they got along fine but they didn't know each other very well. 'He moved to Sydney for uni when I was eight so I've been three time zones away from him for most of my life. I sort of think he judged me for staying in Perth and living with our parents while I went to uni but I saved so much money. It meant I could start making work as soon as I graduated. And the theatre scene in Perth is beautiful. We're so remote so we kind of just mess around and then when something good happens, everyone bands together to get that show on the road. I know I should move to Sydney or Melbourne or, well, I guess, London, but I think I make the best stuff when I feel safe. I don't know how I'd ever feel safe here. London doesn't seem like a place people go to feel safe. Also, how do you go this long without the beach?'

Ada stretched her body as long as it could go and felt the sun on her shins, a breeze fluttering through the hair on her legs that she hadn't shaved since Edinburgh. 'I can't believe you're talking to me about the beach when you get to go home to it for summer. Cruel!' and Sadie said, 'Which one was your beach?' which wasn't a strange question to Ada at all. Ada explained that though she went to high school and uni in Sydney, they lived on the south coast when she was a kid. 'Have you ever been to Austinmer?' and Sadie hadn't, she only really went to Sydney for work stuff so she didn't know about the east coast.

Not all Australians had a beach, that's a lie that Home & Away taught English people. But a lot of them did and Ada did. She talked to Sadie about the mermaid pools near her house where she and her sister paddled after school until Gabby became an inside kid in Year 4. After that Ada went alone with their mum.

'Why were they called mermaid pools?' asked Sadie and Ada wasn't sure.

'I don't know if that was their official name or just what we called them but they were little ocean pools that we could paddle in alone so looking back it was probably just a way of our mum keeping us occupied while she read her book. The sea was pretty rough but we were protected there mostly … although we knew when a storm was coming because the beach would wash into our little baths and rock us back and forth so we banged up against the rocks and those little anemones that shrink away from you. You know the ones that look like Halloween wigs?'

Sadie knew.

Ada told Sadie about the sea bridge that they crossed in the car every day on their way back from school: 'It looked like the end of the earth – we'd fight to sit in the left-side seat so that we could stare out at the surf and see if there was any point taking our boogie boards down today or if it was more of a "sit and chill in the shallows" vibe.'

That was Ada's beach and Sadie told her about hers. 'I still live ten minutes from it and no offence to you east coast folk but your water temperature is pathetic. It gets properly, properly cold for us—'

Ada interrupted, 'Uh, the nickname for where I grew up is literally the Cold Coast! Don't lump me in with, like, Queenslanders.'

They took a moment to roll their eyes at people from Queensland and Sadie went on.

'It'll be like 35 degrees at 6 p.m in Perth and the whole city will be crawling, that kind of sluggish quiet summer energy and then BAM you get in that water and your body wakes the fuck up. I barely noticed how cold it was when I was a kid and I would run in and out. My parents migrated just before they had my brother and I don't think they ever got used to the shock of it. They always told me how brave I was. They still prefer a walk through the water together holding their shoes to full submersion but credit to them, they let my brother and me run wild, which probably scared the old Perth locals. Two little Arab kids tearing up the beach. Then when I was a teenager, I became a baby about the water and the sun and I would go under the rock overhang with my mates and we'd read and then dare each other to jump in and scream.'

Ada asked, 'What about now?' and Sadie said, 'Now it's my secret weapon. Bored, terrified, getting ready for a night out, dragging myself home ... I go to the water and yeah, I wake the fuck up again.'

They were quiet for a while and then Ada said, 'I never really found a beach in Sydney. We moved when I was twelve – my mum got a job with a new council and I think honestly they thought it'd be good for Gabby. It wasn't, but it was OK for me. I started at high school with a bunch of other people who didn't know each other and we'd get the bus to Coogee every weekend but it wasn't really my beach. I mean, I loved it but I couldn't like ... own it like people who grew up there. I think ... I dunno. I think sometimes if we'd stayed on the coast I never would have felt the need to move to London or be an actor, maybe. Like on the coast I was hot shit in our council theatre group; I was a kid acting with adults, you know? And that was when my career as Mary Mother of God started. Sorry, I know that's a sensitive topic for you.'

Sadie laughed and said, 'Yeah, I wasn't white enough for Mary but I brought frankincense like nobody's business.'

And Ada said, 'I'm sure you looked very wise. But yeah, then we moved to Sydney and I had to audition for all the inter-school theatre shit and I started doing vocal training after school and … I don't know. It was probably good for me. Like how unchecked would my ego have got if we'd never moved?'

Sadie said, 'What would you have done on the coast?' and Ada said, 'Nothing? I don't know. I went to Sydney and I sort of … it became like, oh OK this is a city. But it's not the city. London is the city or New York or something. Paris? You know. Cities. Like … if I'm going to be a city person I need it to be the biggest, best one. But maybe if I'd never become a city person in the first place I wouldn't know that, you know? Like when I was a kid and we'd visit Sydney I was shit scared of riding escalators. But then I adapted and … maybe that's just becoming an adult, though, I dunno. I didn't really stay in touch with my primary school mates and I took my uni boyfriend to Austi Beach on a day trip once and he talked shit about it the whole time and … I'd like to go back now though. With someone else who likes beaches.'

Sadie smiled and said, 'You don't even look like someone who likes beaches any more,' and Ada glanced down at her vintage silky playsuit and soft pale chest where all her freckles had faded.

'Beach Girl is my secret identity'.

Sadie asked, 'Did Gabby – that's your sister's name right – did Gabby do the acting stuff with you?' And Ada said, 'She never … or actually yeah, I think she did when we were still on the coast. There are photos of her being Mary actually, when I was still too little. But I don't know, she never did it with me. Like she lost interest by the time I joined up. She wasn't … interested in much, most of the time'. Sadie asked a little more about Gabby which ended up with them look-ing at photos of Hank and Sadie saying, 'Yeah, I think he's cute but not really my thing'. They lay together learning gentle things as the summer sounds burst around them.

They were mostly quiet and at one point Sadie's hand brushed Ada's as she stretched and it wasn't electric but it was warm. Ada was half asleep when Sadie asked, 'Would you ever move back home?' and Ada said, 'I feel like … a longing for it sometimes – most days, really. But no, I don't think so.' Sadie said, 'But the longing?' and Ada said, 'Yeah, I know,' and she thought about explaining that she was better in London, better set in opposition to the things she desired, but Sadie was a thing she desired so she stayed within herself.

At about six, Sadie produced a baggy from her wallet and asked if Ada would like to smoke it. She'd taken it from the girl in Camberwell when she left though she wasn't sure why. 'I don't even smoke that much but I just … saw it when I was packing. I sound psycho right now,' and Ada said, 'We all do crazy things sometimes. You do not want to know the shit I've taken from exes.' She let herself wonder for a moment what it would be like to drive Sadie so wild that she would steal from her, but she suspected that would never happen. Ada had nothing Sadie wanted and that was OK for now.

Ada rolled up for them and explained to Sadie that she'd spent her high school years dating stoner after stoner, always boys, then kissing her female friends at parties and pretending it was for show. 'I had no idea what I wanted because I knew boys liked me and I didn't know what girls thought of me and it seemed easier not to question it,' and Sadie said that she'd liked boys and girls too, which surprised Ada. 'I thought you were one of those mythical young lesbians?' and Sadie said, 'I sort of am? I liked everyone, I was desperately attracted to everyone, but boys never liked me back. Whereas every queer girl I met sensed it in me and I kind of fell into only dating girls and now ... I can't imagine dating a guy. Not all my exes are women but never a cis dude. But I still think they're attractive sometimes, I dunno, in the abstract? My ex-girlfriend and I watched a lot of gay-dude porn together, is that a straight thing to do?' and Ada lit the joint and breathed in. She breathed out and said, 'Boys weren't into you? They're so dumb,' and Sadie didn't acknowledge the flirt but took the joint from her and said, 'Everyone's dumb.'

And that moment was why. That's why hours later, after they'd caught the bus home together, falling against each other and laughing, and drunk a bottle of wine on the floor of their bedroom while eating donuts from Sainsburys. After they'd watched a YouTube compilation of celebrities singing songs from *The Last Five Years* and shared some falafel that Mel had bought and they would need to replace. After Sadie stood up and said she was taking her whisky to the bath. After Sadie did that, and Ada was still lying on the floor with her whisky and her phone, she thought back to Sadie refusing to agree that boys were dumb for not liking her while smoking weed she stole from someone else. That's why after all of that she messaged Stuart.

Fourteen

17/09/2017

Ada Highfield 08:21

Hey, good morning, I'm so embarrassed about last night

Stuart Parkes 08:27

Don't be embarrassed, who among us etc

Stuart Parkes 08:29

But seriously though you should book

Ada Highfield 08:33

I want to! But I'm looking now and it's so fucking expensive.
Isn't Liverpool like just down the road, why is this so expensive

Stuart Parkes 08:45

How much do you know about privatisation

Ada Highfield   **08:46**

I know it's bad

Ada Highfield   **08:48**

Look at us, sexting in the morning

Stuart Parkes   **08:50**

Ada you need to book today, I'm serious. Not trying to be a prick but a man can't live on banter alone.

Ada Highfield   **08:52**

Ew don't say banter.

Stuart Parkes   **08:56**

I'm about to start work, tell me when you've booked

Ada Highfield   **10:18**

OK I've done it, I get in Thursday to Lime Street (?????) (fuck I hope that's the right station) at 11:42am, I guess send me your address and I can walk or bus there or something

Ada Highfield   **10:24**

Train out the next day at 3:30 in the arvo, it was the latest I could get without it getting crazy expensive again (are people really commuting between London and Liverpool that makes no sense)

Ada Highfield   10:42

I'm nervous! But if we hate each other then I'll grab a cushion with Ringo's face on it and be on my way

Ada Highfield   10:50

I can't wait to talk to you about privatisation for 24 hours then never see or hear from you again

Ada Highfield   11:02

Please tell me this is a good idea because these tickets are non-refundable

Stuart Parkes   13:03

This is a good idea

Stuart Parkes   13:05

And you don't have to walk to my house, I'll meet you at the station

Ada Highfield   13:08

You really don't have to, I'm very resourceful

Ada Highfield   13:10

And I love walking around new places on my own

Stuart Parkes   **13:12**

I'm not wasting any time with you getting lost

Ada Highfield   **13:15**

Tell me you're excited

Stuart Parkes   **13:16**

I'm excited

Ada Highfield   **13:17**

OK me too

Ada Highfield   **13:18**

What if I kiss you at the train station like in a movie

Stuart Parkes   **13:19**

What if I let you

Ada Highfield   **13:20**

Thursday is 4 days away, maybe you won't want me to by then

Stuart Parkes   **13:21**

I have to go back to work

Stuart Parkes   13:22

I will want you on Thursday

Stuart Parkes   13:28

I'm going now, don't panic on me

Ada Highfield   13:32

I won't

Ada Highfield   13:42

I can't believe I'm going to meet my imaginary friend

Ada Highfield   13:43

At 'Lime Street'

Ada Highfield   16:02

So Ringo's the guitar one right?

Stuart Parkes   17:06

Drums

Ada Highfield   17:21

Wow it's a good thing I'm going to Liverpool, I have so much to learn

Fifteen

On Tuesday night, only nine people came to the gig and Ada spent twelve of her forty-pound fee buying her and Steven bourbons afterwards, which they sipped moodily at the bar until Clem took pity on them and gave them refills for free.

'Oh shit I almost forgot,' Ada said, 'I won't be here the next two weeks.' Steven said, 'Are you trying to quit because of tonight? We've had smaller audiences!' and Ada said, 'I'm not quitting! I have to go to Florida.' Clem looked up from replacing a keg to say, 'I love Florida!' and this was so surprising that Ada and Steven waited for an explanation that didn't come. 'Right, well I've never been but my sister is giving birth there and the whole family is going for some reason.'

Clem leaned on the bar and looked at Steven and said, 'Wow, the sisterly love is dripping off this one.' Steven said, 'She's told me her sister is kind of a drama queen,' and he and Clem both laughed and Ada said, 'Yes ha ha, even more of a drama queen than me, I get it, my childhood trauma is hilarious.' Clem said, 'So what's wrong with this sister then?' and Ada said, 'Oh, Gabby just takes up so much, like … I don't know. Energy. My whole life it was like, will this make Gabby happy, will Gabby ruin this holiday … I don't know, it's just easier when we're on different continents. And now she's expecting me to drop everything and fly there to witness the blessed event even though I am fucking broke.'

Clem patted her hand and Steven said, 'Maybe I should cancel the gig until you're back,' and Ada said, 'Oh no, what would our thousands of fans do without us?' Clem said, 'You can't cancel, you're the only thing we have on the next two weeks,' and Ada said, 'Clem, honestly, that's ridiculous. This is a great venue in the middle of London! Book more shows!' And Clem looked actually annoyed, not Clem annoyed, and said, 'I am running a bar, I don't give a shit about the thea- tre.' Ada said, 'Maybe I could help?' and Clem said, 'Help me run the bar? You don't even want to work here,' and Ada felt, actually, a little told off. She was thinking about the telling-off, luxuriating in the minor shame, two days later as she jumped onto her train to Liverpool.

Mel had booked Ada a window seat and she staggered to it as the train pulled out of Euston. There was a man in a suit sitting in the aisle. She said 'hi' and tried to gesture with the hand holding her coffee cup but her backpack slipped down her shoulder and she spilled a little on her leg. The man stood up to let her in and she slid past him, backpack jamming her against the seat. She laughed in his direction but he gave no response. By the time she had settled down – backpack at her feet, tray table down with her coffee and her Pret Caesar chicken baguette on it, fanning her face – the man was gone. She was annoyed even though it meant she could put her bag on his seat. She hadn't spilled the coffee on him, after all. She hoped the train would be full and he'd be forced to come back and sit next to her but he never did. She looked at her baguette and remembered that she wasn't eating meat any more but then she figured that not eating the chicken that she had just bought would be even worse for the environment and she imagined Mel saying 'Oh for sure' and rolling her eyes.

When Ada had messaged Mel on Sunday panicking about losing Stuart and the price of the train, Mel had booked the ticket for her without even asking. That hadn't exactly been Ada's intention but she had known there was a chance Mel would do it. A likelihood, even. Ada had thanked her, over and over, and Mel had said, 'What's the point in doing this boring job if I can't help my best friend get laid in every city in England,' and Ada said, 'Your job isn't boring!' then, 'I have also been laid in at least two Scottish cities, please get your records in order.'

When she told Stuart on Sunday night how she'd got the ticket, he said he felt good, like that meant Mel was rooting for them to succeed. But as he was typing that, Mel was coming in their front door, home from her family visit, and gratefully accepting sardines on sourdough toast from Sadie.

'We ate your falafel last night but I replaced it today,' said Sadie and Mel said, 'You *replaced* something you ate? Can you stay forever?' and Ada called out, 'I can hear you! I replace stuff!' Mel popped her head around the living room door and said, 'Sure you do. I missed you!' and Ada asked how much jam her mother had forced on her this time. 'Four jars, all gooseberry,' and Sadie was excited because she'd never had a gooseberry before. Mel declared that they'd have dessert toast with jam after their main course toast with sardines and Sadie said, 'And then we can *toast* each other … with our glasses,' and Mel said, 'And you're a playwright?' So Ada wasn't sure, really, what Mel was rooting for but she didn't tell Stuart that.

They had been messaging constantly since Sunday night, more frenzied even than those first three weeks. On Monday

Stuart had sent her his number, said that Messenger was annoying him and Ada felt there was something formal about the switch to WhatsApp. Two apps both owned by the same company signifying totally different things – she wondered how she'd explain that to her parents.

They only talked about Sadie obliquely. Every night as Ada got ready for bed, Stuart would try to keep her on the line, telling her a new fact about giraffes that he'd learned from his zoology-studying coworker or asking her to describe the best brunch she'd ever eaten (she had been tempted to tell him about the shakshuka recipe she'd been perfecting but then she would be skirting around telling him that last Wednesday Sadie had woken up hungover and they'd eaten it together in the kitchen because Sadie agreed with her that only chilli could fix a hangover and— better, overall, not to mention it). They developed what they called their own personal shipping forecast, where they would predict what time the other would wake up in the morning and how they would feel and then whoever got closest won ten quid though it was unclear if the winnings would ever be collected.

The night before the train, Stuart predicted that Ada would wake up at 7 and be excited and she predicted that he'd wake up at 9 and be turned on and when they both woke up at 8:30 a little nauseous they called it a tie. Then she told him she wouldn't message him the rest of the day. 'it's like seeing the bride before the wedding', 'It's really not', 'oh come on be fun', 'wait are you planning on marrying me today', 'spoilers!' but she'd stuck to it and now she was settled into moulded plastic, racing through grey skies in a white summer dress, legs freshly shaved, feeling every second of her run through the train station in the sweat dripping down her back. She was wearing her Cons and the little socks underneath had slipped down so her left heel was starting to feel raw. She tugged the sock back up and then tried to settle, adrenaline making every movement feel aggressive.

After Saturday, Sadie and Ada had reverted to their usual pattern of not seeing each other outside the house and neither of them suggested another day out. Sadie was busy with meetings during the day and tickets to shows at night and Ada had two gigs and an afternoon repainting a black box theatre as a favour to a friend. They had sex twice in three days and otherwise barely touched, Ada choosing to have Mel braid her hair in front of the TV while Sadie did the dishes.

On Wednesday night Sadie had got home around eleven and found Ada sitting on the kitchen bench in her stage make-up and lacy black cocktail dress, legs tucked under her. She smiled then kept eating a roast beetroot and feta salad out of their big metal salad bowl. Sadie leaned over and said, 'Looks good,' and Ada speared a piece of beet-root on her fork, rolled it around the bowl collecting bits and dressing and then offered it to Sadie. After a pause, Sadie dragged it off the fork with her teeth and made a 'mmm' sound. Ada felt a chill, like she'd done something inappropriate, gone too far, even though that morning Sadie had gagged her with her own underwear to stop her waking Mel. She quickly withdrew the fork and went back to her salad while Sadie boiled the kettle for ginger tea. She held up another tea bag to Ada and Ada nodded so she got a second mug down and it worked so smoothly, they were becoming seamless in this house. Ada thought about Sadie's face as Ada had teased her with her wand and then Sadie's face as Ada had pushed it inside her and then

Sadie's face as she washed the toy and dried it and put it back in its box and then Sadie's face as she said, 'Shit I'm late,' and waved goodbye and slammed the door.

'I meant to say – I can't believe I forgot until now – I'm going away for the night tomorrow. Visiting a friend in Liverpool. Kind of last minute but, you know, I'm going to Florida on Saturday so this was my last chance to see him for a while.' Ada wanted Sadie to ask her more about this friend and why she needed to see him at all but Sadie said, 'That sounds nice. Liverpool is amazing. I did a two-week residency at the Everyman Theatre like five years ago and it was heaps of fun,' and Ada said, 'Oh cool, I've never been. I'm really looking forward to it,' and why didn't Sadie ask? Why didn't she ask why Ada was making her first-ever trip to Liverpool on a whim on a Thursday and who was this friend anyway and wasn't it time they were honest with each other and then they took their cups of ginger tea to their room and drank them while they undressed and moisturised and didn't talk at all.

Ada woke first the next morning and started packing, socks scattered around her looking for pairs. The bed shifted and then Sadie said, 'Good morning.' She sounded awkward, not like her at all, as she said, 'I've been thinking.' Ada looked up but couldn't quite see her, the angle was wrong, Sadie was still settled into the mattress and Ada was on the floor, naked, her butt pressing into the cold wood. She said 'OK' to the base of the bed.

Sadie went on. 'Is it going to be weird for me to stay here when you go to Florida? I love Mel and I'm … trying to be helpful around the place but … is it going to be weird?' Ada returned to her socks and said, 'It won't be weird at all. You'll get the bed to yourself and the room will be tidier but otherwise it's going to be the same. You're not like paying rent with sex if that's what you're worried about,' and Sadie laughed and said, 'No, it's just an unusual situation. I know you said I could stay as long as I wanted and my ticket back is in October so I've been thinking of that as when I leave here, I guess. But if that doesn't work for you at any time I want you to tell me.' Ada stood up to grab a skirt off the hanger and looked at Sadie and said everything was fine with her but they should keep checking in. Sadie made them vegemite and avocado toast for breakfast because she'd been gifted a loaf of homemade sourdough the day before and Ada commented that she seemed just like the kind of person who would be gifted sourdough. Sadie said, 'I feel like you're insulting me but I can't deny it, people love to give me bread.' And then Sadie went out for the day and Ada finished packing and that was where they were as Ada hurtled north.

As the stations ticked away, Ada became increasingly calm though she knew that made no sense. The flurry of the weeks of messaging and the anxiety of the silent days was all going to flatten out now, one way or another. She told herself that this would be a romantic story that they would tell together or a funny story that she'd tell alone. They might not have fun at all, though she doubted that would be the case. Ada was very good at being entertained by exactly the person she wished to be entertained by, a skill that had carried her cheerfully through endless Tinder dates with people she realised, afterwards, that she was desperately bored by. She didn't think Stuart would bore her, but if he did then he only had a day to do it and then she was gone – trains, planes and automobiles, as far away as she could get.

She thought about what they might have for dinner and realised she didn't know what he liked to cook but determined to devour whatever it was. Or maybe he'd take her to a favourite restaurant, somewhere in Chinatown or a pub with a perfect selection of pies. She considered where she'd take him if he were in London, what she'd want her choice to say to him about who she was and who she wanted him to be with her.

The train announced that they were approaching Liverpool Lime Street and Ada wondered, abstractly, if her life was about to change. She wanted to message Stuart and ask if his was about to change but she kept her pledge and stood up, unsticking her dress from her thighs. She pulled her purple zip-up hoodie from her bag, the only jumper she'd packed, and put it on, picked up her backpack and went to the exit.

When she stepped off the platform she headed to the turn-stiles and saw Stuart bouncing up and down on his toes on the other side. His hair was paler than she'd thought, a kind of nowhere brown, and he was wearing a self-consciously scruffy T-shirt that said 'Apples in Stereo' and nondescript jeans. He waved to her and her instinct was to turn and run, get back on her train or any train, it didn't matter which city she got off at, it just shouldn't have been this one. But she put her ticket into the gate and went through and walked straight to him and put her arms around him. He was so much taller than her, which she'd known because she'd asked, but she hadn't really known it until he bent slightly to hug her back. He smelled like salt but she couldn't name the kind.

Ada pulled away from him and looked up into his face and he looked away immediately.

'How was the train?' he said to his left shoulder and Ada felt a dip for just a moment then straightened up and touched his arm.

'Well, a rude man decided he didn't want to sit next to me so it was actually kind of delightful,' and Stuart turned away from her and said, 'I thought we could get some lunch before we go to the gallery.' He was scanning the concourse as though searching for someone else and his hands were furling and unfurling. He scratched his neck and for a moment Ada imagined him as a mangy dog. But what she said was, 'I ate on the train but I can always eat again.' He said, 'OK let's find a cafe,' and walked towards the exit leaving her to follow. She pulled out her phone to message Mel and tell her she was safe and saw that her mother had messaged the family WhatsApp group. She opened it and there was a picture of Gabby, lying sweaty on a stack of pillows, holding a red wrinkled baby.

Ada kept following Stuart as she stared. The message said, 'Look who decided to join us early! Orion Highfield Mathers, 5 pounds 9 ounces but strong and healthy. Thank god we got in last night, I guess he was waiting for us. Gabby will check in when she's had some rest. Love you.' Ada's first thought was, 'Is Highfield his middle name then? Or are they hyphenating?' and she felt ashamed because that wasn't her business really. She realised she was outside now, at the top of a huge bank of steps and she called, 'Stuart.' He was halfway down but he turned back, looked at her properly and saw whatever it was that was running over her face. He called out, 'Are you OK?' and she said, 'My sister had her baby and I'm ... very far away,' and she started to cry.

Stuart ran up the steps – he really was so tall, she thought – and he took her arm and sat them both down at the top. Teenagers sat nearby smoking pointedly and there was a busker singing 'Yesterday' at the bottom but the kind of busker who is selling CDs and has a proper amp. Stuart pulled her into his chest and she felt how sunken it was, all that stretched over him was skin and cotton and she put her hand up next to her face. Placed her palm face down and felt the trace of his nipple. He spoke nervously.

'I'm sorry that you weren't there but I'm glad that you're here,' and she pulled away slightly, ran her hand over her face and said, 'Me too.' She touched his cheek and held it until he kissed her and before she lost herself, she thought, 'That's better.'

Sixteen

From: Hank Mathers
To: Gabby Highfield, bcc: me

To our beloved family and friends,

Please welcome to the world Orion Highfield Mathers, our blessed baby boy. Orion arrived a little ahead of schedule, but as Gabby said, when have we ever done anything on a normal timetable? Our precious little guy was clearly ready to join the party and we're thrilled that he's here.

The labour was a rollercoaster for all of us but Gabby was a superhero and she and the baby are both now as strong and healthy as can be. Special thanks to Gabby's parents who have taken advantage of their jet lag and stayed up with me and Orion all night so Gab could get some rest! I couldn't ask for better in-laws and I hope one day we can eat dinner in a restaurant instead of a hospital cafeteria!

I have never been so full of love in my entire life as I am when I look at little Orion. I'm sure you'll all have questions about his name but try to save them until we see you in person – it's quite a story! We won't be receiving non-family visitors at the hospital but we'll let you all know when we get home so you can come and witness our tiny miracle for yourself. We're so grateful for everyone's prayers throughout this pregnancy and hope that you can keep our little family in your thoughts as we all learn how to be together.

Photos attached – please don't share them to Facebook (I'm talking to you, Mom) or any other social media site. We're trying to keep Orion's face and name offline as much as possible.

Love you all,

Hank (and Gabby and baby Orion)

Seventeen

After the kiss, Stuart's nerves disappeared but Ada realised his restlessness was a feature not a bug and folded it into her understanding of him. He was never still, always scratching at nothing, standing up when it made sense to sit and swiping at her clothes and her arms but never settling on them. She had heard that long bodies 'unfurled' but his unfolded instead, snapping open and closed with every movement.

As they sat on the steps, Ada talked about Gabby and asked Stuart why she felt like she loved Orion already.

'Because he's a piece of your sister and you love her,' he said and she didn't correct him because maybe she did love her sister after all. She knew she wanted desperately to hold this baby and what sense would that make if she didn't love Gabby? So maybe Stuart was right.

'I don't really get the name choice,' she said and Stuart had an idea and stood up. He started walking down the stairs. He reached back to grab her but didn't hold her hand, instead dragging her by the wrist, down down down, and then rounding her up to keep her walking in the right direction. Pacing around her, nudging her this way and that, kissing her on the top of the head when they stopped at a traffic light, then pushing pushing pushing. He was suddenly talking a lot, pointing out landmarks but not slowing to let her see them, and listing places they could eat for dinner without offering much description of the food.

Liverpool was moving around Ada and she couldn't determine yet if the greyness of the buildings was beautiful or sad. It had the same crowded streets and stray grime as every other British city but there was a freshness on the wind that felt different. She guessed it was the air blowing off the water and felt a twist of affection for this new place with a harbour, just like her home. She hoped they could go and see it and when she said that to Stuart he said distractedly, 'The harbour? Yeah later, I want to check something first,' and she allowed herself to be shepherded further along. He stopped abruptly on a corner and she held on to his arm, trying to make herself small to avoid the pedestrian crush.

'Sorry, are you OK? Am I going too fast? I just realised you have no idea where we are,' and he said this to her with real embarrassment in his voice. Ada couldn't have that so she said, 'I'm totally fine. Not knowing where I am is exciting,' and she kissed him on that corner with a street pole pressed against her back and a ticking traffic light letting her know they were missing their crossing. Later Ada would say to Stuart, 'You know that noise at traffic lights to let blind people know to cross? That was invented in Australia,' and he'd say, 'I have no idea what you're talking about, weirdo,' and she'd wonder if she'd heard it at all.

Eventually they stopped in front of a massive, beautiful stone building, the kind that would have floored her before she spent two years drifting around Britain looking at massive, beautiful stone buildings.

'What is this place?' Ada asked and Stuart said, 'It's the library. We're going in but I wanted you to take in this view first.' Ada didn't know what he expected of her but it was definitely something so she said, 'It's great. Very grand?' Stuart let out a grunt of a laugh and said, 'OK, good, wait until you see inside.'

Ada had the same feeling she'd had as a child when a kindly friend of her parents would buy her a puzzle for Christmas. She was a smart kid and did well at school and it only followed that she would enjoy puzzles. But what she really enjoyed was experimenting with lipstick and hanging upside down on monkey bars and *Sweet Valley High* and getting dunked under waves and sneaking downstairs to watch *Buffy* when her parents had gone to bed. As an adult, every man she dated insisted on buying her novels or, if they were feeling particularly superior, biographies of Eleanor Roosevelt. The older ones planned first dates to cafe bookshops and the younger ones read to her from Plath and expected her to relate in ways they never could.

Ada assumed Stuart was on the same track here. Sexily bookish young women were wet as hell for dark musty rooms full of first editions and creaking chairs. Ada couldn't remember the last book she'd finished. It might have been the Ali Smith one that Mel had packed for her that day in July when they went to Cornwall and lay stubbornly on the beach together despite the temperature never quite hitting twenty. On the late-night drive home, Mel said, 'What an awful day,' and Ada laughed and laughed. The next week she got a yeast infection that she swore was from sitting in her damp swimmers on the rock-strewn shore and she blamed the discomfort on 'this pathetic damp country', which Mel took pretty well. Actually, she didn't think she had finished her book that day because she'd decided to learn how to cartwheel again and made Mel watch as she fell over and over, bruising her hands and knees. But here she was in the shadow of a library with an eager artistic boy waiting for her to react.

Still, when they went inside, Ada was impressed. She had assumed that it would be 'lovingly restored' as every building in England seemed to be. But instead the entrance was filled with digital kiosks and noise. Ada looked up and saw suspended metal paths leading back and forth to different floors, spiralling above her like the inside of a shell. She said to Stuart, 'Wow, this is not what I expected,' and he said, 'I know, no one expects it.' She said, 'It feels so … modern,' and he said, 'Liverpool is a very modern city,' and no one in the UK ever bragged that their city felt new so she liked Stuart for doing so. He took her hand again and said, 'I didn't tell you this, but like a week into us messaging our wifi went out at home and none of us knew who to call to fix it and our landlord was being useless. I didn't want to use up my data so I would come here and hang out most of the day using the wifi, applying for jobs and messaging you. I don't know why I didn't tell you. I guess I figured "aspiring artist who spends his days pining in a library" might seem … too much.'

This was the longest Stuart had talked to her while making eye contact and she felt very briefly appalled. She imagined him sitting in this public building waiting on her while she lived her life and she was embarrassed for them both. But she had got on a train to Liverpool so who was she to judge? She took a deep breath and chose romance instead.

'You are too much but that's OK,' and he grinned and said, 'Come on, we're here on a mission.'

They turned down one of the twisty halls and emerged in a round wooden room covered in books and low lighting and spiralled staircases. It looked much more like the boring libraries of Ada's imagination but she forgave that because it appeared in the middle of a modern building.

'This is the reading room, it's very famous,' he said. It was like finding Narnia out the back of a mall and she said that to Stuart, who said, 'I've only ever been in a mall in Australia,' and then he started to wind his way up a flight of stairs.

They reached the upper level of bookshelves, still looking out on the central space filled with readers and writers. Stuart was walking with purpose and stopped in front of a row of leather-bound books. He ran his finger along and pulled out a heavy one, the text on the cover spun in gold. Ada leaned over to see the title but he pulled it away from her. 'Not yet, let me find it first.' He flipped through the pages, not looking up, and Ada had a moment to feel the incongruity of her presence in this warm golden room with this fidgety length of man. 'Here,' he said and she looked.

Stuart was holding the book open and she saw, for a moment, just columns of small print. A little more focus and she realised she was looking at names.

'Is this … a baby name book? And … why?'

Stuart impatiently pointed to a passage halfway down. She read.

' "Orion. Rising in the sky or dawning. The mighty hunter and son of Poseidon. A bright, well-known constellation that lies on the celestial equator." ' Stuart dropped down to the floor, still holding the book, rapidly tucking his legs beneath him and leaning against the shelves. Ada followed him down and leaned in to continue scanning the page then she said, without looking up, 'How did you know this book was here? Do you secretly have a lot of babies that need names?'

There was silence and then Stuart said, 'It's because I looked for you in here.' He flipped the pages back and the book fell open to a list of 'A' names as though it had been bookmarked. 'Ada,' he said, tracing the words with one finger. '"Ada from the Germanic 'Adel' meaning nobility."' Ada put her hands over his and brought it to her heart. He kept his eyes on the page. '"Or from the Hebrew ... adornment."'

'Well,' she said, 'let's go with the Germans on this one.' The light in the room turned suddenly from yellow to blue and Ada looked up as fat drops of rain started to hit the round skylight in the centre of the ceiling. 'Looks like we're trapped here,' she said, as the outline of Stuart's fingers tattooed themselves on her chest and then he kissed her.

When he leaned back, she looked at the book and said, 'Loving Gabby is complicated, but loving a baby I've never even met is easy. Isn't that kind of fucked up?' And Stuart said, 'Why is it complicated to love your sister?' Ada flipped a few more pages of the book, not taking it in, and felt a little embarrassed about criticising someone who had just given birth. But not embarrassed enough to refrain.

'OK, so one Christmas when she was like fourteen, I think, so I was ten or eleven, she got a new bike and she was like really happy about it. She had a kid bike but this was a full adult bike and she liked being alone and doing stuff alone and I guess this made that easier. So it was a nice thing for my parents to do for her. But then after lunch when we were supposed to be cleaning up – OK so she usually didn't clean up anyway, but I thought maybe she would on Christmas – anyway, she got mad at my dad for ... I can't remember. It was nothing, nothing I would ever even think about getting mad at. And she got on her bike and cycled away. She was gone until like ten at night and we spent a big bit of the afternoon calling people, trying not to make it obvious that Gabby had fucked up our day but also trying to find out if she was, like, there and … she came home in the end and she didn't get in trouble really. But then I never got a bike for Christmas after that.' Stuart had watched her talk the whole time and she felt something like pathetic and had a mad brief instinct that she should unzip his trousers, create a diversion. But instead she said, 'That sounds so fucking stupid,' and Stuart said, 'No, she sounds like kind of a mad bint, honestly. No wonder you hated her. But maybe the baby will chill her out.' And Ada cringed at the word 'hate' but she didn't correct him.

They stayed on the floor for some time and turned the pages of the book, pointing out the names of people they knew and names they loved and hated. Ada checked her phone at one point for an update from her mother but found she had no reception and chose not to connect to the wifi. After a while she said to Stuart, 'I feel bad for reacting so weirdly to the baby being born and to his name and everything. Did you think I was nuts?' She asked this as though the incident had been several years ago and miles away rather than that same day and around the corner. But it felt distant to her because that had been before they kissed and more importantly it had been before he had showed her that he thought of her a lot in this library. A message over borrowed wifi, a mention of her name in text.

Stuart said, 'I thought you were nuts from the first time I saw you on stage and you were telling the woman in the front row to leave her husband and run away with you – do you remember?'

Ada didn't really but she always found it safer to flirt with straight women in the crowd than straight men, though safest of all was gay men.

'I sort of do?' she said but Stuart was still talking.

'Everything you've done since has been crazier than the last – you messaged me back and then you decided you liked me and then you agreed to come to Liverpool and then you cried on the steps and then you kissed me. Does any of that sound sane to you?'

Ada considered how little this list took into account Stuart's actions in messaging her in the first place but she moved past it and started to sing under her breath, '"Does that make me crazy, does that make me craaaaazy,"' and on the second crazy she raised her voice slightly and Stuart clamped his hand over her mouth. He was laughing until she touched the tip of her tongue to the centre of his palm and he released a deep, bass sigh. He removed his hand and they breathed at each other. Ada broke first.

'Is there still time to go to the exhibition at the Tate today?' Stuart looked past her and she realised he was checking a clock on the wall. His eyes went straight to it, she noted.

'We can get there for an hour or so if we leave now. That's probably not enough time.'

Ada stood up. 'Can you take me to the water then?' She looked up through the skylight to confirm that the rain had stopped and saw it was clear, a brighter grey.

Stuart walked more slowly this time and tried to hold her hand but he couldn't settle there. He shifted to gripping her wrist, then her waist, then bunching up the base of her hoodie and holding on. He slipped his hand into her pocket then withdrew it like he'd touched something sharp, and at one point he laced his fingers through the split ends of her hair and she wondered if he'd pull. But he took them out again and as the air cooled around them, he pulled her towards him in a sideways tackle of a hug that reminded her of her father.

The streets blurred by mostly without colour, when a flash of red up ahead pulled Ada out of her head. As they got closer, she realised she was looking at Chinatown, not her Chinatown but a Chinatown nonetheless and she asked Stuart about it. He glanced over and said, 'Yeah, we have lots of good food here,' but that wasn't what Ada wanted. She wanted to talk about how there were Chinatowns all over the world, how she'd lined up with her friends on weekends in Sydney to buy Morning Glory notebooks and Emperor's puff rolls. How she'd trawled through London's Chinatown until she found soup dumplings that felt like home and how strange it was for someone who wasn't Chinese and who'd never been to China to seek comfort in their food and places. But Stuart wasn't stopping and she didn't know how to slow him down. He kept walking and on the corner, he popped into an off-licence and she followed him and thought about telling her sister about the beautiful Chinese arch, like and unlike their own.

There was a brief back and forth about whether to get red or white wine. Ada hadn't planned to drink until later but when she said that Stuart thought she was objecting to the choice of red so got a bottle of white too. Ada said, 'Picking the second cheapest bottle, a classic move, I respect it,' and Stuart said, 'What?' and it became horribly frozen between them. Then Stuart said, 'Are you hungry?' and she was so he got two packets of crisps and Ada took them cheerfully, hoping this wasn't dinner. Then Stuart asked if she wanted to split the cost now or figure it out later and she felt fifteen again as the woman behind the counter observed her sympathetically. She paid it all and waved him off when he tried to give her cash and they walked out of the shop, him first, her bumping gently against the swaying rack of Haribo by the door.

There was no ease between them. Ada could put most

people at ease, and that was usually enough to make her feel at ease as well, but she felt that comfort with Stuart was out of reach. He was walking ahead of her again, on, quickly, towards the water, and she trailed behind, apologising to the woman on her phone who Stuart had banged into as he passed. She thought of Sadie and then she didn't.

Stuart stopped abruptly and turned to face her, his palms held out, keeping her slightly back.

'So here it is. Is it everything you dreamed?' and Ada looked around him at the harbour. It was flat and unbothered. Ada realised from the colour of the water that the sky must have darkened and now that she was standing still she felt chilly in her light hoodie. Liverpool summer didn't extend to dusk, she supposed, but she decided to see beauty in the grey. She walked closer to the water and then sat on the concrete edge, her feet dangling. Stuart approached her circuitously, weaving around pylons, seemingly reluctant.

'Come sit!' Ada said, as though she was hosting, and so he did.

Stuart took out the bottles of wine, handed her the white and opened the red. Ada paused to see if there were any cups on this seaside picnic, but when Stuart swigged from his bottle, she followed suit. Stuart opened the crisps and they passed the bags back and forth and Ada distantly remembered her restaurant hopes and felt foolish. She had come to Liverpool to meet him on his level and that was here, by the water, greasy fingers and shared bottles. What else could she need or want from a young artist than to wipe away the crumbs and watch the sky change around them?

They spoke fragilely for a few minutes until Ada asked about his coworker who kept giving his number to customers. They'd mocked this coworker relentlessly in their chats and slipped easily back in. It was as though they'd forgotten their shared history and needed it dragged off their phones into the conversation. Things flowed and the street lights popped on around them and the wine helped.

Stuart drank, then put the bottle down and turned to Ada.

'This feels like ... like I'm meeting a dream. Because I think I slightly ... because I misremembered you. You're how I imagined but you're also ... this is weird but I imagined your messages in your voice so much and you don't sound the way you did.'

Ada clenched her hands and felt she was losing something. 'I guess I use a different voice on stage?' and Stuart said, 'Maybe that's it,' and looked away from her. She needed something from him so she touched his hand and said, 'What?' They were silent and the seagulls overhead screamed. Stuart said, 'I painted you. From memory. And now ... I'm worried I did a shit job.' Ada moved her hand to his hip and pulled slightly. 'Then you'll have to paint me again.'

Stuart jerked towards her, his fingers suddenly on her thigh, and Ada felt desperately grateful. He dug his nails into her skin and she went cold all over. He was still, more still than she knew he could be. Only his eyes moved, from his hand on her thigh up her body to her throat where he stopped. 'I can't believe you're here,' he said to her goosebumped neck, and she said, 'I'm sorry I'm not how you remembered,' and he didn't look up as he said, 'You're better.' And she reached down and pushed his nails in deeper until he kissed her because he had nowhere else to go.

Eighteen

21/09/2017

Melanie Baker   **12:15**

SO HOW IS IT, HOW IS HE, TELL ME EVERYTHING

Melanie Baker   **12:21**

Also not to be too much of a mum but you said you'd message as soon as you got in and you haven't so please check in

Melanie Baker   **12:45**

Ada come on

Melanie Baker   **12:46**

Are you alive?

Melanie Baker   **13:03**

Look I know it's ACAB but if you don't get back to me in the next half hour I will call the Liverpool police

Melanie Baker   13:27

Seriously, Ada! I paid for your train ticket! Please assure me I have not trafficked you!

Ada Highfield   13:33

I'M ALIVE

Ada Highfield   13:35

Sorry mum

Melanie Baker   13:37

Thank god. Everything OK?

Ada Highfield   13:41

All OK! Gabby had her baby! He's early but healthy apparently, he's called Orion

Melanie Baker   13:44

Like the stars??????? That's great though

Melanie Baker   13:47

But how are things with Stuart

Melanie Baker   13:58

Helloooooooo

Melanie Baker 14:02

You're gone again aren't you, OK have fun you crazy kids

Ada Highfield 19:17

He's just gone to find somewhere to pee. We're down at the harbour and I think I love him

Melanie Baker 19:19

OK thanks for the update babe, use a condom

Ada Highfield 19:20

Mel I'm serious

Melanie Baker 19:28

OK love, I'm happy for you then

Nineteen

Ada woke up and it was dark and she became aware of a soft sound off to her left. She rolled and saw the shape of a laptop, open but blank, its battery humming insistently. She didn't know where she was so she raised herself on to her elbows and saw Stuart's head at the other end of the bed. It seemed they were sleeping top and tail and before Ada could consider this further, she became alarmingly aware that she needed to pee. She eased herself sideways and stood in the room, trying to orient herself enough to find a door. As she spun slowly, her body told her she was naked and so she got on her hands and knees and crawled until she found her sundress. She pulled it on without a bra or underwear and tiptoed to a wall. She ran her hand along it until she found a door and after a little more exploration she hit the knob, turned and eased herself into the hallway.

The hallway was dark too but as Ada creeped unsteadily down it, she could hear a laugh track issuing from one of the rooms. A vague memory emerged of a housemate popping his head out to say hello when they'd got home – Tom? Was it Tom or did she just think every white British guy was called Tom? – and then disappearing again with an oven pizza and some beers.

Ada reached a door tucked under the stairs and pulled it open, finding a cupboard filled with the miscellany she associated with student living. An iron attached to nothing, upside down. Empty boxes, partially crushed so unusable but also unrecycled. Wrapping paper spotted with damp. Chargers on cables on cords. Ada realised this was the Harry Potter cupboard Stuart had joked about in a message to her weeks ago, saying she could move in there and cast spells on his housemates. She then pretended she'd never read Harry Potter, claiming it never came out in Australia. Stuart had then spent a full day attempting to explain the plot to her before she folded and said there were actually two copies of each book in her parents' house because she and Gabby wouldn't share. They lost part of the next day to debating whether they could ever read the books again, what with the issue of the author, before Ada guiltily admitted she and Mel had watched the movies one weekend when they both had throat infections. 'They mostly hold up,' she'd said, 'and did you know Dean Thomas grew up hot?'

Ada closed the door to the cupboard and continued her hallway exploration, taking in the mould creeping down the walls in a foggy sort of spread. She pulled open another door and there was a toilet and sink, grim in the darkness and grimmer still in the buzzing light after she pulled the switch. Ada closed the door behind her, found no lock and lowered herself onto the slick, damp seat, hiking her dress up with her right hand while gripping the door handle with her left. She pissed and grinned.

Ada picked through her memory to figure out how she'd ended up lying at the wrong end of the bed. They had started by the water. Stuart had pulled her up and she'd thought they were walking home but they only made it a few feet. She was pressed against the closed shutter door of a Food and Wine when Stuart had surprised her by very quickly pushing his hand under her dress, urgent like a teenager who didn't have a private room to go to. He had pulled back, seeming equally surprised at himself, and she had grabbed his hand and put it back, right at the top of the inside of her thigh. He kept it there while he kissed her and she felt his sweat or hers run between his fingers. He groaned every time her body shifted and she responded by angling herself until the tips of his fingers were grazing the damp outside of her cotton underwear. She always wore plain cotton on a first date, a lack of artifice that was all artifice.

Stuart made a fist and his knuckles grazed her as she rocked over him. Within a minute she was gasping into his mouth but she found, as she often did, that this moment disappeared quickly, leaving her desperate to reach it again. But Stuart pulled back and stared at her, in one light looking horrified and in another amazed. He lifted his hand close to his face and asked, 'Did what … I think happened … I mean,' and she said yes and pulled him to her, wanting to climb him, to keep climbing, scale him like a cliff face, and he said flatly, 'Well, wow, I mean good for me.' Then he stared at her, took her hand and laid it on him and she felt the disconnect again between his body and his disinterested words and he asked if they could actually go home now.

The walk took half an hour and they each finished their bottles of wine, barely touching and only talking when Stuart gave directions. Ada considered his awkwardness, which she knew she could take away with her body, but that he held between them all the same. Her comfort in her body startled partners and she had noticed it sometimes had this effect, of drawing them further into themselves, an equal yet opposite blah blah, whatever the science thing was.

She remembered a man she met when she was temping at a construction company who worked as their in-house lawyer and spent five nights a week at the gym and cringed when Ada stepped on his shirt which had landed on the floor. When they were done – lights off – he put on a full set of pyjamas before going to sleep, and when he woke to find her naked in bed he asked if she'd been that way all night. The only partner she'd had who matched her was a yoga teacher she spent a weekend with in Essex after opening Tinder on the Central line. They revelled in their shared nakedness but Belle didn't drink and Ada felt certain she'd start smoking just to spite her if they stayed together, so the weekend was enough.

When they reached Stuart's house – the same kind of house as every other on the street but, Ada thought, kind of romantically worse – he unlocked the door and told her the bathroom was upstairs. It was clean and well stocked with shampoos and shaving caddies and now that Ada was sitting in this downstairs buzzing toilet cell she thought it was considerate of Stuart to have sent her to the other one first. Ada had looked at herself in the mirror, fuzzy at the edges but sharp around the eyes and felt ready.

She'd come back downstairs and found Stuart grabbing glasses from the kitchen, chatting to Tom, who waved his hand at her in a vague sort of way but who she felt watch her as they left the room. They went into Stuart's bedroom then and he turned on the fairy lights that were strung over his mantlepiece and around his curtain rod and then also the lamp with the greying shade next to his bed. 'Very seductive lighting set-up,' she said and he looked uncomfortable and said, 'The overhead light blew and it has some weird bulb situation so only the landlord can replace it but fucked if we can get him to answer an email.' Ada was at risk of feeling very silly and said, 'Oh, I bet you use that landlord line on all the girls,' and she sat on the bed while Stuart stood, hovering, in the middle of the room before deciding it was OK to sit next to her.

Ada reached for him and he jumped up again, opening his laptop on the other side of the room. 'Will you pour us a whisky?' he asked without turning around and Ada picked up the bottle on his bedside table, noted its presence, wondered if it always lived there or was a concession to her visit. She free-poured into their tumblers, took one and waited. Music started to play softly from the laptop and he came back to her, picked up his glass and sat on the bed and looked at nothing in particular. Ada was on the verge of something – screaming, climbing out a window – when she realised the song that was playing.

'This is that song … this is the song you said I reminded you of,' and Stuart said, 'I've been listening to it every day,' and the laptop sang about a woman who can't stop leaving and Ada swallowed the last of her whisky and laid Stuart down. She hummed the music as she unbuttoned his fly, staring at his face while he looked at her and away and at her again. She took her time to touch him and watched his whole body clench with anticipation. She pulled down his jeans and then his underwear and then she looked at him and he looked at her looking at him and she felt a pass of melancholy because they would never quite have this moment again, these seconds before. The track changed to 'One Crowded Hour', another Australian song, and she realised he'd made a playlist for her, had crafted it out of the songs of her teenage years, and she leaned down and put her mouth on him at last.

Ada remembered the end, remembered how he had touched her hair while steadying his breath and not rushed to bring her up to him. She remembered leaning back so she was facing him and then, she didn't remember this bit, but then she must have gone straight to sleep. And that is how she had come to wake, desperate to pee, with her head in the wrong spot and his feet by her ears. She considered that he must have made the choice to stay that way rather than sleep at the wrong end of the bed with her and wondered if he was compulsive. She wiped and flushed and ran her hands under the water, noted the lack of soap but wasn't concerned by it.

When she stepped back into the hallway, Ada heard the front door open and two voices coming in and considered whether this was the right time to meet more Toms. The two men rounded the corner and looked briefly so similar to Ada that she wondered if they were twins then she realised they simply had the same short hair and particular northern paleness that often confused her senses. They stopped and were suddenly silent until one stepped forward and said, 'All right, love, sorry, are we in your way,' and Ada laughed and said, 'Yes, please step aside, I have somewhere to be.' She realised she was still very drunk but said, 'I'm Ada,' and the quieter one nudged the first one and said, 'Stuart's girl,' and they introduced themselves and Ada didn't take in either name. There was an awkward shuffling and some nice to meet yous and she eventually passed them and slipped back into Stuart's room where he was snoring in a staccato way.

Ada dropped her dress back to the floor and considered Stuart's back, which had the same kind of paleness as his flatmate's and the slightly rounded spine of the reluctantly tall.

It was beautiful and as she looked Stuart whined a little and scratched his side in his sleep, looking again like a mangy dog, this time dreaming of a rabbit. He looked malnourished, full of need, though he was probably stronger than her. He was so like the exact idea she had of an English artist that it was like she had cast him. She climbed into bed next to her sniffling stray and as she wrapped herself around him, he shook awake. 'It's Ada,' she said, and he shuddered a little then whispered, 'You're in my bed,' and then, 'Stay.' They both went back to sleep.

When Ada woke, his pale grey curtain was lit up from the outside and she was in the exact same position, wrapped around a sleeping Stuart, their bodies damply clinging. She ran her hand down Stuart's chest, feeling the dent in the middle, and he murmured and moved back against her. She tapped out a rhythm lightly, wanting him to wake, and a growl emerged that she could feel under her hand. She didn't know if he'd meant to make that sound or if something stirred in his ribs but she tapped at him again. All at once he turned to her, and a moment later, he was on top of her and she was surprised to see he hadn't put his underwear back on last night; she hadn't figured him for the type.

He reached over her head to the drawer in his bedside table and his armpit dangled above her nose. She breathed him in, knew from experience that this scent would become a stink if they were together long enough, considered the science of partners growing to resist each other's smell. He sat back, eased himself off her briefly and she saw he was holding a condom. He looked at her, a question, and she answered 'hurry' because she was desperate for his weight. He pulled the condom on and climbed back on top of her and without guidance they locked together and even though she had been waiting for it the sensation was a shock. They moved in a frenzy and after seconds or minutes – some time had passed – she took his right hand in hers and pressed it between them so he was rubbing her as he moved. The speed with which she came drove him somewhere else and he bent to her neck and bit down as he came too, digging his way into every part of her at once. He gave her everything. She took it all.

'I'm sorry,' he said to her throat and she could feel him breaking it, the heavy code of their bodies; he was trying to break it way too soon. He was drifting out of his body again and she stroked his hair and said, 'Don't say sorry to someone who you just fucked unless you fucked them wrong,' and he said, 'You actually talk like that?' and she said, 'I actually do.' And then he looked up at her and smiled.

'So you liked the playlist then?' and Ada said, 'Yes, the Aussie music knowledge is deep.' Stuart said, 'Months of bar work in Brunswick will do that,' and Ada said, 'So were you in Melbourne the whole time you were there?' And Stuart shrugged a little, said 'mostly,' and it occurred to Ada then that he never wanted to talk about his time in Australia. She wondered if he'd gone with a girlfriend or if he'd had one out there. Maybe she reminded him of her. Maybe that's all this was. But then he took the end of her hair and chewed it for a moment, the animal in him coming out, and she pitied whatever girl he'd left in his past.

'Can I show you something?' he asked and she knew this was the bit where they looked at his art. With musicians it's better to see them at a gig first because then you avoid the moment where you're sitting on their bedroom floor and they bring out a guitar – or worse, when they do it at a party. Actors don't usually subject you to monologues unless they are preparing for an audition, but that does mean you have to go to a play, and the secret, Ada had realised, was that a lot of plays were bad. Poets were the worst because poetry could happen anywhere, anytime. You could be blindsided by a poet. She'd only dated one dancer and she hadn't seemed interested in making Ada watch her dance, so Ada bought a ticket to Sadler's Wells and watched her glide and flip across the stage, then waited at the stage door after, and the dancer seemed annoyed that she'd come and didn't message her again.

So Ada was prepared for this bit and as Stuart eased off her, put on a pale green, stained dressing gown and opened a case on his floor, she sat up and waited. He pulled out a canvas which had been stored carelessly, she thought, and he said, 'These aren't ... these aren't my finished things, they live at my parents' place because this house is a shithole,' and Ada said, 'Oh come on, some of this mould is artisanal,' and he didn't respond because he was looking at the canvas. He carried it to the bed and lay it before her then said, 'I'm going to make coffee,' and walked straight out the door. And on the bed in front of Ada was a painting of Gabby floating in the sea but then she looked again and saw that it was her.

Twenty

22/09/2017

Sadie Ali   **10:00**

Hey you're back from Liverpool in time for dinner right? Thought I'd cook a going away dinner before your Floridian jaunt

Ada Highfield   **11:48**

Sorry just got this! Yes I reckon I'll be home by like 7? But don't go to any trouble

Sadie Ali   **11:50**

No trouble! Mel says she's in too and she'll pick up drinks

Ada Highfield   **11:51**

Ah you two are the best, what should I bring

Sadie Ali   **11:53**

Nothing! You eat eggplant right?

Ada Highfield   11:53

Fuck yeah I do

Ada Highfield   11:55

But it's aubergine darling, eggplant, so gauche, so colonial

Sadie Ali   11:56

Call me colonial one more time, didn't your family come out with the bloody convicts

Ada Highfield   11:58

Yes hardened bread stealers, the lot of them. Eggplant sounds great!

Sadie Ali   12:02

It's capers you hate right?

Sadie Ali   12:03

I'm menu planning

Ada Highfield   12:56

Oh no I missed this message

Ada Highfield   12:57

Yes capers are satan

Ada Highfield 12:58

Please no capers

Sadie Ali 13:01

Nothing but capers, got it, a caper fiesta

Sadie Ali 13:14

OK, have a good trip back, see you at dinner!

Ada Highfield 15:48

Yep I'm on the train now! Can't wait to puke capers all over you!

Ada Highfield 15:56

OK fine I'll puke on Mel instead

Ada Highfield 18:03

Pulling into Kings X home soon!

Twenty-one

Stuart came back with the coffee and said, 'Sorry, we only have filter and there's no milk,' and Ada pointed at the painting and said, 'She seems nice.' Stuart handed the mug over and got back on the bed. 'I painted it when we weren't talking, I hope it's OK,' and she said, 'I did not give you permission to make an art of me!' He looked up and said, 'Fuck, I thought you were serious for a second,' and she said, 'Why would god give me great tits if not to be painted,' and he said, 'You're kind of ruining the moment,' and she said, 'Sorry I'm a shitty muse.' Then she asked, 'Why didn't you paint it when we first started talking?' He drank his coffee then said, 'I wouldn't have had time, I was messaging you like every five minutes.' She said, 'And job hunting I guess,' and he said, 'Would you believe that took less time than thinking of interesting things to tell you?'

He was staring at the picture now so she stared at it too and saw the figure's dark hair winding under the surface and wondered at the broken-doll quality of the legs, knees not pointing quite the way knees do. She thought about asking him but what if he just wasn't good at painting knees and she embarrassed him? She put the picture aside and sorted through the canvases below it, mostly of objects around the house and one she recognised as a room at the library. They were good, she thought, kind of academic, like exercises more than pieces.

She looked up and saw him watching her, so she said quickly, 'Oh, the boy's actually good at this art thing then.' And he said, 'Why wouldn't I be?' and there was no way of answering that question without giving him a full history of her romantic partners and, probably, the western world. So she said, 'Have you painted me again?' and he said no and she said, 'Do you think you will?' and he said, 'I don't do people, much.'

And she hated that answer, so she put her mug gently on the bedside table then did the same with his. And she picked up the canvas and placed it on the floor and then she crawled across the bed to where he was sitting, his back against the wall. She opened his filthy green dressing down and climbed inside it, onto his lap. Her breasts were in his face and then she dipped low and kissed him. He tasted like the coffee she tasted like and there was no space between them at all. The kiss was long and then it was short and then they were simply pinned together, his face in her breasts again. He said into her chest, 'Thank you ... for being here,' and she didn't want to cry. So she climbed off him and started getting dressed. And he didn't ask why but he did look annoyed as she pulled on her bra and then her black tank top with the neckline she privately considered miraculous.

'Don't you want to shower?' he asked as she shook out the pink paisley midi skirt that she probably should have hung up. 'No, I'm good, I don't want to lose the whole day!' and so he got off the bed and started to dress too, pulling on the same jeans from the day before but taking a fresh, wrinkled T-shirt out of his top drawer. Ada pushed her few remaining items back into her backpack, then said, 'OK, I'll just pee and we can go,' and he said, 'Go where?' and she said, 'I don't know, this is your city!' When he didn't respond, she said, 'Ooh, I want to see where the Beatles live,' and he said 'lived' and she said, 'OK, where they lived,' and he said, 'They didn't all have like a big house together, you know,' and she said, 'See, this is exactly the local knowledge I need. Back in a minute.' She went to the cell bathroom and waved goodbye to one of the housemates in the kitchen and then they were back outside in the watery sun, too warm for her jumper while they were moving and then freezing cold the minute they stood still.

Stuart waved down a bus and as it was pulling up, she said, 'How do you pay for the bus here?' He looked at her holding up a card and said, 'It's cash only.'

'Well, I don't have cash,' and he sighed deeply and said, 'I can get your ticket,' and they got on together. After he had bought the tickets, they sat down and she said, 'Who carries *cash* any more,' and he said, 'Who doesn't,' and she thought about explaining that she was joking, that she actually often had cash because she got paid with it for most gigs. But then he put his head on her shoulder for a moment, which took a lot of effort because his neck was too long, and so she tried silence for the rest of the journey.

When they got off the bus, Stuart took her hand and lead her down a side street and then another and he said, 'Here we are!' She looked at the grimy laneway which was inexplicably full of people and said, 'This is ...' and he pointed at a sign that said the Cavern Club. She looked at it and said, 'Maybe too early for shots,' and he sighed again and let go of her hand and shifted between his feet.

'The Cavern ... where the Beatles were like ... discovered. Ring any bells?' and Ada said, 'Seems like a weird place to live,' and he said, 'Ha ha, so do you want to go inside?' She held out her hand for him to take again. They went into the darkness, her eyes adjusting slowly as Stuart headed down a winding flight of stairs.

Ada sniffed the air and said, 'It does have that authentic piss smell,' and Stuart said, 'Well, you know, teenage girls used to piss themselves when they saw Paul.' Ada sniffed again, performatively this time, and said, 'So do you think they hire teenage girls to come in here occasionally to piss, you know, keep things fresh?' Stuart still didn't laugh but said, 'Doubt they'd be pissing themselves over Paul these days,' and Ada said, 'Yeah, isn't he dead?' Stuart said, 'I really don't know if you're joking or not,' and she said, 'And you never will,' then she tracked through her brain trying to remember which one was the dead one. When they got to the bottom, they found a dank bar covered in memorabilia and they walked around in silence, looking at the gold records on the walls, the framed guitars. Stuart said, 'I haven't been in here in years, it's only really for tourists now,' and Ada said, 'Thank you for bringing me.' After a while Stuart headed to the exit then said, 'Sorry, are you ready to go?' and she said, 'Oh sure,' and they headed out. When they neared the top, he said, 'If you wanted teenage girl piss these days I reckon you'd do well to follow that Harry Styles around,' and she said, '"That Harry Styles", OK grandpa,' and he said, 'You're one to talk, old lady,' and then he was kissing her right there in the street surrounded by boomers taking photos of each other next to the glowing red sign.

Ada thought about suggesting food – she hadn't eaten since those crisps. She realised she had wine and coffee rolling round her system with nowhere to go, but it was so good to be kissing again and she didn't want to slow them down. They turned a corner and Stuart pointed to a falafel place and asked if she was hungry and she felt so in sync with him. She ordered a wrap and he said to make it two and then he said, 'You can get mine, you owe me for the bus ticket.' She had already forgotten about the bus ticket and she had certainly never intended to pay him back but she allowed herself a lie as she said, 'Of course, I was planning on it,' and she wondered at his internal ledger. Where did she sit on it now? How much debt was she in? She remembered the wine the night before, the way she'd waved him off, and figured if this was any other stage she could tease him about his cheapness, with only a little malice, or maybe they could even fight about it – but she had no fight in her, not on a day washed in beginning.

They ate their wraps on a metal bench in the street, seagulls screaming overhead, and she saw that he ate like he did everything else, gracelessly, as though he didn't have the requisite body parts to complete this task. She loved him, she realised, as garlic sauce covered his hands and he used the only napkin they had between them. She pulled her metal water bottle out of her backpack and poured some day-old water out of it onto her hands and he watched her do it then held out his hands too. And she washed them, there in the street, until they were clean and there was no water left.

They realised they had two hours left until her train and she asked if there was anything to do near the station.

'I get kind of anxious if I'm too far away when I have to catch a train,' and he said, 'I can't imagine you anxious.' He decided they should go to the museum near the station, which he said was mostly natural history stuff, and she decided not to mention the Tate because he didn't, and they started walking again, not holding hands this time but chatting a little and it was mostly easy.

When they got there Ada realised they were right next to the library and she thought about suggesting they go there again but didn't want to touch that memory so soon. Maybe in ten years they would go in there together and talk about when he had shown her a name and they'd laugh at how young they'd been or maybe she would go there alone and remember love. But either way today was too soon, so they went into the museum and passed the time. Stuart was still being too serious so Ada asked him loudly which items Britain had stolen and he shushed her but he laughed. He said, 'Yeah, look, Liverpool is all lefty today but we were a big colonial port,' and she said, 'Your tour-guide skills need work,' and he laughed again and took her hand.

Ada pointed to a sign and asked what 'horology' meant and Stuart said that it was a really good bit, so they headed to the collection and Ada learned that horology meant clocks. She wouldn't personally have said this was a 'really good bit' but then Stuart recited most of 'Funeral Blues' except he couldn't remember how it ended so Ada substituted the 'I'm just a girl' speech. They debated the best Richard Curtis movies and Ada shrieked loudly, so loud, when Stuart made a case for About Time and he screamed, 'Oh, come on,' when she wouldn't budge from Notting Hill. A security guard glanced at them and then looked away. Ada waited for the mood to fade but it didn't this time.

They went to the insect house which Ada had expected to be filled with dead things but found instead that things were creeping and crawling in cases around them. Only the butterflies were dead – 'RIP,' Stuart said and crossed himself – but the spiders were scuttling up well-lit branches and Ada felt goosebumped and in love. A millipede she was watching gyrated and she shuddered and Stuart said, 'Are you OK?' and she said, 'Yes look, it's so disgusting,' and they leaned their faces close to the glass together. There was silence and then Ada whispered, 'This is hot,' and Stuart laughed and said, 'Oh yeah baby, look at that worm thing go,' and Ada mimed throwing cash at the millipede and it was the best day of her entire life, probably, or it felt it in that moment.

Ada checked her phone and saw more messages from Sadie, who she had been answering every time Stuart wasn't looking. She put her phone back and said, 'I think I have to go to the station,' and Stuart turned to her and said, 'Or you could live here forever,' and Ada said, 'In the bug house?' and he said, 'In my bug house,' and she touched his cheek and said, 'Gross.' They walked to the station together, holding hands for sure this time, neither of them pulling away. They got to the top of the steps and Stuart said, 'Could we sit for a little bit?' and Ada had half an hour left so she said yes.

They sat and looked at each other and he held on to her hands, massaging them between his, moving moving moving. Ada said, 'Maybe you can come to Florida,' and he said, 'I'm not much of a hot weather person.' Ada said, 'What a disgusting thing to say, hot weather is the best,' and he said, 'Why are you in England again?' And Ada said very earnestly, 'The truth is that I'm a Beatles mega fan. I was so sad when Paul kicked it,' and Stuart said, 'Oh shut up,' and he kissed her lightly and then they held each other and she wondered if he would cry. Instead, he stood up and pulled her up and said, 'Come back here when you're back, yeah?' Ada said, 'Why don't you come to London instead?' and as she said it she knew it was wrong, the sentence fell out of her mouth and they watched it tumble down the steps and break its fucking neck. And she said, 'Sorry,' and he said, 'Well, will you be … living alone then? I mean apart from Mel?' and she said, 'I don't know. I don't think so,' and he said, 'I don't sleep well on a couch so let's stick with Liverpool for now.' Ada said, 'Of course,' and he said, 'We have to get you to your train.'

They walked into the station, up to the ticket barrier and there were eight minutes left and Ada wanted to stay but he said, 'I think that's your train there already.' She had everything to say to him and nothing. She wanted to give him so much and berate him for asking her to and also murder him if he ever stopped wanting it all. She said, 'I had a wonderful time. I think I like your life here,' and he said, 'You didn't see my life,' and she said, 'You don't go to the Cavern every day?' He laughed but like he'd forced it and then he held her shoulders, tight, and kissed her. She felt trapped and he felt hard. It was perfect.

He released her and she said, 'Message me when I'm on the train?' and he said, 'I'll message you tomorrow, if that's OK,' and she said, 'Of course, of course.' And he chucked her under her chin but because the angle was wrong it sort of grazed her instead and he said, 'Thanks for coming, pet,' and she said 'of course' again and turned to go through the barriers. She found her carriage and turned back to wave at him but he was looking at his phone. She called his name and then she called it louder so everyone boarding the train looked at her. He looked up too and he grimaced and waved her on to the train. She blew him a kiss and he made the waving gesture again and she got on.

She found her seat as the train started moving, window again, facing forward, Mel was so thoughtful. An older woman sat in the aisle seat reading her Kindle and she smiled at Ada and moved her legs to the side as she climbed over her. Once she was seated, her backpack propping up her feet, her jumper across her lap, she pulled out her phone and saw a message from Stuart that said, 'I couldn't wait until tomorrow.' She checked the time stamp and realised he was writing it when she called out his name. He was being romantic and she had ruined it and she wrote back, 'Sorry I yelled in the train station,' and he said, 'You're fucking nuts lol,' and they were safely back in their little boxes.

Twenty-two

From: Diana Highfield
To: Ada Highfield

Hello baby,

Just confirming that you're on the 11:15 a.m. flight from Gatwick NOT Heathrow, I know I have said this a few times but I would hate for you to go to the wrong one and miss it. You will land at Tampa and Dad and I will meet you at arrivals. Don't worry about texting when you get in, your father has a flight tracking app that he's honestly a bit obsessed with. I caught him tracking a plane to Sweden the other day and we don't even know anyone there. We are both so looking forward to seeing you, little one, I can't believe it has been so long. Gabby is so excited for your arrival too, though obviously she is mostly focused on breastfeeding and sleeping right now. I had forgotten how 24/7 the newborn phase is! But we are having such a special time and it will be so wonderful having everyone together again. Let me know if you need anything. Hank says he has sent you all the flight details but for your old ma's sake, please check them again. See you tomorrow, baby. Love you. Mum xoxo

Twenty-three

Ada had been so hungry when she got in to London that she'd stopped at the M&S at the station to buy crisps for the tube and then, on a starving whim, had picked up a Colin the Caterpillar cake too. So she sat on the tube and then the Overground pouring salt and vinegar into her mouth with one hand and balancing the cake box with the other. By the time she reached the flat she was sweaty and felt covered in the grime of the city, of both cities, and all the trains.

She let herself in and dumped her backpack on the floor then headed to the kitchen where Sadie was stirring lentils and Mel was peeling an orange. Sadie turned to her and said, 'Welcome home,' and Ada almost said, well, yes, this is my home, did you forget, but then Mel said, 'Missed you!' and Sadie said, 'Mel made me watch some British game show for nerds.' And Ada laughed and said, 'University Challenge?' and Mel sniffed exaggeratedly and said, 'I apologise for trying to raise the intellectual level of this household,' and Sadie said, 'Don't go to Florida, she'll try to make me smart.' And it was good to be back and she felt sad about leaving again so soon. She brandished the slightly squashed cake and Mel said, 'Oh hey, Colin!' and then made Ada an old fashioned and Sadie kicked them out of the kitchen so she could finish cooking.

In the living room Ada caught Mel up on Stuart, quietly, so the words wouldn't travel and Mel kept saying, 'What? He went where?' until they gave up. Ada said she'd tell her later though she didn't know when. They set the table and Sadie served them eggplant stuffed with lentils and pine nuts and a salad with shaved raw broccoli and something sour, and a buttery rice with fruit running through it. Mel poured wine and Sadie asked about Liverpool and Ada told them about the bugs at the museum. Sadie said, 'It must have been nice to see your friend,' and Ada said, 'It was nice,' and Sadie said, 'Shame it was such a flying visit,' and then Mel asked if she was packed for Florida.

Ada said, 'I'm obviously not,' and Mel said, 'We're going to do a packing party, aren't we.' Sadie said, 'I don't know what that is but I feel like I can guess.' Mel explained that in all the time they'd lived together, no matter how long the trip would be or where it was to, Ada would leave her packing until the morning she was leaving. After months of this Mel told her that it stressed her out and asked what she'd have to do to make Ada pack the night before and Ada said, 'You pack with me!' And since then, they'd had a packing party ritual, where Ada chose some music and drinks and Mel begged her to pick some underwear and overall they managed not to kill each other.

Sadie said, 'Sounds fun!' and they looked at her and she said, 'I'm kind of drunk already, is this the right energy for a packing party?' and Ada said, 'Yes!' and Mel said, 'No,' and they all laughed and kept eating. Ada said, 'This will be a very special packing party because Colin is invited,' and Sadie said, 'Who's Colin?' and Mel said, 'The caterpillar, Sadie,' and Sadie said, 'The one at the museum?' and Mel and Ada laughed as they tried to get the word 'cake' out. And Sadie said, 'Oh the cake! The cake is a caterpillar!' and she joined them and they were laughing and laughing together.

Sadie offered to clear up so they could start the packing party and Mel objected because Sadie had cooked but Sadie stage-whispered that she was trying to be late for the party, and they went their separate ways. Once in Ada's room, Ada tried again to catch up Mel on the Stuart of it all but once separate from him she couldn't quite explain the romance of his dingy mouldy house and the eroticism of cheap wine under seagulls.

She said, 'It felt kind of … terrifying to be with him,' and Mel said, 'God I hope you mean in a good way,' and Ada said, 'Yeah, no I can't … describe it really.' Mel asked if the sex was good and Ada said yes and Mel asked if his art was good and Ada said well she only saw a few pieces but they seemed good. Mel also asked if she was planning to tell Sadie about the trip and Ada said, 'Why?' and Mel said, 'Because you like her?' and Ada reminded her, again, that Sadie was leaving.

By the time Sadie joined them they had opened Mel's shiny red suitcase and placed eight pairs of plain cotton underwear inside ('But you're going for ten days', 'I don't know what to tell you, this is all I have clean') and drunk half a bottle of supermarket Côtes du Rhône. Sadie sighed and sat on the floor next to them, proffering her empty glass while Ada opened her laptop.

'That doesn't look like packing,' Sadie said and Mel said, 'She's choosing music, it's part of the process.' And after a moment 'Low' by Flo Rida started playing and Sadie said, 'This is a banger,' and Ada said, 'And it's on theme. Flo Rida. Get it?' and Mel said, 'Wait, Flo Rida means Florida? How did I never see that before?' and they listened to a Flo Rida playlist on Spotify while Sadie paired socks and Mel collected toiletries and Ada grabbed her flimsiest dresses. 'Finally going to be hot enough to wear these without leggings!' she said and Mel said, 'See, there *are* good things about Florida,' and Sadie said, 'Apart from the obvious. Seeing your family,' and Ada said, 'Is that the obvious?'

They finally finished and the wine was gone and they agreed that Flo Rida's output was not consistent. Mel said good night and promised to get up to say goodbye in the morning and Ada and Sadie looked at each other. Sadie walked to her and Ada wasn't sure what her plan was but she raised her arms for Sadie to pull off her dress. As she did, Ada said, 'Fuck,' muffled into the material in front of her mouth and Sadie said, 'What?'

'I haven't showered today, I was in sort of a rush this morning,' and Sadie took her hand and they walked to the bathroom.

Ada finished undressing and found that Sadie had undressed too and she held her finger to her lips. Ada understood. While Mel was aware they were having sex, it was something that existed so entirely in her bedroom that there was something illicit in taking it down the hall. If Mel was forced to acknowledge their relationship, they might be forced to acknowledge it too and it seemed too fragile to withstand collective scrutiny. So Ada mimed zipping her lips and Sadie turned the shower on.

Ada climbed in and found it lukewarm, not the close-to-scalding she usually chose so she turned the tap. Sadie followed her, started at the heat, and turned it back slightly, then Ada ducked her head under. She poured shampoo into her hands and started to rub it through her hair and Sadie turned her back to her to get under the water too. Ada watched the muscles move at the base of Sadie's neck where her hair was starting to grow kind of mullety and she realised for the first time that Sadie was shorter than her.

Sadie soaped and rinsed her pits and then stepped out of the stream, watching Ada run the shampoo through the lengths of her hair and then she gestured for Ada to get into the water. Ada did, feeling sick though she didn't know the source – there could be so many places in her gut and her brain for her nausea to originate – and she started to rinse out the shampoo. Sadie knelt in the bath and nudged Ada's legs further apart and pushed her face in. Ada leaned further into the water until it was running over her face, stinging her eyes; she found it hard to breathe and Sadie probably did too but she pushed her mouth in further, faster, no teasing or build-up; and Ada came with half her brain on the possibility of slipping and killing them both on the porcelain. Sadie stood back up and Ada pulled their bodies together for a moment then started to move her hand down Sadie's body but Sadie took it off.

'I have a moon cup in,' she whispered, and Ada nodded and affectionately patted Sadie's breast instead which made Sadie smile. She put her hand over the outside of Sadie and said, 'Should I?' and Sadie shook her head then kissed Ada without restriction.

Sadie pulled back, picked up the conditioner on the edge of the bath and turned Ada around and rubbed it through her hair, twisting the ends around her fingers and lightly tugging which brought the nausea flooding back. Then Sadie stepped out of the shower and wrapped herself in a towel, gave a wave and left, leaving Ada to rinse. She did, grabbing a comb from the sink and dragging it through, dropping her dead hair in the drain and steadying her breath. It felt so normal. Her hair, the drain, and the stranger who lived in her room. She realised that she hadn't cleaned herself after

Stuart, before Sadie, which didn't seem possible because Liverpool felt a decade ago. She turned off the taps.

Ada dried herself and joined Sadie in the room, who was slipping a bra into Ada's suitcase, a black push-up with lace across the top. 'Sorry, I realised you hadn't packed any so you'd only have whatever you wore on the plane,' and Ada said, 'And who knows, maybe I'll meet a Nascar driver and need my "fuck me" bra for our date,' and Sadie said, 'Exactly, that too.' Ada looked at her phone. It was 1:48 a.m. and she had to get up at five. She was clean and ready and she set her alarm and fell straight asleep.

When her alarm went off, Ada opened her eyes and found herself in the exact position she'd been in when she closed them. Sadie stirred slightly and Ada cuddled up to her but she didn't smell of herself, probably due the midnight shower. Ada closed her eyes and woke again to Mel banging on her door at six.

'Ada, you have to go!'

She rolled out of bed and pulled on the outfit Sadie had folded for her the night before – a stretchy blue jersey jump-suit that she had bought from a sustainable fashion brand she'd seen on Instagram that looked like pyjamas on her but was comfortable enough for flying. She put her demin jacket over it and pulled on her Cons and Sadie opened her eyes and said 'good flight' then closed them again. Ada looked at her and looked away.

She opened her bedroom door and pulled her bag out and Mel was pacing the landing between their rooms. Ada rubbed her face and said, 'I'd planned to eat before I went but—' and Mel said, 'Your hair looks insane,' and Ada touched it and realised she'd slept on it wet and it was flat on one side and flying out on the other. She pulled a hair elastic out of the pocket of the jumpsuit and pulled it into a ponytail and the effort of it made her want to die.

'OK, I really have to go, I think it's a bus to Finsbury Park then Victoria to Green Park then Jubilee to London Bridge and my train goes at eight? Is that right? Hang on—' and Mel said, 'you are stressing me out, I'm booking you an Uber.' Ada looked at her and said, 'To Gatwick? You're insane,' and she said, 'No, to London Bridge. You look like you're dying, I can't handle the idea of you walking that tunnel at Green Park trying not to throw up,' and Ada said, 'I love you so much.'

She felt barely conscious when Mel put her in the Uber, Mel who came out into the street in her pyjamas and a pair of Ada's sandals she'd left by the door. Mel waved her goodbye and she slept again immediately, only waking when the driver said they were there. The rest of the morning was a blur of ticket machines and a train station croissant and sleeping in a moulded metal chair and then sleeping on the train and then security and an airport coffee and then sleeping in the departures lounge and splashing water on her face over and over and finally boarding and she leaned against her window seat to sleep and realised she hadn't messaged Stuart since dinner the night before.

Ada took a selfie with the safety card and said, 'Hoping I get to try the big slide!' and Stuart wrote back, 'Don't joke about that! Aren't you superstitious at all?' She said, 'Wait aren't you at work? How do you have your phone?' and he said, 'I sneaked it into my pocket, didn't want to miss saying goodbye before you took off.' And then the flight attendants came to check the seatbacks and their tray tables and she said, 'That's cute. About to take off, I'll message when I land!' and he said, 'I miss you,' and she said, 'I miss you. Now go serve those hungry people!' And she fell asleep again.

Ada was out of rhythm with the rest of the flight and after lunch, her seat mates went to sleep while she stayed awake and watched old episodes of *Always Sunny* and drank ginger ale and Diet Coke. When she had an hour left of the flight, she suddenly became aware that she was about to see her parents. She had missed them for so long that it had become background noise and now that it was about to end, the volume was turned way up. She was going to do the crossword with her dad and watch cooking shows with her mum. Her dad would buy experimental beers based on the fancy label, then declare them undrinkable and give them to her, and her mum would suggest they all watch a movie together after dinner then fall asleep on the couch once it started.

Ada wanted to hold them so much that it hurt in a way she hadn't let it hurt for so long. She had never had trouble with her relationship with her parents and she sometimes wondered if that meant she felt less passionate about them than Gabby. She had always got good marks, starred in the school play and been passably good at netball. She partied in high school in ways that didn't impinge on their view of her, always pulling up fine the day after, never bothering to bring the person of the week home to them. She didn't think of this as dishonest so much as a contract they had all entered in to, not to bother or be bothered by each other and to love each other as much as they could. Gabby never signed that contract and Ada sensed that she viewed the family equilibrium the other three achieved with disdain.

When Ada told her parents she was taking advantage of her mother's Irish passport and moving to London for a while, they seemed to take this as an inevitability. They had done the London thing in their twenties, as had the parents of half the people she knew, and they figured she'd be back within a year.

It had been over two years now and they had come to visit her once, a year ago, staying in a flat in Islington and going to every Ottolenghi restaurant. They had told her how proud they were of the life she had built there, and Ada put that mostly down to timing. Their trip coincided with her longest consistent acting job outside of the Fringe, a two-week run of a modern ghost story at an independent theatre. British people loved putting ghosts on stage and Ada didn't much care for it but it had felt good introducing her parents to her friends in the foyer after their sold-out opening night. They didn't sell out any other night of the run but she could see why her parents felt proud.

The plane was landing and Ada thought about how much her parents would like Sadie.

Twenty-four

23/09/2017

Stuart Parkes   **11:15**
I didn't know you were such a stickler for the no phones policy

Stuart Parkes   **11:16**
Narc

Stuart Parkes   **11:31**
You're definitely in the air now, FINE I'LL PUT MY PHONE AWAY

Stuart Parkes   **13:01**
OK I'm on my lunch break

Stuart Parkes   **13:02**
You still flying? I guess America is far

Stuart Parkes 13:05

Shit I just googled your flight time, 9 hours is shit

Stuart Parkes 13:58

Going back to work now

Stuart Parkes 18:17

Finished work, had to lock up

Stuart Parkes 18:30

I guess you're still up there, wow I have forgotten how to waste time on my phone if I'm not talking to you

Stuart Parkes 19:11

My housemates are going to the spoons and want me to come with

Stuart Parkes 19:20

OK I'm going out but message me when you land

Stuart Parkes 20:48

You have definitely landed now helloooooooo

Stuart Parkes 21:03

How are your ma and pa and the wee one?

Stuart Parkes 22:17

What time is it there

Stuart Parkes 22:29

OK I'm going home, hope you didn't die in a plane crash

Stuart Parkes 23:04

Man I fucking miss you so much, is that weird

Stuart Parkes 23:05

I'm home and fucked but I'm going to stay awake until I hear from you

Stuart Parkes 23:11

I can't believe I have to work tomorrow

Stuart Parkes 23:13

I said that's why I was going home but my housemates saw me checking my phone

Stuart Parkes 23:15

Tom thought you were hot

Stuart Parkes 23:16

Maybe I should paint you again

Stuart Parkes   23:17

So I don't forget you

Ada Highfield   23:34

SORRY SORRY SORRY

Ada Highfield   23:35

Didn't die but phone doesn't work here no internet on it

Ada Highfield   23:36

Back at the house dropping bag so using wifi but going to meet
baby now will be back sorry

Ada Highfield   23:37

Paint me!!!!!!!!

Stuart Parkes   23:39

She's alive!

Stuart Parkes   23:48

Shit you're gone again aren't you

Stuart Parkes   23:54

All right I'll paint you

Stuart Parkes 23:55

I'll put you in the water again

24/09/2017

Stuart Parkes 00:02

Ada?

Stuart Parkes 00:09

Shit I have to go to sleep, message me when you can

Ada was tired, too tired for this and she tried to remind herself that she was white and cis and many of her friends went through far worse than this to travel but she was too tired to acknowledge her privilege right now either. She would acknowledge it later when telling this story though, she knew that already. She smiled at the man in the booth, staring expectantly at her, enjoying the power imbalance, and said, 'I really can't think of anything right now.' And he said, 'What about Shakespeare?' so she dug into the recesses of her mind and said, ' "Puppet? Why so? Ay, that way goes the game—".' The immigration officer handed her passport back to her and said blandly, 'You're good. Next!' and she walked out, through, until she saw her parents waiting for her.

Her mother was dressed just like her, she noticed, a wide-legged jumpsuit and her hair pulled back. She was checking her phone. Her father waved frantically, ecstatically, when he saw her, and he nudged her mother who looked up and smiled at her baby. Ada ran to them and pulled them in to her, noticing that her always tiny mother appeared to have shrunk even more and deciding not to mention it. They chatted about the flight and the weather and her dad pulled her bag for her and then her parents argued about which level the car was on and then they were off down the Florida freeways.

Ada watched the billboards and the cars without much interest and started to close her eyes but her mother said, 'We'll drop your bags and go straight over to Gabby's, OK? I said I'd pick up dinner so we can all eat together, then leave them to try to get some sleep.' Ada said, 'Sure, I mean, we could just go over in the morning? I don't want to make a big fuss if they're tired,' and Ada's dad looked at her in the rear-view mirror and said, 'No, we'll go today. You only have ten days, we don't want to waste it.'

'Exactly,' said her mum, looking at her phone again, 'Hank didn't fly you out here to lounge at home.'

'Is he nice?' she asked, because it seemed like the right question, and her mother started talking about Hank and his wonderful cooking and his boat that they could use any time and his kind but shy parents and how much he 'loves our Gabby'. Ada looked out the window again.

This is how her parents had always coped with her and Gabby, as though they were actually very close, two people who would definitely choose to spend time together even if they weren't related. They didn't acknowledge the resentment Gabby felt towards Ada even when it was overt, even when it was screamed in their faces. They couldn't or wouldn't accept how exhausted Ada was by Gabby, how long ago she'd given up reaching for her approval. They watched them leave the house for school together every day and then didn't see that Gabby would take a different, longer route to the train station to avoid walking with Ada. The best they had ever got along was when Gabby moved to Melbourne for university and Ada had the school to herself and their parents to herself and they texted each other happy birthday and exchanged books at Christmas.

Their father had been a lonely only child and their mother was one of six, which came with so much internal politics that they seemed to forget to hate each other. Ada thought of the family photos of her and Gabby when they were small, dressed in matching outfits and holding hands, repeated attempts by their parents to convince the world and the girls themselves that they were best friends. The alienation didn't make sense to them, so they insulated themselves from it and they were doing it again, right now. People with their eyes open would never have thought that Gabby wanted Ada to fly over to meet her baby. They would never have thought Ada would do it. But Hank had paid for it and Ada wondered what Gabby had said about her. Gabby had said 'I hate my sister' so many times, often in Ada's presence, but Hank didn't seem the type to hate people. Especially members of his family. So maybe Gabby softened it with 'we just aren't close' and maybe that was the truth now anyway. They just weren't close. Any hate was historic.

Ada's mother looked over at the car's display and said, 'Rich, something's flashing,' and her dad looked down and said, 'Fuck, we need petrol.' He smiled at Ada in the rearview and said, 'The rental place only had these gas guzzlers,' and Ada said, 'I'm guessing Florida isn't really up on the whole climate-change thing,' and Diana said, 'Actually, baby, there are some very progressive pockets! Such an interesting state.' Ada felt that Diana would never criticise the place one of her daughters had chosen to live unless they said it first.

Ada looked at the flat scrub off the freeway and said, 'So is this the south?' and her father said, 'Technically yes,' and Ada said, 'My friend Brandon is from Missouri and he says you know you're in the south when there are more churches than fun things to do,' and Diana said, 'He sounds funny.' Ada thought about Brandon, who had directed a workshop she took part in last winter and had a sexual focus on her butt to the exclusion of everything else, and she said, 'He is funny.'

They pulled into a 'gas station', as Diana said in a terrible American drawl, and Richard got out to fill the tank. Diana unbuckled her seatbelt and whispered to Ada, 'Should I sneak us some treats?' and Ada didn't know if her mum was play-acting nostalgia or really feeling it but she said, 'Yeah I think you should.' Diana got out of the car and did an exaggerated sneak into the shop and Ada saw Richard see her and shake his head affectionately. He treated his body, as he put it, 'with respect' and as her mother put it, 'too seriously', so for as long as Ada could remember, she and her mother would binge on junk whenever Richard wasn't around. They got bolder as time went on and started doing it in his presence and booing if he tried to object and Ada appreciated this throwback. She wondered if her mother snacked alone now.

Diana got back to the car with packets upon packets of American treats – Twizzlers and Twinkies ('they're terrible, you have to try one') and Flamin' Hot Cheetos ('please don't open them in the car') and Milk Duds and Reese's. The two women passed the packets back and forth over the muted objections of Richard for the rest of the ride, agreeing that Americans really weren't good at chocolate but were masters of everything else. They turned off the freeway into the Sarasota suburb they were staying in, camping out in Hank's parents' house, around the corner from Gabby and Hank. Ada took in the strip malls and pointed to a sign that advertised 'Guns and Ammo' and Diana said, 'Yes, the gun business is terrible, I try to tune it out.' They pulled into a gated community, Richard waving his fob at the sensor in an embarrassed sort of way, and parked in the driveway of an all-white, one-storey house on a block of land that would contain a hundred London flats.

Diana said, 'We can just take your bags in and be on our way,' but Ada said, 'I need to check my email if that's OK,' and then added, 'work stuff,' and Richard and Diana nodded because yes, work stuff did usually happen on email. They went into the house and Ada was surprised to find it tiled all the way through. White walls, white freezing cold floors, air conditioning blaring. Her house in Sydney was all floorboards and ceiling fans and she felt the two approaches to heat signified something but she couldn't grasp at what.

She went to open a window and her mother stopped her, saying the mosquitoes were something else, so she settled under the cold blasting air con at the high kitchen bench. Richard retrieved the wifi password for her and she connected, skipping over everything apart from Stuart's messages. She felt guilt and pleasure as she read them and she was about to reply when her mother said, 'Sorry to hurry you, darling, but I said we'd be at the house by six,' and Ada dashed off a reply and stepped back into the world.

They stopped at a strip mall on the way and picked up sandwiches – 'We're eating sandwiches for dinner?', 'They're called po' boys, darling, they're very good, your father has gone a bit mad for the whole concept of frying an oyster' – and then they were on their way to Gabby's. Just as Ada had felt longing for her parents as she closed in on them, now she felt a retro anxiety at the idea of dealing with her sister.

A memory drifted in of watching Gabby circle her eyes with dark liner, getting ready to go out with friends when she was fifteen and Ada was twelve. She was usually thrown straight out of Gabby's room but tonight was receiving the silent treatment instead which felt like a hug. Ada asked, 'Gabby, do you have a boyfriend?' and Gabby said, 'None of your fucking business,' then stopped circling her eyes and said, 'Why, do you?' And Ada had felt like they were starting a real conversation so she had said, 'I think so? A boy called Peter catches the same train as me and he asked his friend to ask me to be his girlfriend and I said OK but only if he asked me himself and so I think on Monday he's going to ask me.' And Gabby looked at her, really appraised her then, and said, 'Well. Good for you.' She turned back to the mirror and said, 'Can you get the fuck out of my room?' and Ada did.

They parked on the curb outside a two-storey pale yellow house with a neat lawn and a flag pole though, Ada noticed, there was no flag on it. Her parents hopped out and hurried to the door, her mother holding a magnum of pale pink wine (she said that's how they sell them here and her father said they sell regular bottles too and her mother pretended not to hear him), her dad with the takeaway bag banging against his legs. Ada followed them and hung behind them when they rang the bell.

Hank answered the door and Ada's first impression was that rarely had photos so well captured a person. He was exactly as she had imagined him, his angles as predicted, the size and weight of him oddly familiar for a stranger. He hugged both her parents then said, 'Ada, I assume!' and squeezed her lightly and she suppressed a strange urge to touch his biceps. He led her into a cosy living area, still mostly lit by the setting sun outside, and in the centre of a sagging dark green sofa was her sister and a baby.

Gabby was breastfeeding and looked at Ada and said, 'Get over here! I can't get up,' and Ada walked to this person who seemed less known to her than Hank. Ada had always thought of herself as the softened version of Gabby. Round-cheeked where Gabby was angular, both with dark hair but Gabby choosing a heavy fringe. Privately Ada thought Gabby should have been the actor because while Ada was prettier and people loved to look at her, Gabby had A Look. Her bones made themselves known while Ada's were undercover.

The woman feeding the baby had hair lighter than Ada's and Ada realised it was the colour hers used to go in the Australian summer while Gabby stayed indoors. Her body was soft at the edges and her smile creased around her eyes. Ada felt they had never looked more similar, although Gabby was somehow more Ada than Ada – she had taken her freckles and sprinkled them on her own cheeks. It took growing and birthing a baby for Gabby to acquire the body that Ada had gained as a teenager and she seemed to wear it so naturally. Ada sat next to her and didn't know how to hug her without disturbing the baby so she leaned her head on Gabby's shoulder and Gabby said, 'This is Orion.'

Ada looked down at the child's closed eyes and dark sticky hair with scatterings of dry skin underneath and realised that she had never been this close to a newborn before. Orion didn't look like a baby exactly, had none of the pudgy healthfulness that she was used to. He wasn't a toddler with a running nose or a five-year-old kicking a ball or a nine-year-old with earnest questions or a teenager slamming a door or her sister sitting beside her. He was papery skin and legs like a frog sticking out from his polka-dot onesie. It was like someone had dressed an alien and tried to pass it off as a human. She felt something stir inside her that she recognised as love but she couldn't make sense of it. She didn't even recognise him and he wasn't hers. He was still attached to her sister and she realised she had been looking at a breast for quite some time but Gabby didn't seem concerned by it.

'He's beautiful,' she said and Gabby said, 'I think he's pretty weird-looking, but you know, they all are,' and then, 'He reminds me of you when you were born. You had all this hair too,' and Ada realised she had never, not one time, thought about Gabby meeting her when she was this small.

'How's the whole … boob thing?' and Gabby shifted a little so Ada sat back up and Gabby said, 'It really fucking hurts.'

And from the other side of the room Diana said, 'Yes darling, I'm sorry, I'd forgotten how it hurts at the start. I promise it feels totally normal after a while,' and Gabby said to Ada, 'The cheer squad over there didn't mention the bleeding nipples,' and Ada felt she was in the TV version of her own family. She whistled and said in a faux southern drawl, 'Introducing Florida's most distressing punk group, the Bleeding Nipples!' and Gabby laughed a little but not enough for Ada to keep the bit going.

Hank came out of the kitchen then with a big water bottle with a straw in it and some apple slices and Ada watched as he knelt in front of Gabby and held the bottle for her to drink. He then took one piece of apple and placed it gently in her mouth and she gave him the thumbs up and he took his place on the other side of the room. Gabby chewed and swallowed and said, 'It's all very dignified as you can see,' and Hank said, 'She's doing so amazing,' and he sounded like he might cry and Ada did not see what she contributed to this place.

Hank asked her questions about her flight and she remembered to thank him for booking it but he waved her off. And as Gabby switched Orion to her other breast – leaving the first one hanging out for something like a minute until she reclipped the bra, which no one reacted to at all – Hank asked her thoughtful questions about where she lived and the show she had done in Edinburgh. He told her he had been on several business trips to London but had always stayed close to the Shard which he understood wasn't real London and maybe when Orion was a little older they could come to visit. 'I'd love to eat somewhere that isn't Soho and with someone who wasn't my boss!' and she laughed politely as she tried to imagine Hank catching a show at the Bethnal Green Working Men's Club then crossing the street for a curry.

Orion finished feeding – he simply took his mouth off and everyone accepted that he was done but how did he know?

How did any of them? – and Gabby said, 'Would you like to hold him?' Ada held out her arms as this fragile bumpy creature was laid in them and Gabby said, 'This is your Aunty Ada.' The child blinked and looked at nothing in particular, closed his eyes, rolled a tiny fist in and out. Ada felt a vibration in his stomach and said, 'I think I can … feel him digesting? Is that crazy?' and her mother said, 'No, you probably can. They're just guts at this point,' and Gabby said, 'The miracle of life. Turns out it's mostly shit.' But she was looking at Ada holding her baby like it *was* a miracle and for the first time Ada considered whether Gabby was the one who planned this trip after all.

When she got home that night she messaged Mel a photo of her with Orion and then sent it to Stuart. He asked her what it was like meeting the baby and she didn't know how to answer him and she was so tired so she just said, 'It was a lot.' She climbed into bed and realised it had been weeks since she'd slept alone, she spread herself sideways and felt relief. She asked Stuart about his day and he told her about some sort of shift-swapping drama at the cafe and she fell asleep before she could reply.

Twenty-six

25/09/2017

Stuart Parkes 20:45

How was Camp Baby today?

Stuart Parkes 21:27

I think you should be getting home soon but time zones are confusing

Stuart Parkes 21:30

I'm a simple artist who makes good coffee, I can't understand 'hours ahead'

Stuart Parkes 21:33

I've finished sketching the new painting I think

Stuart Parkes 21:33

Of you

Stuart Parkes   21:40

Your new painting, if you want it

Stuart Parkes   21:41

Then when I become famous you can sell it

Stuart Parkes   21:44

Or we can hang it in our mansion together

Stuart Parkes   21:45

I assume you'll move to Liverpool if I get a mansion

Stuart Parkes   21:47

Fuck socialism if there's a mansion on the line

Stuart Parkes   23:36

I wanted to wait up for you but I'm fading

Stuart Parkes   23:38

I'm an old man!

Stuart Parkes   23:44

I know you think of me as a toyboy but my ancient bones need
rest

Stuart Parkes   **23:58**
Good night xx

26/09/2017

Ada Highfield   **00:32**
I'm so sorry, it's 7:30 here, just got home

Ada Highfield   **00:38**
Baby Camp going well, my dad and I got sent out to Trader Joes for supplies and that place is a wonderland. So many ways to spice a nut!

Ada Highfield   **00:41**
Oh also our local megachurch is doing pet blessings???

Ada Highfield   **00:43**
There's a big sign up saying to bring pets to church on Sunday for their annual blessing

Ada Highfield   **00:44**
Can you imagine being a cat

Ada Highfield   **00:45**
In church

Ada Highfield 00:46

Surrounded by dogs and like birds you can't eat

Ada Highfield 00:47

I almost want to disguise myself as an evangelical and sneak in

Ada Highfield 00:51

I think Hank's family might be that kind of Christian???

Ada Highfield 00:52

But they're pretty nice, we met them today

Ada Highfield 00:53

But I dunno, they were like … weirdly positive about everything but like nothing behind the eyes

Ada Highfield 00:54

And like you live in Florida Mr and Mrs Mathers, how happy can you be

Ada Highfield 00:56

And that's exactly the kind of negative shit you can NOT say at Baby Camp

Ada Highfield 01:11

Gonna watch a movie with my mum now

Ada Highfield 01:13

She's opened another MAGNUM OF WINE

Ada Highfield 01:14

I take it back, this country is perfect

Ada Highfield 01:21

We're watching *The Proposal*, my mum will agree to anything with Sandra Bullock and she asked me if I thought she was pretty which is my mum's regular reminder that she knows I like girls and she's VERY FINE WITH IT

Ada Highfield 01:23

Sandra Bullock is obviously hot

Ada Highfield 01:24

And she has a toyboy in this movie

Ada Highfield 01:25

Stars, They're Just Like Us

Ada Highfield   03:28

I'm getting ready for bed, miss you x

Stuart Parkes   07:48

Morning! Hank's last name is Mathers? Like Eminem?

Stuart Parkes   07:50

OK teach Orion to rap

Stuart Parkes   07:53

I'm a baby yes I'm a real baby all you other little babies are just imitating etc

Stuart Parkes   07:56

Hmm can I unsend a message

Stuart Parkes   07:58

Sorry I just woke up

Stuart Parkes   08:13

I'm going to visit a friend in Manchester today, did I tell you

Stuart Parkes   08:14

Uni mate

Stuart Parkes   08:23

Anyway have a good day at Baby Camp

Stuart Parkes   08:27

Maybe we'll catch each other later

Ada Highfield   12:47

I will definitely teach the newborn the rap as soon as he stops
puking so much

Ada Highfield   13:50

OK back to Baby Camp

Ada Highfield   13:51

Hope Manchester is fun!

Twenty-seven

The days in Florida were bright and beautiful and mostly the same. Ada and her parents went to the yellow house around nine every morning to take Orion for an hour or two while Gabby went back to bed and Hank was supposed to go back to bed but he would tidy and host instead. On the third morning, after making everyone's coffee and toast, he had sat on the couch and fallen straight to sleep and Ada had held Orion and watched him and whispered, 'That's your daddy, he's a good daddy isn't he,' while Orion stirred and grizzled. Gabby usually rushed to Orion when she woke up, but this time she saw Hank asleep and went to curl up next to him, leaning on his side for a few minutes before collecting the baby for a feed. When Hank woke up a little later he was so apologetic and Gabby said, 'You're allowed, honey,' but Hank shook himself off like a dog that had jumped in a creek and headed into the kitchen to fix some snacks.

Around lunchtime, Ada and her dad would get in the car and go to buy groceries and stuff for dinner. On the first day they passed a turnoff for a beach and Ada told her dad she was desperate to go swimming. So from that day on they would go to the beach on the way back from the store. They'd hit the freeway then detour across a narrow bridge to Siesta Key.

Diana had packed one of Ada's old Speedos from home, so she would pull it on hiding behind the car door in the car park while her dad held a towel and looked the other way. They would head across the hot, white sand and into the flat sea. Ada and Richard occasionally tried to catch waves but it wasn't that kind of water, so mostly they drifted, looking up at the sky, until one of them would say, 'We'd better get back,' and they'd head in to shore.

After two days of this Diana started to make slightly snippy comments about the beach trips and Gabby said, 'Mum, I am begging you to go with them, Hank and I can handle two hours alone!' so after that Diana joined them and made them put sunscreen on in the car. Ada grumbled but had in fact noticed pink patches round the edges of her swimmers so was pretty sure her mum was right. They would swim until Richard said, 'We'd better get back before the car cooks those groceries for us,' and Diana rolled her eyes at his caution while knowing he was right. They would head back to the house and take turns showering in the all-white bathroom with baby blue accents, Ada making note of which sham-poos and body washes she was using so she could replace them at Trader Joe's.

The grandparents would hold Orion or take him for a walk around the block if the sun wasn't too hot and Hank would be on nappy standby. When Orion fussed, Hank bounced with him on a yoga ball they'd bought during Gabby's pregnancy and sang nineties grunge classics in soothing tones. When Ada expressed surprise at 'Black Hole Sun' becoming a lullaby, Hank looked embarrassed and said, 'I'm realising I don't know any kid-appropriate songs.' Ada felt bad, she hadn't meant to shame him, so she knelt next to the yoga ball and sang, 'My baby son, won't you come, and wash away the rain ... see it works!' and Hank smiled at her and she smiled at him and Orion farted and everyone relaxed.

Ada had noticed that a burp or fart from Orion was the pivotal action upon which the whole household hung. Gabby would watch anxiously as he was walked up and down by someone else – walking was still a challenge for her with her stitches, she said, and Ada tried not to visibly cringe – as Orion fussed and writhed until he let out a sound at either end. The first time Ada got him to burp, she felt like she'd just scaled a mountain while learning an instrument at the same time and when he followed up that burp with a light rain of white vomit she said calmly, 'Ah, could someone get me a muslin?' and didn't even gag. She had never heard the word muslin before this week and now they were the most important items in the world, these little scraps of fabric, and Ada felt like she'd entered a secret club of infant knowledge.

Ada fell into the habit of making dinner, the old recipes that had been the first her parents taught her. Roasting a chicken with three kinds of vegetables, spaghetti bolognaise, leftovers fried rice. And always a big, fresh salad, the kind it was hard for her to make when it was just her and Mel and a sad bag of Sainsbury's rocket. Hank said everything was delicious and she really believed him and Gabby ate more than she'd ever seen her eat before. She said nursing made her starving and she'd had heartburn for most of her pregnancy so it was so good to fill her tummy again. After their early dinner they would eat fresh pineapple and watermelon, sometimes a little yoghurt, and then Hank and Richard would draw the mosquito nets down and the day was mostly done.

Hank's parents came over for dinner every two days, always with a new item for Orion, a rattle or a squishy book or a bath toy that he didn't need because he wasn't taking baths yet. Mr

Mathers would get close to the baby and say 'Atta boy!' and then try to engage Hank in conversation about something to do with Trump. Ada had been grateful to discover the Mathers were anti Trump and when she said that to Gabby the next day she'd said, 'Duh, Ada, they're not hillbillies,' then had said, 'Though you never know,' and Ada realised Gabby had probably worried about the exact same thing.

Mrs Mathers would hold Orion until he made any sort of move or sound at which point she'd say, 'Oh bless him, he wants his mummy,' and hand him back to Gabby while saying, 'Little boys always want their mummy!' This drove Gabby mad, Ada could see, and after Mrs Mathers had made her fifth comment of the night about giving 'that little boy' (she didn't call him Orion) a bottle, he was obviously very hungry, Ada said, 'Oh, but he wants his mummy, you see,' and Gabby smiled at her. Ada knew that they were giving Orion a bottle here and there – Hank had told them a story about spilling half a tin of formula in the kitchen in the middle of the night – but they had all decided without discussing it that that information wasn't to be shared. Mrs Mathers wasn't in the club.

One morning, Gabby complimented Ada on an orange shirt dress with huge purple flowers on it and Ada said, 'Thanks, a charity shop find,' and Hank said, 'Oh, you should go to the big Goodwill! The snowbirds always donate a tonne of stuff.' Gabby explained that snowbirds were people from the north who came down to Florida when the weather got cold there and Hank said, 'They drove me nuts as a kid but when I was living in New York, I really understood it, you know? Those winters are brutal,' and Ada said yeah, she knew. She asked Hank if he missed New York and he said, 'I never planned to move back here but when Gabby got pregnant ... no, I don't think I do. The pizza maybe. And my friends. The job is the same anywhere but the people aren't. Maybe I do miss New York,' and Gabby said, 'It's OK if you do.'

So that afternoon, between the store and the beach, Ada and her parents went to a Goodwill the size of Ada's primary school and she picked out dress after dress from the $5 racks. Sequinned mini dresses and floaty seventies kaftans and a couple of vampy cinched-waist ones for the cabaret night. When she went to pay, her dad offered to get them as an early Christmas present and she said yes and then they took them home to show Hank and Gabby.

That night the Mathers came for dinner and Ada said she couldn't believe how many great dresses had been donated. And Mrs Mathers said, 'Well, no one wears dresses in Florida apart from religious extremists,' and then she speared a piece of her steak, held it up to the light to examine it and then put it in her mouth. The next day Ada said to Gabby, 'Would you like a biscuit with your tea?' and Gabby said, 'Of course not,' very rudely, and Ada felt a rising barrel of stress, and Gabby said, 'Only religious extremists eat biscuits in Florida,' and it was great. Ada said, 'Are they on you about getting married?' and Gabby said, 'No, they save that shit for Hank.' Ada said, 'Is it kind of weird that they live so close?' and Gabby said, 'Not for me but maybe for Hank. He was gone a long time and I think it's ... different now. He seems to want them around more but when they're here I think he hates it,' which Ada hadn't noticed.

One morning a clatter of women came over, five of them, none of them, Ada noticed, in dresses or skirts. Gabby had told her that some friends were coming but these women seemed to mostly know Hank, from high school, Ada figured. They were in blousy tops and capris and two of them carried babies of their own but they fussed over Orion and Gabby like they were the first babe and mother to ever exist. Ada had made an Earl Grey teacake for the occasion, though there had been no loose-leaf tea at Trader Joe's so she'd had to tear the little bags apart to make the batter and she was worried it would be flavourless. Only one of the women commented, though, to say it was interesting, which Ada decided was a compliment.

When Gabby told the group that Ada lived in London – they didn't already know this basic fact, Ada observed – they tripped over each other to say how exciting that sounded. 'My Lord, you're brave, girl, the things we hear about knife crime over there,' said orange capris while bouncing Orion and Ada said nothing about guns, which she thought was very discreet.

'At least we're not worried about alligators!' she said instead, pathetically, as grey capris said, 'I went to London with hubby after our honeymoon in Paris and it's a nightmare to drive through. Tell me, have you found the English to be particularly bad drivers?' but Ada said, 'I've never really driven there,' and soon the morning tea was over. When they left Gabby said to Hank, 'That went OK, right?' and he said, 'It was great hun, they love you,' and Ada realised she hadn't had the worst morning.

There was wifi at the yellow house and Ada asked for the password on the first day and Hank said, 'Of course, I'll get that for you,' and then Gabby had asked for a breast pad and he had been distracted. Ada didn't ask again after that. So every night they'd get back to their stark, tiled palace and Diana would open a bottle of wine and she and Ada would share whatever snacks they'd snuck into the shopping that day ('they will put peanut butter in anything here baby, it's innovative really').

And Ada would read the messages from Stuart and reply with any funny stories she could remember from the day. But her days weren't very funny so sometimes she would send photos of the beach or the weird snacks or the baby. The only ones he replied to were the snacks. She told herself that babies weren't for everyone though she felt, maybe, that this baby should be of some interest to him.

Ada also messaged Mel every night – selfies with Orion, photos of her mum asleep on the couch, thoughts about Gabby and Hank and Florida in general. She told her that in diners they top up coffee constantly so when she and her parents went out for breakfast one day when Gabby had a hospital visit she ended up getting so buzzed on caffeine that she wasn't sure she should hold the baby. Mel told her about her day and Ada tried to ask about Will, the guy from work, and Mel was vague so she left it. Ada asked about Sadie too and Mel said she was seeing less of her, she was out most nights, but she'd showed Sadie some pictures of Orion and Sadie thought he was very beautiful. Sadie had liked the Instagram post of Ada holding him and that was all they'd heard from each other.

On the fourth night, Stuart was still awake when she got home and he told her he'd gone out and got 'mashed' and she 'should have been there' so she suggested they FaceTime. She took a glass of wine into her echoey tiled room and climbed onto her high stiff bed and called him and he answered from his own bed, mostly in the dark. She tried to ask about his night and told him to turn a light on so she could see him and he said, 'You don't need to see me,' and she said, 'I do,' and then he went quiet and she realised he'd fallen asleep. She held on a little longer then hung up and went back into the living room. Her mother asked who she had called and she said, 'This guy … artist guy that I'm sort of seeing,' and her father said, 'An artist! So boho. Is he any good?' and Ada said, 'Yeah, I guess.' Stuart messaged when he woke up saying he didn't remember hanging up and he was really sorry but she was asleep when he sent it.

At the yellow house the next morning Richard said, 'Ada's dating an artist!' and Gabby said, 'Oh, what discipline?' and there didn't seem to be malice behind the question so Ada said, 'I guess painting mostly. Though he won a sculpture prize once,' and Hank said, 'That's impressive!' Diana said, 'Our girls have always been attracted to artsy types, I mean they're both so creative themselves,' and Hank said, 'I assume I'm the exception that proves the rule,' but Diana wasn't listening. She said, 'Do you remember when your boyfriend … Gabby, what was his name, that boy you were dating in high school and he came to see you both in the dance concert and sat next to us while you two performed?' Ada knew this story was all wrong, Gabby quit dance when she was ten, it was Ada's concert only, Ada's boyfriend. Gabby was forced to be there and brought a book and afterwards she referred to the boyfriend as 'a creep'. But present-day Gabby was focusing on Orion, rubbing a damp cloth over his milky chin and said vaguely, 'I don't remember, what concert was this?'

Then Hank said, 'Speaking of art, you should really go to St Petersburg,' and Ada said, 'In Russia?' and he laughed and said, 'Sorry, no, the one near here.' And that's how Ada learned there was more than one St Petersburg. Hank explained that it was an art district and he said, 'And actually my parents are coming in the afternoon today instead of dinner so … you could go this afternoon.' Ada saw the weight of the two families on Hank and said, 'OK, I'd love that.' She asked Gabby if it was OK and Gabby said, 'Yes, I think I'll plan a nap around three.' Ada said they'd pick up take-out for dinner and Gabby gave her the address of a Mexican restaurant – 'and they put Coke in their sauces, it sounds crazy but it's so fucking good' – and then Ada and her parents left for St Petersburg.

It took about an hour during which Diana drove and Richard read them the full St Petersburg entry in the Florida guidebook Hank had given him. When he said the museum there housed the biggest Dalí collection in the world Ada said, 'Fuck off. In Florida? Why isn't it in Italy?' and Diana said, 'Well, first of all baby, Dalí was Spanish,' and Ada said, 'OK but still.' Richard said, 'Turns out Dalí had some rich American mate who bought a bunch of his stuff and now here it is,' and Ada said, 'I need a rich American.'

St Petersburg was built around the water, like all the best places in Florida, and when they got out of the car Ada was hit with a sense of incongruity. They were surrounded by art and by galleries and the sun was lazing above them and the water was light and glinty. They turned a corner and saw the Dalí museum, rising out of a deep green lawn, concrete and undulating glass. Ada said to her mum, 'Well, the Tate Modern can get fucked,' and her mother laughed and they went inside. As they moved through the levels, crossing winding concrete bridges, Ada felt a sense of déjà vu, and when she looked up at the spiralling crosswalks she realised that it was like the library in Liverpool. She took a photo and then spent ten minutes connecting to the museum's wifi and then sent it to Stuart saying, 'This museum copied your library!' When they left she checked her phone and saw that the message had sent but not the photo and she thought about going back inside but her parents were talking about their favourite pieces and she realised she hadn't absorbed a single one.

They got gelato and walked along the wide footpaths together and her father said there was one other gallery they had to look at. An artist called Chihuly, who Richard said was the most important glass-blower in the world, and Diana laughed and said, 'Well, what a claim to fame,' and Ada was struck, as she was every so often, by how much she was her mother. They reached the gallery and stood on the footpath finishing their gelatos, her father smugly spooning his from the cup into his mouth while Diana and Ada licked the runny bases of their cones.

Inside was like an alien planet, technicolour rivers of glass somehow spiralling upwards all around them. Ada stood under a piece called *Tumbleweed*, hanging neon blue spirals that buzzed and hummed so slightly that you had to lean close to catch it. There were glass sea creatures filling waterless tanks and Diana said, 'Like the Barrier Reef!' and Ada remembered when she and Gabby snorkelled off a boat, staying close together as their parents went further out. Ada tried to take photos but nothing captured the colour and she remembered when she and Mel took the Eurostar in the middle of the week and stayed in a crappy Paris hostel for three days. And on the second day they had gone to the Louvre and lined up with everyone else to see the *Mona Lisa* and Ada said, 'Oh, it really is just like in pictures,' and Mel said, 'I tried to tell you.' This buzzing room of rainbow glass was the opposite of that.

At the gift shop, Ada got a tiny snow globe with a Chihuly miniature inside for Orion and that night, over enchiladas, she showed it to Gabby. 'Sorry if you don't want this, I realised after I bought it that you can go to St Petersburg any time,' and Gabby said, 'I love it, it's like a decoration for a hot Christmas,' which was exactly what Ada had thought when she bought it.

Twenty-eight

29/09/2017

Ada Highfield   **00:47**

How was work today? Did you have work today, I've lost track

Ada Highfield   **00:49**

Kind of crazy news, I think Gabby and Hank might move to Australia

Ada Highfield   **00:53**

I think Hank's only been there like once for a wedding but they seem to be really thinking about it

Ada Highfield   **00:56**

Which would be so good for my parents

Ada Highfield   **01:01**

Like they never complain but I think it really sucks for them having both of us overseas and they're retired and I know they have other stuff on but a baby would fill some of that time!

Ada Highfield 01:02

Babies fill a LOT of time I'm learning

Ada Highfield 01:05

It's just kind of crazy because they seem pretty happy here

Ada Highfield 01:07

But apparently they can both 'work anywhere' according to my dad

Ada Highfield 01:09

And I'm like oh sure yeah they'll work anywhere doing their jobs that I fully understand what they are

Ada Highfield 01:13

Anyway there's reruns of The Amazing Race on here and I'm going to talk my mum into watching with me, wish me luck

Ada Highfield 03:48

OK going to bed! Xx

Stuart Parkes   08:14

Didn't have work yesterday, going in today though

Stuart Parkes   08:16

Cool that your sister might move

Melanie Baker   08:35

EXCUSE ME I DID NOT GET A BABY PHOTO YESTERDAY

Melanie Baker   08:36

PLEASE SEND AT YOUR EARLIEST ETC

Melanie Baker   08:38

Also I don't know if this is weird or you want to know or whatever but Sadie didn't come home last night

Melanie Baker   08:40

I guess I'll … mention it when I see her? Or that might be weird

Melanie Baker   08:42

Anyway thought you might want to know

Melanie Baker   08:43

Love you

Twenty-nine

The yellow house was quiet when they got in on the sixth morning and Hank was sitting on the couch alone. 'Where's Gabby?' Ada asked and Hank gestured upstairs. He looked worse than she'd ever seen him and seemed to be wearing the same T-shirt as when they'd left, though all of his T-shirts looked basically the same to Ada. Hank told them that they'd weighed Orion the night before and he hadn't gained enough weight – he used quotation fingers around 'enough', which seemed out of character – so Gabby had spent a lot of the night on breastfeeding forums. Ada said, 'Like ... on Reddit?' and Hank said, 'Yes, Reddit mostly,' and Diana said, 'Isn't that the one with all the terrible sexists? What do they know about breastfeeding?' and Ada said, 'There's a lot of other stuff on there.'

Richard said, 'So what is Gabby doing now?' and Hank explained that one of the suggestions to boost supply was to take a 'nursing holiday' which meant staying in bed with the baby for two days straight and letting them latch on you as often as they wanted. He said, 'I thought we were doing fine ... we were supplementing, you know ... but Gabby seems really ...' and Diana said, 'She'll be blaming herself, which is very silly but here we are.' Ada asked if she could go up and Hank shrugged and so she did.

When Ada opened their bedroom door, she saw Gabby lying on top of the covers in only her underwear, Orion lying next to her, cuddled in but asleep and not feeding. Ada could see Gabby had been crying. She sat on the end of the bed and asked, 'How's the nursing … holiday?' and Gabby said, 'Why did you say it like that?' and Ada said, 'Like what?' and Gabby said, 'Oh come on, you said it like "nursing holiday",' and Ada said, 'I really don't know what you mean, how else should I say those words,' and Gabby said, 'Can you get the fuck out of my room,' and Ada stood up and left and walked down the stairs.

Hank tried next, carrying up Gabby's water bottle, but he was sent away too. He said to Ada, 'When she was pregnant, Gabby didn't even want to breastfeed,' and Ada said, 'Women, am I right?' and Hank didn't respond. Diana went up next and lasted the longest and while she was gone Richard did a deep clean of the kitchen and then started on the downstairs bathroom. He popped his head out and waved a rubber-gloved hand when Diana came back down and said, 'Should I?' and she shook her head so he went back to scrubbing at the grout.

Ada realised they probably weren't going to the beach today and she went from room to room, blazing and hurt, and then she saw an iPad on a bookshelf in the living room. She asked Hank to connect to Hulu and he did and didn't ask why and she took it upstairs. She walked back into Gabby's room and Orion was feeding now and Gabby was still mostly naked and lying on her side. Ada carried the iPad over and opened it in front of Gabby. Gabby said, 'We don't want screens around Orion,' and Ada said, 'He's not looking, Gab, he's focused on your boob,' and Gabby looked down at him then back up. Ada said, 'Did you know *Top Model* is streaming here?' and Gabby said, 'You mean the new ones?' and Ada said, 'Nah, the old ones. Peak crazy-Tyra.'

Ada opened up season five – 'Cycle five, Tyra didn't do seasons,' Gabby said – and hit play and Gabby watched and Ada watched and then Ada came downstairs to make dinner. They hadn't gone to the store today so she went through Hank's huge walk-in pantry and pulled out beans and tins of tomatoes and said, 'Everyone OK with a veggie chilli?' Hank said, 'Yum!' and she could see how hard he was trying. She said, 'Hank, you should go upstairs, I think she'd like company as long as you're quiet,' and Hank went, clearly grateful to have been told what to do. Ada put on a podcast about Lean-In culture and started chopping a slightly soft red onion and zoned out until the food was done.

Everyone took their bowls upstairs and ate on the floor of Gabby and Hank's bedroom and Gabby said to Ada, 'I don't know if I should have this much spice while I'm nursing,' but she ate most of her bowl. Diana cleaned the dishes, and Ada watched the cycle-six makeover episode with Gabby while Hank scrolled his phone in the corner and their dad did the mosquito guards. They said good night and went back to the tiles. When they settled on the couch, Diana poured Ada a glass of wine and said, 'You were so wonderful for your sister today,' and for the first time in the entire trip Ada wanted to go back to London. She sent Stuart a photo of her kissing the open magnum of wine and then said 'miss you' because she had nothing else to say to him right then.

Ada opened Tinder while her mum set up *The Amazing Race* on the TV (once she'd realised it was a show about travel and not athletics, she'd been surprisingly amenable) and poured stuffed pretzel bites into a big bowl for them to share. Her phone took a moment to calibrate and figure out where she was. The first option to come up was a Gloria, forty-two, divorced, looking to make friends.

Ada stared at Gloria, tanned and glossy blonde, smiling over a bright blue cocktail that matched her eyes. She tried to imagine being fucked by Gloria and found that Gloria was too gentle and fumbling. So she imagined fucking Gloria and that worked a little better but then she wondered if Gloria really was just trying to make friends. If she was then this whole fucking-a-woman thing was a terrible misunderstanding and Ada could only apologise. She swiped left.

Ada continued swiping through Go Gators and big cars and a MAGA hat and an 'I AM A DEMOCRAT, MAGA NEED NOT APPLY' bio but they were all men. Maybe Gloria was the only queer woman in Sarasota and Ada had written her off too quickly. She considered why she wasn't considering men and decided it had something to do with Stuart but not much to do with Sadie. Ada swiped a little more and saw 'they/them' in the profile and a cute face under a sweatband. She paused and then saw that the person in question was only nineteen and decided it was time to change her age range. 18–50 was probably too wide a net when all genders were fish.

Ada realised that even if she matched with someone, she'd be unable to meet them. The rental car wasn't insured for her and anyway she was terrified of driving on the wrong side of the road after two years of not driving at all. There were no buses and hardly any footpaths outside their gated community, so she reflected that unless there was a very bored housewife she hadn't noticed three doors down, this was probably a non-starter. She was trapped in the cold tiles with her wonderful parents and she might go insane. Maybe access to public transport had been all that held her together as a teenager, and she felt a little wave of sympathy for American kids.

Her mother sat on the couch and put the bowl between them and Ada messaged Mel and told her about the Tinder offerings. She wondered how Gabby had made friends here and figured they must all be Hank's old friends, 'which must be THRILLING,' she wrote to Mel. Richard walked into the room and looked at the pretzel pieces and said, 'What are *those*,' and Diana said, 'Oh, they're very gourmet, they pair beautifully with this Californian chardonnay,' and Richard said, 'We have got to get your mother out of Florida.' Ada scrolled Twitter a bit while she watched the TV.

Ben had got the role he'd auditioned for and now all of his tweets ended with #rehearsallife and Ada dutifully liked them. The show was an all-male production of *A Doll's House* and Ada had said to Sadie that she felt uncomfortable about it but the production team was all queer so maybe it was interesting to, like, queer the domestic in that way. And Sadie had said, 'I know you have to say that because your mate is in it but I honestly think it's total shit. That is a show about like … the feminine and the masculine in a deliberately trad sense, I just don't get how you'd, I don't know, make that work. I mean all power to the team; I guess we'll see if they pull it off.' Ada said, 'It opens after you leave London unfortunately but I promise to send you my most scathing thoughts about it,' and Sadie said, 'Make sure you do,' but this whole conversation happened a couple of weeks ago now.

Ada had assumed Sadie had forgotten about it but the night of the packing party she'd said, 'How's your mate's gay Ibsen going?' Ada had shown her some of Ben's tweets and Sadie had said, 'Wait, the children are being played by adult men too?' and Ada said, 'Yes but they're extremely twink-adjacent.' Sadie had laughed and then said, 'OK, do not say that outside this room.'

Ada opened her Messenger app and scrolled to Sadie's name, the last messages between them from days ago, on the train coming home from Liverpool. She copied a tweet of Ben's that said 'lunch breaks with my little dollies #rehearsal-life' and pasted it in then said, 'How many of these dolls will be fucking by opening night do you think?' She paused then sent it and felt secure because Sadie was definitely asleep so she didn't need to expect a reply.

Diana patted Ada's leg and pointed at the television. 'You're missing the man yelling at his wife about a map!' she said and Ada said, 'Which man with which wife?' and Diana said, 'I haven't learned any of their names, I'm sorry.' Ada looked at the TV and then at her mother watching the fighting contestants and wondered how she really felt about Gabby's day in bed. Diana had never seemed particularly interested in babies – she told Ada that kids didn't get interesting until about five and that Richard had been the baby-friendly one of the two of them. But Ada had never considered until now the labour that went into keeping an infant alive and wondered if her mother's view was shaped by her general listlessness. Ada sometimes felt she had inherited this trait, but sometimes felt her work ethic exceeded her mother's – it really depended on the project.

When Ada was growing up, particularly after they moved to Sydney, she watched other mothers bake intricate concoctions for the school fundraisers and run the City 2 Surf every year looking to improve on their time. These Sydney mothers sewed delicate hair pieces for dance recitals and had strong views on the lunches that were available in the school canteen.

Ada's father resembled these mothers in a lot of ways but they were wary of his interest. Ada had assumed as a child that these women didn't have jobs, but as she grew up she saw that often wasn't true. They worked for money but they worked at being professional mums too.

Diana, by contrast, pursued a life without friction. She enjoyed her job at the council, developing projects with local artists and reading endless funding proposals. But she was gone by 5 p.m. every day, if not before, and she would often take long lunches to walk or swim or eat eggs at an all-day breakfast cafe. She had the kind of sunny disposition that put people off scolding her, and as far as Ada knew she had resisted any suggestions at career advancement precisely so she could stick to her comfortable pace.

Ada always had a hair piece for her recital but it was bought, usually by her father, or sometimes gifted to her by a sympathetic mum who viewed her own mother's neglect as something other than benign. Diana was unbothered by these intrusions into her maternal space, telling Ada that if they were going to waste their time, she may as well benefit from it. Though they had moved to the city, Ada saw in her mother a coastal resistance to escalation, and while it annoyed her on occasion, she had come to view it as something like radical. Why shouldn't a life be lived for pleasure? Why shouldn't a woman be coddled?

There was something in Diana now that Ada had never seen before. A fierce desire to be near Orion, a seeming willingness to orient their lives towards him. But was it him or Gabby, this new Gabby who was so much easier to love?

On the third day, Ada had asked Gabby about Orion's name, saying immediately, 'It's so beautiful just I guess I've never met anyone who's actually called that.' And Hank said, 'Well, on our first date we went star gazing—' and Gabby said, 'Hank, you don't need to tell them the bullshit we told your parents, we can tell them the truth.'

Gabby explained that the first time she saw Hank naked she discovered a series of moles on his lower back. 'And I told him they looked like Orion's belt,' and when she said this Hank looked slightly awkward but said, 'No one had ever got that close to them before I guess.' Ada said, 'Oh!' and Diana said, 'You were a virgin, darling?' and Gabby said, 'Mum! No!' And they had all laughed until they were gasping, Gabby saying, 'I can't believe you just said virgin to Hank,' and Diana shrugging in her easy unbothered way. Ada wondered now what her mother would alter to keep Gabby laughing like that, and where Ada fitted in.

She looked up again and Diana was asleep on the other end of the sofa so Ada watched the end of *The Amazing Race* episode because Diana would want to know who was eliminated. While she was watching her father came over and picked up their empty pretzel bowl, taking it wordlessly to the kitchen. She poured herself another glass of wine from the bottle on the table, kept chilled by the air conditioning, and she stayed awake just long enough to see the fighting couple go home.

Thirty

30/09/2017

Stuart Parkes **07:45**

Sorry I didn't message much yesterday, I'm finding this distance thing rough

Stuart Parkes **07:46**

I know we were always a distance thing

Stuart Parkes **07:48**

But now I know what it's like having you in the same place as me it kind of fucks me up more when you're not in the same place as me

Stuart Parkes **07:49**

And we don't know when you will be

Stuart Parkes   **08:11**

I don't know how to say this really but like it's fucking hard being the one who is just at home and living my regular life and you're off on an international holiday

Stuart Parkes   **08:14**

Sorry I'm walking to work, this is a bad time to be doing this

Stuart Parkes   **08:16**

But I need something from you

Stuart Parkes   **08:20**

Like I need you to tell me this is something and this will be something

Stuart Parkes   **08:22**

I don't need monogamy yet

Stuart Parkes   **08:25**

Maybe I never will I don't know

Stuart Parkes   **08:26**

But I need to know that I'm not making an idiot of myself here

Stuart Parkes 08:29

Anyway I'm clocking on

Stuart Parkes 08:31

I meant to say I can't believe you went to the Chihuly gallery

Stuart Parkes 08:32

That guy is such a fucking sell-out

Stuart Parkes 08:33

No offence but liking his stuff is very basic of you

Stuart Parkes 08:35

I can teach you about good art, don't worry

Stuart Parkes 08:37

And you can teach me about the things that you're good at

Ada Highfield 11:46

What things am I good at

Ada Highfield 11:47

I'm going to assume you mean sex but I can also definitely improve your cooking

Ada Highfield   **11:48**

Maybe I move in with you and provide sex and food and in return you paint me all the time

Ada Highfield   **11:49**

Although you should know that I would leave you for Chihuly in a second

Ada Highfield   **11:50**

A sell-out is exactly what I'm looking for

Ada Highfield   **11:51**

And think of how fancy our crockery would be

Ada Highfield   **11:55**

Ah fuck

Ada Highfield   **11:56**

I sent that without scrolling up

Ada Highfield   **11:58**

I don't know what I can offer you in the way of assurance

Ada Highfield   **11:59**

I like you so much

Ada Highfield 12:01

I like being with you and talking to you

Ada Highfield 12:03

I like drinking with you and having sex with you and I like thinking about you

Ada Highfield 12:04

I don't know man

Ada Highfield 12:07

Yesterday I wanted to talk to you so much and you were asleep so I watched an old interview on YouTube with John Lennon just to hear a voice that sounded like yours

Ada Highfield 12:08

I guess if you were going to do that you could watch *Neighbours* or something

Ada Highfield 12:09

I want to offer you what you need but I don't know what it is

Ada Highfield 12:11

I think you want me to send Sadie away but then you say you don't want monogamy so like what would that achieve

Ada Highfield   **12:12**

Or you don't want monogamy YET

Ada Highfield   **12:14**

What am I supposed to do with that?

Ada Highfield   **12:16**

I wish we could just talk about this

Ada Highfield   **12:18**

Could you stay up tonight maybe? I can try to get back early and call you?

Ada Highfield   **12:20**

I guess like a bit after midnight your time? It'll be a bit after 7 for me?

Ada Highfield   **12:21**

I have to go to Gabby's place now

Ada Highfield   **12:22**

Sorry I just woke up

Stuart Parkes   **13:01**

I think Chihuly is dead

Stuart Parkes   **13:03**

Wait no Wikipedia says he's alive

Stuart Parkes   **13:04**

But married, sorry

Stuart Parkes   **13:05**

And old

Stuart Parkes   **13:06**

And you only date younger men

Stuart Parkes   **13:07**

I'll stay up for your call tonight

Stuart Parkes   **13:08**

I can't promise I'll be sober

Thirty-one

When they returned to the yellow house, they found Gabby sitting in the living room with Orion on her chest, looking showered and freshly dressed. Hank was in the kitchen making banana pancakes – 'Don't get excited,' Gabby said, 'it's just banana and egg, not real pancakes. It's a throwback to his paleo days' – and everything was as it was before the day in bed.

Gabby let Orion finish feeding then handed him to Richard, grabbed a pancake off the plate and ate it on the way up to her nap. Hank told them they'd all had a relatively restful night and now he felt energised enough to go outside and mow the lawn, explaining that he had to get out there early before the bugs got bad. Diana asked Ada what she was thinking of making for dinner and Ada said, 'Well, I don't know, are we going to be allowed to go shopping today or will Gabby be having another breakdown?' And Diana and Richard gave her a look she hadn't seen in years and then continued discussing dinner options. So maybe things weren't exactly as they had been.

Ada was angry with them and she had forgotten the sensation of being angry with her parents. She let it roll through her body, deliciously dripping into all the open spaces, the vacuums she'd been ignoring. She felt like she was built to contain this rage, no need to explode when you have endless plains inside you for the malice to scream through like a windstorm in a desert.

These people and their denial disgusted her. Couldn't they see that a tan and a baby hadn't changed Gabby? And poor Hank didn't know, couldn't possibly know the hurricane he had trapped himself inside. Destruction, that was all Gabby wrought, and no one here could see it but Ada. She remembered when she was ten and Gabby had stopped eating chocolate for a whole year so Ada's birthday cake had to be vanilla and how she, Ada, pretended that tasted just as good and she pitied Orion growing up in this house. And then she drank some water straight from the kitchen tap, tipping her head underneath and letting it run into her mouth and then she said, 'I could grill some fish? What kind of fish is good here? Something white, I've kind of gone off salmon,' and she was complicit too.

They went shopping and to the beach and Ada swam away from her parents until she couldn't hear their chatter about one or the other of Ada's uncles. She rolled onto her back and closed her eyes, the sunlight so bright that it burned through her lids. She thought about Stuart. She couldn't not think about him.

After his messages this morning she had read back over their exchanges this week, holding Orion in her arms and scrolling over his head. They weren't even exchanges, really, just thoughts they were having at each other, picked up too late to make sense. And she realised his had been getting shorter and shorter. If she'd been in London she would have showed Mel and they would have pored over them for signs of what was wrong, of where her offence lay. But she was here, for Gabby, and she had let her vigilance slip and now maybe Stuart was letting her go. She couldn't let that happen after how hard she'd worked to get him back onside after the Sadie revelation.

Ada rolled over so she was treading water and opened her eyes. Her parents were back on the sand, sitting with their feet in the shallows, her mum having retrieved her large straw sunhat and put it on her head. Their section of the beach was quiet apart from a pair of mothers with three young children between them and a man sunbathing who Ada had seen every day. He was either twenty-five or sixty, she had never got close enough to figure it out, and his skin was glossed and sheened and the colour of rust.

She knew, really, that Stuart was playing some sort of game with her, becoming distant for a couple of days and returning with a list of demands. She didn't begrudge him that the way she had begrudged him ignoring her when she first told him about Sadie because he had earned it, a little, now. Their relationship was still amorphous enough to absorb these lumps and disappointments and she knew that whatever happened next would be shaped by how completely she could prostrate herself. She knew from experience that he wanted debasement and she was willing to give him that. Hadn't she been giving that to Sadie all along? Maybe it was his turn. Or maybe it was nothing to do with Sadie and the comparison wasn't fair.

Ada paddled towards shore and stopped when she could stand in the water. The tide was barely perceptible here, unlike the violent riptides of her childhood. It could get boring, she thought, this affectless ocean, but only if you gave it time and she would be gone in two days, back to the stinking canals. She remembered being thrown to shore with her junior boogie board still strapped to her legs and coughing up salt and phlegm into the sand. Coming home with her cheeks and shins rubbed equally raw by the bottom that the waves dragged her over repeatedly. She thought that if she could still do that every day maybe she wouldn't be so restless or maybe she would smoke a lot more weed or maybe both.

Mel had said that Sadie hadn't come home one night and then she didn't come home the next night either and Ada didn't know how to feel about that but she settled on 'suspicious'. She didn't assume it was for someone else, only because Sadie seemed driven by desires Ada couldn't access. She felt sure that Sadie expected so little of her, wanted to possess her only in fractured moments that felt like they lasted forever but in reality disappeared when both of them were spent. Ada was a rebound that would never have lasted this long if London Airbnbs were cheaper and that should bring her shame, probably. But she stood in the warm, flat water and she felt that she was simply smarter than other people. Why question something good that moves into your bed when you can instead enjoy it until it goes away again?

Ada sensed she was being dishonest with herself but she didn't know in which direction so she ducked her head under the water and opened her eyes. The salt stung them but the reward was a bumpy base of sand that she disturbed with her big toe, breaking the pattern that had formed overnight and would form again tonight until someone had the sense to rub their toe through it tomorrow. She came up for air then ducked under again and held her eyes open longer, feeling the pale green light draining the anger out of her hidden places and replacing it with salt.

When Ada came up again, she called out to her parents who looked up and waved to her. 'Watch this!' she said, and she ducked under again and went into a handstand, her legs bent awkwardly at first, her knees not pointing quite the way knees are supposed to. And then she straightened them and walked on her hands through the sand, disturbing more and more of it, the tiny white particles floating around her face and clouding her view. She came up for air and her parents applauded her and one of the small children stood up from her sandcastle to applaud her too. And Ada thought of nothing except how much she needed to blow her nose.

They headed back to the house and Gabby was watching *Top Model* on the big TV downstairs, Orion sleeping on her chest. Diana said, 'I'm glad you've given up on the whole screen thing, darling, honestly that baby can barely see ten centimetres past his nose right now.' And Gabby said, 'Yes, though if anyone is going to infiltrate a newborn's subconscious it's Tyra Banks.' Ada lay down next to her and gently stroked the top of Orion's head. 'Are you going to learn to smize little guy? Do you wanna be on top?' and Gabby started to laugh and tried to hold it in so she didn't shake and wake the baby. Ada had made her laugh and she watched two episodes with her sister before going into the kitchen to make dinner.

Hank showed Ada how to turn on their outdoor barbecue but he called it 'firing up the grill' and she let it heat while she made some brown rice. She steamed some broccoli and pan-fried some leftover sweet potato chunks. She put salt and pepper on her snapper fillets and then added a dash of Old Bay Seasoning, which she had only seen mention of in rambling American food blogs. She grilled the fish, three minutes each side, and put together five perfect plates. A scoop of brown rice, slightly wilted broccoli, gooey sticky sweet potato and hot fish. She squeezed lemon over the fish and brought a wedge to the table in case anyone wanted more.

Everyone came to the table and Orion immediately started crying. Gabby tried to leave to feed him but Richard said, 'It's

OK, eat first,' and took the child out the front of the house to stand on the even lawn. Gabby shoved a couple of bites of everything into her mouth – 'Breathe,' said Hank and Gabby ignored him – then pushed her chair back and went to collect her wailing baby. Richard rejoined the table and everyone sat, tense, until the sound from the next room quieted and then they could eat. 'What's on this fish?' asked Diana and Hank said, 'Old Bay Seasoning! A secret of the south,' and he winked at Ada. She pierced a piece of broccoli, felt repulsed and spooned the plain rice into her mouth instead. When Hank had finished eating, he carried Gabby's plate into the living room and fed her tiny pieces while she fed Orion and eventually the plate was cleared.

Gabby smiled at Ada and said, 'I really appreciate you doing all this cooking,' and Ada said, 'It's no trouble, I do most of the cooking for my flatmate too,' and Gabby said, 'You'll make someone a lovely wife one day.' Ada felt her stomach twist, not at the words but at how obviously Gabby was joking. Because why couldn't she do that? Why shouldn't she.

When Diana had cleared the plates, they said goodbye, and as he let them out Hank said, 'Tomorrow is your last full day, isn't it? What will we do without you,' and Ada said, 'Maybe your parents will come over more?' Hank said, 'Ah yes, your sister would love that,' as though the three of them were sharing a funny secret, and Ada wondered if Hank knew this was the first secret she and Gabby had shared in their entire lives. In the car she realised Hank had mentioned a brother in his email and she hadn't seen or met this man. She asked her parents about him and Richard said, 'Matthew! We met him at the hospital. Does something in retail, can't remember what,' and Ada thought maybe Hank understood her and Gabby after all.

Ada walked into the tiled house and her phone lit up and the most recent message was from Stuart. He said he was waiting up and she realised she'd forgotten they were supposed to talk. This wasn't like her – Mel described her as 'obsessive' and sometimes 'love addicted' – and she considered that maybe her entire personality would be different without the internet. Maybe everyone's would, even people like Sadie who set themselves up at least partly in opposition to it.

Ada pulled a bottle of rosé from the fridge and poured a large glass and said, 'I'm going in to my room to make a call if that's OK.' Diana nodded and didn't turn around from her spot in the pantry. 'Don't be surprised if these are gone when you're done ... whatever these are ... almond-butter almonds? So the almonds have ... almond butter on them. OK, I have to try this,' and Ada felt briefly pulled to a seat on the couch and a handful of those atrocities. But she carried her wine into her all-white room and climbed up onto her all-white bed and spilled a spot of rosé on her pillow case and picked up her phone to call.

Stuart answered and he was also sitting in bed, his face lit under the fairy lights like a canal boat, speckled and lovely. She raised her glass of rosé and said 'hi' and he raised a tumbler of something dark and said 'hi yourself' and then he said, 'Could I turn my camera off?' and she said, 'No?' and he sighed deeply. Ada asked him about his day and he told her about going for a late breakfast with his flatmate Paul, who was recently dumped by his boyfriend and suddenly wanted lots of company in the middle of the day.

Ada said, 'Wait, I didn't realise any of your flatmates were queer?' and Stuart said, 'You met Paul with his boyfriend the night you stayed over. Don't you remember? I was asleep, I guess.' Ada remembered the two pale men she had run into who she hadn't read as partners at all. She tried to explain this, that she had thought they were both straight, and Stuart said, 'Why would you assume that?' She knew he was poking her, provoking her, trying to question her politics and her sense of her own identity. She didn't know what he'd get from that but she met him halfway and said, 'I guess I'm prejudiced against northern people,' and he said, 'Everyone from the south is,' and she said, 'Yeah and Australia is way south,' and then they were mostly back on track.

Stuart said after breakfast they'd gone to see the exhibition at the Tate that Ada had been so interested in and she thought this might be provocation too or it might just be insensitivity, which she had long learned not to take too seriously when it came from men. Perhaps that was sexist of her, she had said to Mel, but it was also kind of survival. You can engrain sensitivity into men over time but expecting it from them up front would narrow your dating pool pretty substantially. And Mel said, 'And we're against narrowing dating pools?' and Ada said, 'Yeah, fair point.' But anyway, Stuart was young.

Ada asked questions about the Tate exhibition and Stuart seemed to be put off-kilter by this and that's how she knew that mentioning it had been bait after all and not guileless-ness. He told her about an older trans artist who did a piece addressing the legacy of the AIDS crisis and a young lesbian artist working with found objects. And she said, 'All sounds very earnest, I guess I'll stick with my commercially success-ful glass-blowing,' and he said, 'How do you get away with saying the stupidest shit?' and she said, 'Because if you say it confidently people assume you're actually smart under all that.' Then she said she was going to put him face down on the bed so she could go and refill her wine glass and he said, 'No, show me the house,' and then he said, 'Anyway, shouldn't

I be putting you face down on a bed?' She thrilled a little and didn't say that it could actually go either way.

Ada took her phone for a walk through the cold tiles, angling it down so he could see her toes, painted a shiny coral, crossing the floor. He said, 'Woah, fancy feet,' and she said, 'Yes, we had a bit of time to kill a few days ago so Mum and I went to a beauty place in a strip mall and got pedicures.' She pulled the phone back up so he was looking at her face and he said, 'Say strip mall again, I don't know what it means but it sounds hot,' and then she turned into the kitchen where her father was eating olives at the bench. She waved the phone in his face and said, 'Stuart, Richard, Richard, Stuart,' and Richard said, 'Nice to meet you,' and returned to his olives and his news app.

Ada poured her wine and headed back to the room and when she settled in, Stuart looked annoyed. 'You didn't tell me I'd be meeting your dad, I'm wasted,' and she said, 'Trust me, my dad is used to meeting my wasted friends and lovers,' and he said, 'Wow, you can make a guy feel so special.' Ada held the phone away from her, turned it to the window and said, 'Look at that sunset, the sky goes fully postcard-pink here,' and he said, 'It's nice. Sorry I'm being weird.' She turned the phone back to her face and said, 'It's OK, I know it's late there.'

Stuart didn't ask any questions about the baby or her family but he was interested in what she'd bought from the Goodwill and even a little in what she'd been cooking. Then he asked her what she thought she'd work on when she got back to London and she said honestly, if a job doesn't come up soon she might need to temp for a while. He said, 'Or you could move in with me. Imagine how cheap the rent would be on my shitty little room if we split it,' and she said, 'Don't joke, I might do it if I get desperate,' and he said, 'I'm not joking, are you?'

And then Ada lay on her side, holding her phone close to her face as the room got darker, her glass of wine balanced precariously in front of her on the bed. 'What do you want us to do, Stuart?' she asked and he inhaled and she thought an onslaught was coming but then he let the air out and didn't say anything. She said, 'What do you want me to say to you? Are you looking for guarantees?' and he said, 'It's normal to look for guarantees.' Ada was quiet for long enough that he asked if she was still there and then she said, 'I think it is normal, but isn't this too soon for that? We've been talking, what, a month? And we've spent one night together.'

Stuart said that wasn't that basically how her sister had got together with Hank. 'They fucked once and then they decided to be together.' And Ada said, 'Yeah but they're older than us and anyway what, do you want to put a baby in me? Because I don't know that your flatmates would like that.' He said, 'Do you want a baby some day?' and she said, 'With you?' and he said, 'Any baby,' and she said, 'No, I don't want just any baby.' Then silence again.

Ada noticed Stuart's eyes fluttering and asked if he needed to go to sleep. He said he did but 'before I do, can we make a plan?' Ada said sure, maybe, I don't know, what plan? And he said, 'Any plan. I need to know that there is a plan we could make together, like in the future.' And Ada said, 'OK how about this, how about I guarantee that within two weeks of me getting back, we can see each other. It's expensive coming to Liverpool, though.' Stuart said, 'Then clear your bedroom for me,' and Ada said, 'I can't just clear out a person, she's not a broken chair.' More silence and Stuart said, 'We'll go somewhere else then,' and Ada said OK and then she watched as he fell asleep in front of her and then his phone tipped forwards and everything was dark. She hung up.

It was getting late now but Ada headed out to get another glass of wine. She heard her dad brushing his teeth in the bathroom and wondered what he had thought of Stuart. Nothing much, probably. She had barely told them anything about this guy except that he was an artist in Liverpool and from that they had likely surmised a lot of accurate things about his life. She hadn't talked about Sadie because 'a playwright from Perth' wouldn't sum her up as neatly and she couldn't face telling these people who loved her about inertia and how she had hurtled towards someone who would neatly step out of the way.

Ada sat on the couch next to her sleeping mother and noticed there were two almond-butter almonds left in the bowl. Ada knew her mother's appetite, so like her own, and felt moved at the willpower it would have taken her to leave some behind. Ada popped one in her mouth and felt it roll around, tacky and sweet. She decided to decide. It was Stuart, who had asked her to choose, while Sadie, she was sure, never would. And so, inevitably, it was him.

Thirty-two

01/10/2017

Sadie Ali 08:48

Hey! You're back tomorrow, right?

Sadie Ali 08:49

I want to make sure I'm in when you get back

Sadie Ali 08:51

I went into the Turkish grocer near the station for the first time and they sell proper vine leaves, why did you never tell me?

Sadie Ali 08:52

Anyway I thought I'd make dolmades if that sounds good to you

Sadie Ali 08:54

I somehow have a whole free day, why not stuff some leaves

Sadie Ali   **08:57**

Anyway I hope you've had an amazing time! I can't believe how cute your little nephew is.

Sadie Ali   **09:01**

I was waiting for a response on the dolmades and just realised it's like 4am there

Sadie Ali   **09:03**

Anyway see you tomorrow!

Ada Highfield   **12:23**

Good morning! Yes I'm home tomorrow, will I be hugely jet lagged who knows?

Ada Highfield   **12:24**

Dolmades sound great though

Ada Highfield   **12:25**

If I fall asleep on the couch either you or Mel has to put them into my mouth and make me chew

Sadie Ali   **12:27**

We'll scissors paper rock for it

Ada Highfield   **12:28**

Hi!

Sadie Ali 12:30

Hi! Looking forward to getting home?

Ada Highfield 12:32

I don't know, yes I guess? It's always hard leaving the folks

Sadie Ali 12:33

And the baby I'm guessing

Sadie Ali 12:35

Last time I stayed at my brother's place in Melbourne I was ready to kill him by day 2 but my nieces are perfect angels

Ada Highfield 12:38

Maybe that's why we have niblings, it's nature's way of making adult siblings talk to each other

Sadie Ali 12:40

Lol yes maybe

Ada Highfield 12:42

Speaking of, I'm going over to my sister's place now, I'll see you tomorrow!

Ada Highfield 12:44

I should be home by like 8? Depending on security? So might be a late dinner, sorry

Sadie Ali   **12:46**

No worries, I guess message when you're leaving Gatwick and I can get stuff going

Ada Highfield   **12:48**

Thanks, that's really nice of you

Sadie Ali   **12:49**

My pleasure honestly

Sadie Ali   **12:50**

And maybe Mel will invite Will over again!

Ada Highfield   **12:51**

Wait what do you mean again?

Ada Highfield   **12:52**

Ah fuck I have to go

Ada Highfield   **12:53**

TELL ME WHAT YOU MEAN BY AGAIN

Sadie Ali   **12:54**

Aaaah fuck um maybe ask Mel

Ada Highfield   12:55

EXCUSE ME MELANIE DID YOU HAVE A BOY STAY OVER
WHILE I WAS GONE?

Ada Highfield   12:56

I AM GOING TO GABBY'S BUT SEND A FULL REPORT FOR ME
TO READ WHEN I GET BACK TONIGHT

Melanie Baker   14:33

Shan't. I'll tell you when you get home.

Stuart Parkes   14:46

So I've been thinking about where we should go

Stuart Parkes   14:48

And looking at my bank account

Stuart Parkes   14:49

And coming up with no ideas

Stuart Parkes   14:51

But I miss you

Stuart Parkes   14:53

And I'm going to figure it out

Thirty-three

Gabby didn't go for her usual morning nap on Ada's last day and when they were discussing going to the shops to buy lunch she said she'd come with them. Diana said, 'Oh darling, it's OK, you don't need to do that,' and Gabby said, 'Please, I am so stir-crazy.' But it turns out deciding to go somewhere with a newborn creates a whole mission. By the time they had packed Gabby's car with nappies and cloths and three changes of clothes for the baby and one change of clothes for Gabby and Hank had checked Orion's car seat was secure ('For the millionth time,' Gabby said apologetically, though Ada noticed she was watching pretty carefully) and Orion had got a fresh nappy and then Gabby had fed him and he'd needed another nappy and then everyone was hungry so Ada quickly made them ham and cheese sandwiches and they ate them standing up in the kitchen and then Orion needed another nappy change – by that time, the sun was higher in the sky than it usually was when they left.

Hank drove and Gabby sat in the back seat of the car with Orion. Ada looked out the back window of their rental and saw Hank's car crawling down the street, fading back even before they hit the freeway. When they got to the grocery store, Ada and her parents sat in the car for twenty minutes waiting for the new parents to arrive. At first, they tried sitting with the doors open but the air was so hot that they resorted to closing everything up and turning on their air conditioning. Richard casually said that he could see how Americans were destroying the planet, their cars were basically their homes, and Diana started to disagree with him out of loyalty to Gabby's chosen home and then said, 'They really should have more trains, though.'

Eventually Hank pulled in and parked near them and he got out of the car but Gabby stayed behind because, as he explained, Orion was asleep in his seat. Diana and Richard went over to look at him and, after a pause, Ada followed them, the tarmac warm even through her canvas shoes. They looked through the back window at Gabby looking at Orion who was looking at nobody and Richard said, 'Will they be too hot in there?' and Hank, looking slightly affronted, said, 'The air is on.' Then he quickly rearranged his face into a smile. They headed into the store and Hank touched Ada's arm and said, 'Don't worry about cooking tonight, we can pick something up, you shouldn't have to go out of your way on your last night.' So Ada trailed behind him as he picked up formula and apples and wondered why she'd come.

They packed the boots and headed to the beach but Ada was feeling slightly spotty behind the eyes from so much time in the overheating car. When they pulled in, Gabby eased Orion out of the car seat and strapped him to Hank in a complicated carrier that they had mastered over the last two weeks. Hank almost tiptoed towards the sand, holding a parasol over the sleeping infant. He looked incongruously dainty and Ada felt a rush of something warm towards this man who she realised, for the first time, would be in her life forever. Even if he and Gabby broke up, he was the father of her nephew and she would never ever be rid of him and that felt OK.

Ada headed straight to the water, sensing that this might be a quick visit, and tried to quash the resentment she felt. Because this was her last swim, in so long, and no one seemed to appreciate that. Her parents would be back in Sydney soon and Siesta Key would be here waiting for Orion to grow up on. Or maybe he wouldn't because maybe her sister was going home.

Ada swam out, moving strongly, kicking frenetically. She was doing a casual sort of freestyle but holding her head under for longer than she should, taking breaths sparingly, letting her chest start to hurt a little before turning her cheek. When she hit deep water, she stopped and looked at her family. Her father was swimming too, but staying closer to shore, and Hank was hanging back with Orion in a small patch of shade near the edge of the sand. Gabby and Diana were sitting with their feet in the water and Ada vaguely remembered Gabby saying she couldn't have a bath until her stitches healed. So she probably couldn't swim, either.

Ada drifted for a precious few minutes until she heard her mother calling her name. She looked back to shore and saw them gesturing for her to come in, so she started to swim, more slowly this time, imagining them waiting for her, imagining refusing to get out. But she hit the sand eventually like she always did and Gabby said, 'I'm sorry, I didn't want to cut your swim short, we need to go back but I told Mum and Dad you could stay.' Richard was drying himself and said, 'But it's your last afternoon together!' and Gabby and Ada looked at each other and Ada didn't know what she saw in her sister's face. She wrapped her towel around her and sat in the back of the car, her hair dripping on the hot leather seat.

They got back to the yellow house and Gabby took Orion away to feed and Ada showered and then didn't know what to do with herself if she wasn't cooking dinner. She pulled her book of theory out of her bag and opened to a chapter about triggering sense memory to enhance your acting and put the book away again. Hank found her sitting in the court-yard with her green cotton dress pulled up to her underwear, letting the sun warm her legs.

'Not going to have much of this back in London I'm guess-ing?' Hank said, gesturing to her glowing shins and she was suddenly aware of the hair that she'd let grow out there though he gave no indication he noticed or was bothered by it.

She said, 'We might have a little summer left – though, yeah, not much sun,' and Hank said, 'I'm going to pick up dinner, want to come with me?' There was nothing she could pretend to be doing in this house that wasn't hers so she stood up and followed him out.

As she buckled herself into the front seat of Hank's enor-mous car, Ada asked, 'Where are we going for dinner?' and Hank said, 'Oh, somewhere very fancy,' and winked at her, then said, 'Popeye's,' and she said, 'That's chicken right?' Hank pulled out of the driveway and said in a mock-offended voice, 'Chicken? It's so much more than chicken, it's a southern institution!' Then he said, 'And your dad is going to hate all that grease but luckily Orion is still young enough for us to pull the baby card. I'll tell him fried foods boost breastfeeding antibodies or something,' and he smiled at her then turned his eyes back to the road.

Ada allowed herself, for a few minutes, to do the thing she had avoided doing since she arrived in Florida, and consider what her life would be like if she loved Hank and he loved her the way Gabby loved Hank and Hank loved Gabby. He was funny, Ada hadn't expected that, and Gabby was funny when she was with him. They had this ongoing bit about the movie *Scream* that Ada didn't really understand. At one point Gabby said, 'I should have known Ada was bi when we were kids, she was way too into Drew Barrymore,' and Hank said, 'I'm a Neve man myself.' So, also, his comfort with her queerness was more than she had expected. Overall, he was so much more than she had expected.

If Ada loved Hank and Hank loved Ada, she would move to Florida for him and cook with him in the big yellow house and swim while he worked because there would probably be nothing for her to do here. Or maybe she'd get a job in St Petersburg, become a shining star in the Sarasota arts community, a big fish with a cute accent in a small, supportive pond. And her hair would lighten and her freckles would come back and they would shower together at the end of a sweaty day. They would Skype her family back home and Gabby would look at the man on the screen and think, I wonder what it would be like if that man loved me and I loved him. And she would stay in Melbourne and she would be alone.

Ada wondered how she and Hank would meet – maybe he'd spot her in a bar on one of his business trips to London or, better, she would tour in a show to New York and he'd be in the audience. And everyone would agree they were an unlikely pair, the money man and the artistic girl, and Ada would wave her cocktail glass in the air and say, 'It's a tale as old as time! I'm Kirsten Dunst in that movie and he's the grandad from *Gilmore Girls*!' And Hank would smile indulgently at her and say, 'I'm not *that* much older than you,' and she'd say, 'Oh, pour me another, you filthy old man,' and she'd never have to pay rent again. But then there would be no Orion because any baby Ada had would be no Orion and that suckling, squalling, perfect infant was inevitable, Ada could see that.

Ada knew the fashionable thing to say was that she wasn't interested in men like Hank but the acute truth of it was that they were not interested in her.

Ada asked Hank a few questions about growing up in Sarasota and he told her that he had mostly drifted through school with a few close friends – 'I wish you could have met them but most of them have moved away' – and then left for college planning never to come back. While he was away, his parents inherited the yellow house from a grandparent and told Hank it was his, clearly thinking it would persuade him back. 'But it didn't,' he said, apologetically she thought, though she had no stake in the matter at all. 'I moved to Chicago to be with my college girlfriend and rented it out. And when we broke up, I stayed in Chicago and then moved to New York when a job came up and then I met your sister.'

'And now you're back here,' Ada said and Hank turned on the indicator and swung them into a line of waiting cars at the Popeye's drive-thru.

'And now I'm back here.'

Ada asked, 'What happened with you and your college girlfriend? Sorry for the personal question but I'm like, really nosey, I'm sure Gabby told you,' and Hank laughed and said, 'She never mentioned that actually. But Madison and I broke up because I wanted to have kids and she didn't. Well, I dunno, that was the reasoning at the time but I guess it turned out not to be true. We were together nine years and didn't get married and now we've been apart five years and she's married with two kids and I have one so I guess actually who knows why we broke up? But thank god we did.'

Ada didn't know what to say to this so after a pause she

said, 'Are people really called Madison then? I thought that was like a joke name,' and Hank said, 'Oh yes, there are a lot of *Madisons*,' and he said it with such an over the top drawl that Ada accepted him, forever. And then he said, 'Are there really people called Crocodile where you're from?' and she stared at him before realising he was joking and then she said, 'I actually dated a Crocodile,' and then he stared at her until he realised she was joking and she saw a flash of decades of them being exactly like this together.

When they got to the window, Hank ordered what sounded like an immense amount of food and when they picked it up Ada was delighted to see that it was. She was hungry, starving suddenly, and Hank said to her, 'Look in the bag for the popcorn shrimp, I got that as a little car snack. A reward for us hunter-gatherers.' Ada pulled out the greasy paper bag and said, 'Is this it?' and Hank said, 'Have you never had popcorn shrimp before?' and they ate the whole bag in under a minute. It tasted like indulgence and love. Ada said to Hank, 'We actually have a whole fried chicken culture in London too,' and he said, 'But this is *Nashville* fried chicken,' and Ada said, 'When I get rich I'm going on a fried-chicken-of-the-world tour. I'll start in Korea.' Then Ada laughed and Hank said, 'What?' and she said, 'I forgot I'm vegetarian.'

They were about to turn into their street when Hank said, in a rehearsed sort of way, 'It was really nice having you here. I think Gabby ... she worried you wouldn't want to come,' and Ada felt annoyed that Gabby had intruded on their time. But there would be no time with Hank without Gabby and she said, 'Why wouldn't I want to come?' Hank glanced her way then said, 'Sure, that's what I said,' and she realised he knew everything. She wanted to redirect that knowledge, explain it all from her side, but she didn't know what Gabby's side was. There was a villain and a victim between them, Ada had always felt. And Hank had chosen villain, though maybe he didn't believe that. And maybe it wasn't like that really anyway, Ada told herself, but she knew her gut couldn't follow her there.

They got into the house and Hank unloaded the food onto big aluminium platters. Hot chicken pieces and cajun-spiced fries, individual servings of mac and cheese and one coleslaw between them which was more than enough. Also biscuits, those savoury American scones that Ada had been ordering at diners and that she now dipped into gravy-covered mashed potato, letting the hot carb seep into the other hot carb and heat every part of her on the way down. She was surprised to see Hank eat like this and he said, 'Oh no, you've seen through my classy disguise,' and Gabby smiled at him and smiled at Ada.

Everyone sat down to serve themselves except Hank who started dumping ice in the blender and then free-poured tequila and an acid-coloured margarita mix in. 'Start!' he said to them as he poured out drinks for the women (Richard had sighed and said, 'I'll drive,' as soon as the tequila appeared) and himself. Orion was sleeping in a soft sling on Gabby and as she picked up her lurid icy cocktail Ada took out her phone and took a photo. Gabby laughed and said, 'Please submit that photo to the Mother of the Year awards,' and Hank said, 'I'd vote for you.'

As they ate and drank, Ada pretended to be a waiter at a fancy restaurant. 'The tartness of the elegant drink pairs beautifully with the crisp spice of the carefully seasoned chicken,' and Diana took a long sip of her drink and said, 'Ah yes, a complementary pairing.' Orion stirred but didn't wake up and after Gabby finished eating she held up her hands and

Hank dampened a paper towel and wiped them for her. And then Richard and Hank wound out the mosquito covers, Hank slightly pink in the face, and it was time to leave.

They all walked to the door and Diana and Richard headed out to the car to let their daughters say goodbye. Ada looked down at the sleeping Orion. 'I wish I could hold him one more time,' she said and Gabby said, 'I don't really want to wake him, sorry,' and Ada said, 'Duh of course, I wouldn't expect you to. Let sleeping nephews lie.' Hank hugged her, full body, and he smelled of grease and old sunscreen, the smell of every boy she dated in high school.

Ada turned to Gabby and wondered when she had last hugged her like that or if she ever had. Maybe when she was little like Orion her parents had laid her in Gabby's arms and Gabby had felt an uncomplicated love for her. But more likely she had felt responsibility – don't drop the baby – and maybe an urgency to get up and go play, do something more interesting than hold this puking pale blob that had moved into her house.

Ada couldn't hug Gabby like that now, anyway, because of the sling on her front and it was a relief. She put an arm around her big sister's shoulders and squeezed slightly, from the side. Gabby said, 'Thank you for being here and for doing so much cooking and everything. It really helped. I don't know what I'll do when you're all gone and Hank's back at work,' and Ada said, 'Popeye's every night?' and Gabby said, 'Not a bad plan.' Ada touched the tip of her index finger to Orion's soft head and said, 'Goodbye, little guy, I don't know when I'll see you again,' and Gabby said, 'Maybe back in Sydney?' And Ada said, 'Maybe,' and then, 'OK, I'll leave you to your long baby night.'

She squeezed Gabby one more time and Gabby said, 'Have a safe flight,' and Ada crossed the lawn. When she got to the car she turned back and waved goodbye to her softened sister and the tiny centre of her world and her large, American almost brother-in-law. And Hank called out, 'Safe flight, Ada! Love you!' like it was an easy thing to say. And Diana stuck her head out the window and said, 'We'll be back tomorrow after we take Ada to the airport,' and Gabby said, 'OK, thanks Mum, see you then,' and she closed the door and they pulled away.

Back at the house Ada packed, a light buzz from the margaritas easing the process along. She had washed her jumpsuit on the first day and would be wearing it home and she looked at her rumpled, sweaty sundresses crushed into her bag and knew that it was over. Tomorrow she was going home. She thought about talking to Stuart about it but she felt too tired to explain so she sent him a selfie lying next to her open suitcase and a plane emoji and then she went back out to her mum.

Thirty-four

02/10/2017

Ada Highfield   **19:11**

I'm at Gatwick! Back on British soil!

Ada Highfield   **19:13**

I am extremely very tired but looking forward to eating (and seeing you and Mel I guess)

Ada Highfield   **19:15**

Going through security now

Ada Highfield   **20:05**

OK that took fucking forever

Ada Highfield   **20:07**

I will be home laaaaate

Sadie Ali   20:11

Don't stress! It'll be a midnight feast!

Ada Highfield   20:12

Tell Mel to go to bed! She has work tomorrow!

Sadie Ali   20:13

She says to please stop bossing her around MUM

Sadie Ali   20:14

She said to capitalise Mum

Ada Highfield   20:21

OK cute cute, I am getting on the Gatwick Express now, I will
be with you sooooon

Sadie Ali   20:22

I'll get the mushrooms going

Ada Highfield   20:23

MUSHROOMS

Ada Highfield   20:24

I don't even care what you're doing to them, I am so hungry

Ada Highfield   20:32

My flight was at like buttfuck o'clock and I ate what I guess???
Was lunch??? On the plane like 10 hours ago

Ada Highfield   20:41

Anyway you are probably cooking, SEE YOU SOON, food first
hugs after

Ada Highfield   20:42

Guess who's back, back again

Stuart Parkes   20:43

Hey my girl is in my timezone, that's cool

Ada Highfield   20:44

Ugh being in the same country at the same time, isn't that a
little too intimate

Ada Highfield   20:45

(I'm joking, hello!)

Stuart Parkes   20:46

How was the flight?

Ada Highfield 20:47

OK don't laugh but I watched 27 *Dresses*

Stuart Parkes 20:48

I'm not laughing but I am breaking up with you

Ada Highfield 20:49

Because of the bad wedding movie?

Stuart Parkes 20:50

Yeah I'm just not sure I'm ready to get married 27 times

Ada Highfield 20:52

Ugh she doesn't get married 27 times, she's a bridesmaid 27 times and if you weren't such a gross boy you'd know that

Stuart Parkes 20:53

How many times have you seen this movie?

Ada Highfield 20:54

I plead the fifth

Stuart Parkes 20:55

America changed you man

Ada Highfield 20:56

I'm going home to eat and collapse, it has been a long fucking day

Stuart Parkes 21:01

OK have fun

Ada Highfield 21:02

Ah come on you can't get weird every time I mention going home

Ada Highfield 21:03

I do it almost every day

Ada Highfield 21:04

It'll get tired

Ada Highfield 21:09

I was thinking I might have a chat with She Who You Will Not Talk About though

Ada Highfield 21:10

If you want that

Stuart Parkes   **21:11**
Like a chat about the weather or what

Ada Highfield   **21:12**
I guess a chat about me and you?

Stuart Parkes   **21:13**
Do you want to do that?

Ada Highfield   **21:14**
Will it make things better for you?

Stuart Parkes   **21:16**
I guess I can't answer that until it's happened

Ada Highfield   **21:18**
OK well … I'll keep you posted

Ada Highfield   **21:19**
What are you doing tonight?

Stuart Parkes   **21:21**
Paul and I are in a YouTube hole

Ada Highfield   **21:22**

He's still using you as a substitute boyfriend huh

Stuart Parkes   **21:26**

I guess it's nice to feel wanted ha ha see I wrote ha ha so you'd
know I'm joking

Ada Highfield   **21:27**

Very convincing

Thirty-five

No matter where she lived, Ada loved the feeling of walking up her own street. She didn't know her neighbours at this place – why would you know your neighbours in London, there's so many of them and a lot of them suck – but she felt like the corner she turned and the pedestrian crossing that a lot of drivers ignored and the foxes joyfully fucking in the bushes outside the Anglican church were the neighbours that she needed. The footpath was covered in scattered crisp packets and dog shit and sometimes human shit too. But it was her street, this was her spot and she had earned it.

Ada got off the bus and walked, wrapping her jacket tightly around her as she dragged her bag. The seasons had started to change in her absence but she was still warm enough, just, when she was in a hurry and two light layers. Some people loved this time of the year when the edges of the evenings got crisp and Ada firmly believed they were experiencing mass delusion. The same people who claimed to come into their own when their cardigans came out would be depressed out of their mind come February but every year they celebrated the onset of autumn like a kind of amnesia.

Ada was no amnesiac and she resisted their propaganda at every turn. She had never encountered the Autumn Girl in

Australia because in Sydney at least autumn had very little shape to it. She might get away with skipping sunscreen some days but otherwise the heat ebbed out gradually and the light remained. It was only in true winter that the sky went from almost painfully bright to simply golden, a slightly softer blue. Whereas autumn in London meant moving drinks inside to the corners of pubs, dark ales that made everyone drunk in a way Ada found unpleasant. Dark corners and dark ales and dark leather chairs belonged to men and she thought they could have it, though Mel said she shouldn't cede that ground. It meant rain and sludge and two days of vibrant leaves before they became brown slipping hazards as she got on and off the bus.

Mel had struck a 'neutral about autumn' position in the flat, partly to stave off Ada's seasonal madness but Ada sensed this year she would have an ally in Sadie. Sadie, who was choosing the get-the-fuck-out-of-winter dodge, to go back to radiance. A double-up on summer, gorging on the sun. Ada found she couldn't imagine Sadie in winter but she was sure she would wear a very cool, structured coat, the kind that Ada couldn't pull off. And she would probably be sad too. But Ada knew she wouldn't be sticking around long enough for that.

Ada passed her most important neighbours, the Turkish guys who ran their local 24-hour shop who she had seen almost daily for two years and who would never acknowledge that they knew each other. She remembered the night of the Brexit vote when she had gone in there to buy overpriced gin and five kinds of chocolate at 11 p.m. and they gave no sign that they knew anything of significance was happening. Or when she went in at 3:30 a.m. the night Trump was elected to buy another bottle of wine because there were three friends staying over and they were running out.

The friends had come over for an all-night election party to celebrate the first woman president – they would have voted for Bernie over her but hey, a woman, that's something – and the party had become a wake around 1 a.m. but they couldn't make themselves sleep. So she went down the road in pyjama bottoms and a coat and grabbed a cheap and familiar Rioja, and when she went to pay for it with the card slipped into her pocket, the man at the store asked her for ID. She was clearly over eighteen and she didn't think many teenagers were out for a bottle of red in the middle of the night and most importantly, this same man had sold her hundreds – possibly, best not to think about it, but possibly thousands – of bottles of wine. And here they were, engaged in a strange stand-off as the world collapsed around them. So Ada called Mel, who came to the shops in her own pyjamas and waved Ada's ID, and they paid for the wine and as they walked home Mel said, 'Good to know some things won't change,' and they laughed and then when they got back everyone cried a little more.

Ada waved through the shop window and was ignored and it felt great. Anonymity! What a drug! She reached their building and headed inside and when she opened the door to the flat she heard Sadie saying 'gigantes' and Mel said 'gigant ass' and Sadie laughing. Ada left her Cons at the door and headed into the kitchen and the clock on the wall said 10:17 p.m., but here were these two friends of hers, waiting up.

Ada hugged Mel who said, 'I missed you! Sadie is making us giant ass beans,' and Sadie said 'gigantes' and laughed again. Then Ada turned to Sadie expecting a smile and Sadie put down the wooden spoon and came to her, hugged her with both arms and kissed the corner of her head. It would have thrown Ada off but it was so warm in the kitchen and Mel had poured her a glass of cava while explaining that, sorry, most of it was gone and instead of resisting Ada melted into the night ahead.

They didn't set the table but ate in the kitchen, around the stove, Ada and Mel sitting on the bench and Sadie perched on a stool. They had the beans and the messily rolled dolmades – Sadie said she wasn't a very delicate cook but Ada said they were as delicious as they were ugly. There was halloumi-stuffed mushrooms and lemony potatoes and when the cava was gone there was the kind of sharply acidic sauvignon blanc that supermarkets favoured and Ada associated with this flat.

They asked question after question about Florida and Sadie was so interested in St Petersburg and jealous of the pure white sandy beach. And Mel wanted more diner stories, of the pumpkin pancakes that tasted of pure sugar and the gruff men at the next table who Ada overheard union organising. Ada said she'd assumed they were Trumpy before she heard the union stuff and Sadie said, 'Union guys can definitely be Trumpy,' and Mel said, 'See, that's so confusing to me, I don't understand anything any more,' and the others agreed that none of them did.

Sadie wanted to know about Orion, how his feeding was going, had his weird belly-button nub fallen off yet – it had and it was a horror show, Ada said. Mel asked about Hank and Ada struggled to explain him.

'He's like … every stereotype of like a too clean American that I could have come up with but he's also kind of cool? He's really funny and he … I mean, he's a good dad obviously. And hot!' And Sadie touched her arm and said, 'A word of advice? Don't fuck your brother-in-law,' and Ada said, 'Well, they're not married so he's technically not my brother-in-law,' and Sadie said, 'Ah well, in that case go with god!'

Then Mel asked about Gabby and whether they had got along OK and Ada said yes, mostly, 'although as I'm sure you can imagine, when the family's most precious girl has a baby, she will milk the attention for all she can get.' And Sadie said, 'Doesn't everyone do that when they have a baby?' So Ada told a few mildly exaggerated stories about her cooking and her cleaning and Gabby's day in bed but she couldn't strike the right tone, she sensed, so she pivoted back to Hank. And Mel said she needed to go to bed. Ada said, 'But I haven't caught up on Will news!' and Mel said, 'Tomorrow!' and slid off the bench. Ada called after her, 'Why won't you tell me stuff! I need gossip to live! Oh god he's not—' and Mel called back, 'No, he's not a Tory. Good night!'

Ada turned to Sadie and said, 'So what's happening with this guy? Are they, like, a couple?' and Sadie said, 'I don't know much more than you! He seems nice. Hard to know if they're casual or relationshippy.' Ada said, 'I've never known Mel in a relationship, could be kind of weird. But nice, right?' and Sadie shrugged, which Ada took to mean that it wasn't for her to say.

Ada had a quick shower while Sadie cleaned up, though Mel had offered to do it in the morning. Then she dragged her bag into their room and emptied the contents into the leopard-print laundry basket from Sadie. She sat on the bed in her towel and considered whether she should be naked if she was going to talk to Sadie and then she considered if she needed to talk to Sadie at all and she had come to no good conclusions when Sadie came in with two glasses and a brand-new bottle of bourbon.

Ada decided that staying in a towel was a mid point between naked and not and meant she could put the conversation off a little longer or maybe forever. Sadie poured them both something like a double and pulled her own clothes off down to her underwear and pale grey crop-top bra. She sat beside Ada on the bed and said, 'I know it's late but I want to talk to you about something,' and Ada wondered what she knew or what she suspected.

Ada sat up and crossed her legs and faced Sadie and Sadie mirrored her and they sipped their drinks and Sadie began.

'Mel probably told you that ... I was gone a couple of nights while you were away. I'm guessing. Maybe she didn't?' and Ada said, 'She did,' and thought, Oh, this isn't going to be the conversation I thought it was, and observed that fact with some control.

Sadie said, 'I went to this talk at the Barbican, it was being recorded for Radio 4, Mel is the one who got me tickets actually, but she didn't come, I think she was with Will. Anyway, afterwards everyone had some drinks and I started talking to someone. She's a journalist. I don't know how much of this you want to know.'

Ada said, 'It's OK, keep going,' so Sadie did.

She and this journalist had chatted until they were thrown out of the Barbican and then Sadie had got home and found her on Twitter. She'd DMed her and learned she lived in Ealing and Sadie had said she'd never really been to west London so the next night she went over that way for a drink.

Ada interrupted to say, 'You went to Ealing?' and Sadie said, 'I did, it is far,' and Ada told her to continue. Sadie faltered a little, then said they had spent two nights together and had been messaging ever since and this woman knew about Ada but Sadie didn't want to go any further without talking to Ada so here they were.

Ada considered the story, though the details she picked over were not, she suspected, the ones Sadie was anxious about. A journalist, the kind who went to talks at the Barbican. In her thirties, it sounded like, based on the fact that she lived in her own flat in Ealing (in Ealing!). But the main thing that Ada rolled around was that after they met, Sadie found her on Twitter. The DM slide had been Sadie's and Ada considered, once again, that in every story Sadie told, she was the pursuer and yet if she ever told the story of Ada it would be the reverse. But maybe she wouldn't tell their story very much. Maybe neither of them looked good in it.

Ada waited but Sadie was evidently done and so she said, 'I guess I have a few questions. The main one is … What do you want me to say about this? You haven't done anything wrong. We didn't say we were anything apart from friends, and the sex complicates that I guess, but also it doesn't have to. Do you want to date this woman?'

Sadie paused like she hadn't thought about this when Ada was sure this was all she had been thinking about, otherwise why the special dinner and the new bourbon and the careful little chat.

Sadie said, 'I mean … she lives in London and I'm going back to Perth soon. There would be no point in pursuing anything serious with her. But I guess I would like to see her again.'

Ada thought about this very serious woman on the other side of London and said, 'Does she want to see you given that … you're seeing me? Or living with me. Fucking me, whatever,' and Sadie said, 'She thinks it's kind of a weird arrangement but she doesn't seem particularly bothered by it. I wasn't … specific about us though. I said that we're friends and we're sleeping together and I'm staying with you and then we kind of decided to hold off on anything else until you got back.'

'That's pretty specific,' Ada said and Sadie shrugged and said, 'As specific as I can get, I guess.'

Sadie put her empty glass on the bed and took Ada's hand then and Ada was so put off by the unfamiliar gesture that she sort of shook it in return. But Sadie held it there and said, 'But Ada, if you would prefer we were … monogamous, I guess … until I go, that's OK. You're allowed to ask for that. It wouldn't be unreasonable. And if you want me to go stay with this woman instead, if you're angry at me, that's OK too.'

Ada said, 'Thank you so much for that permission to feel things,' and Sadie looked sad and Ada realised they had to have the other conversation after all.

Ada said, 'I didn't expect us to be monogamous, Sadie. Because I … haven't been,' and Sadie said, 'Did you sleep with someone in Florida?' and Ada said, 'Literally who would I have slept with in Florida.' And as she said that, she thought of Gloria, sweet forty-two-year-old Gloria, recently divorced and discovering herself via Ada's mouth and she realised Gloria would probably feature in her fantasies for some time. And then she told Sadie about Stuart.

She told the story chronologically and without many bells, figuring this was the time for baldness and starkness and unpretty things. She explained that he knew about Sadie but she had never mentioned him because, she didn't know really but mainly because there was no real thing to mention until she went to Liverpool. And then after that the timeframe was tight and she left and she had never thought that Sadie wanted to know these things about her life. They shared a bed and a kitchen and a few quiet hours in the park, but Stuart seemed to want more from her and Sadie? Much less.

So Ada said all of this, with as little judgement in her voice for herself or for Sadie or for their whole situation as possible.

And Sadie stopped looking at her about halfway through, instead choosing the maddening point behind Ada's head that she always found when Ada most wanted her to look her in the face. And when Ada was done, Sadie stood up and walked to the window seat and sat there, as far as she could get without leaving the room.

There was nothing to say exactly then, even though in a broader sense they had everything left to say to each other. But Ada waited and finally Sadie said, 'Why didn't you think … this would matter to me?' It was a fair question coming from another person but coming from Sadie, who made it very clear to Ada every day that she was incidental, it was unfair and Ada said as much. Sadie finally looked at her then and said, 'In what way are you incidental? We share a bed,' and Ada said, 'Yeah, because you needed somewhere to stay,' and then Sadie looked away again and said, quietly, 'You're not the only person I know in this city.'

Ada said, 'Was I the only one who'd sleep with you though?' and it was so disingenuous, pretending that it was Sadie who wanted her desperately and not the other way around, that she thought it was kind of a joke but Sadie said, 'That's a fucked up thing to say.' Then Sadie said, 'Do you want a relationship with this guy in Liverpool? Does he want one with you?' and Ada said, 'God, why are we talking about this, you've clearly decided you want to go to Ealing, don't make this about Liverpool.' And Sadie said, 'I hadn't decided anything,' at the same time as Ada said, 'You're leaving anyway,' and Sadie said, 'That's true, I'm leaving.' Then added, 'I wish you'd told me, Ada.'

Maybe that should have been it, Ada thought later, but she was tired and reckless and she said, 'I don't owe you anything, Sadie, and you don't owe anything to me'. She took off her towel and climbed under the covers, noting that the sheets felt clean, figuring that was Sadie's doing. She closed her eyes and Sadie said from the other side of the room or maybe she didn't say, maybe this was in Ada's mind, but someone said, 'I don't like to live like no one owes anyone anything.' Ada went to sleep and when she woke up Sadie was sleeping next to her and the curtains were closed but Ada could tell it was raining.

Thirty-six

Ada Highfield   **09:11**

What about Brighton

Stuart Parkes   **09:12**

Good morning

Stuart Parkes   **09:13**

What about Brighton?

Ada Highfield   **09:14**

What about we meet up in Brighton? Isn't that sort of between us?

Stuart Parkes   **09:16**

It isn't. It's south of you so that means very south of me

Ada Highfield   09:18

OK but what if I could get us free accommodation?

Stuart Parkes   09:20

That would be interesting I suppose

Ada Highfield   09:21

OK leave it with me

Stuart Parkes   09:22

My girl is so mysterious

Stuart Parkes   10:11

OK seriously what is happening

Ada Highfield   10:44

OK do you want to go to Brighton this Thursday and Friday night?

Stuart Parkes   10:46

And stay where?

Ada Highfield   10:48

A comedian friend lives there in a studio flat but I remembered he's on tour so I asked if we could use it

Stuart Parkes   10:49

And he said yes?

Ada Highfield   10:51

He did and then he called me a top shagger

Stuart Parkes   10:52

No argument from me

Ada Highfield   10:53

So are we going to do this?

Ada Highfield   10:54

His neighbour has a key to let us in

Stuart Parkes   10:57

This is all happening very fast

Ada Highfield   10:58

Book a ticket!

Stuart Parkes   11:01

Why don't you just come to Liverpool again?

Ada Highfield   11:02

I mean I can I guess?

Ada Highfield   11:03

I thought this seemed fun

Ada Highfield   11:04

And you wanted us to plan something

Ada Highfield   11:06

I'm taking the initiative

Stuart Parkes   11:11

Did you talk to her?

Ada Highfield   11:13

I did

Stuart Parkes   11:17

Care to elaborate

Ada Highfield   11:18

I'll elaborate in Brighton

Stuart Parkes 11:21

Why does this feel like a hostage situation all of a sudden?

Ada Highfield 11:24

Come on, I'm sick of us wasting time going back and forth, let's do something fun and romantic and stop all this shitty piece by piece stuff

Ada Highfield 11:26

Book a train ticket

Stuart Parkes 11:30

OK

Ada Highfield 11:31

OK?

Stuart Parkes 11:32

Yes freak I said OK

Ada Highfield 11:33

It's going to be great

Ada Highfield 11:34

Rob's place is kind of a dive but it's super near the water

Stuart Parkes   **11:36**

You stayed there before?

Ada Highfield   **11:37**

Yeah once

Stuart Parkes   **11:38**

… no further questions

Ada Highfield   **11:41**

OK I've booked, I get in at 12:15 on Thursday

Stuart Parkes   **11:52**

Wow this ticket is like a week's wage

Stuart Parkes   **11:53**

2 changes? Christ

Ada Highfield   **11:54**

I'll pay for everything once we're there

Stuart Parkes   **11:56**

With what money, my unemployed little freak

Stuart Parkes   11:58
OK booked

Stuart Parkes   11:59
I get in like 2 hours after you

Ada Highfield   12:01
I'll be waiting

Thirty-seven

Sadie stayed in bed most of the morning. Ada was in the kitchen when she heard the toilet flush and she headed back into their room to finish the conversation from the night before. She had no ideas yet on how to resolve it, she only knew that she wasn't giving Stuart up and Sadie presumably wasn't giving up Miss Ealing Journalist. But she was sure Sadie would want to clarify things further or fight, maybe.

But Sadie was packing a backpack when she got in there and she said hi without looking up. Ada watched Sadie fold a pair of underwear and put it into the bag then grab her deodorant from the top of the drawers and drop that on top. Sadie looked serious and affected in a way Ada wasn't used to and she remembered a morning about a week before she left for Florida.

Ada had woken up to Mel's alarm, made the tea and come back to bed and looked at Sadie, lying flat on her back, her breathing even, her eyes closed. It had been hot the night before so they'd taken the duvet out of its cover and were using the cover as a sort of top sheet. They'd agreed that this country needed to learn about top sheets and Sadie had said, 'It makes me feel kind of dirty sleeping under just a doona,' and Ada had said, 'Duveeeeet,' and Sadie had said, 'Don't you My Fair Lady me.'

So Ada had looked at Sadie in a quiet early light, the duvet cover bunched around her knees where it had fallen when Ada got up. Her breasts sat neatly, straight up, not slipping sideways like Ada's did when she lay on her back. When Ada looked closely, she could see the slightest wrinkling at the centre of her chest, where the hard met the soft. Sun damage right there felt like home to Ada, like every woman she had loved in any capacity.

No expression passed over Sadie's face, there was an absence that Ada felt, just then, that she might try to fill for the rest of her life. Her want made a fool of her. This flatpack woman didn't need her intervention. But she was selfish so she would offer it anyway.

Ada had climbed onto the bed, pulled the duvet cover further down and rolled Sadie's leg slightly out. She kissed the inside of Sadie's thigh and felt Sadie shift slightly, opening herself up more fully, her eyes still closed. Ada kissed her again and the humid morning funk of Sadie hit her and she wanted to climb inside her and sweat it out. But she paused, raised her head, saw Sadie looking at her through half-opened eyes. She lowered her mouth and kissed her one more time and then she left her mouth there, barely touching.

There was silence and though Ada didn't move at all, she felt Sadie's body wake up. She felt she could hear every bit of water inside her rushing towards the point Ada hovered over and she wanted to keep Sadie like this forever, wanting, for once, wanting her. And then Sadie said, 'Ada ... please,' and Ada couldn't bear to leave her for one more minute and she climbed desperately between her legs and pushed her tongue into her and Sadie said, 'Ada, please,' again and again. Ada tried to pull back but found that she couldn't. When Sadie came, she laughed so hard that the tremors of pleasure mixed with some other kind of primal shaking and then Ada laughed too.

She was still laughing when Sadie reached down and sat her up so they were both seated and facing each other. Sadie was still giggling, breathless, and she traced a finger down Ada's ribs and said, 'Does that tickle?' And Ada giggled too and then Sadie reached lower and tickled her some more. And then after they had been inside and around each other, Ada had got out of bed to shower and as she did Sadie had taken her wrist and held it for a moment before letting her go.

And Ada thought about that now as Sadie packed with her eyes averted and Ada wondered why she hadn't stayed in bed that day. And all she could think, when she assessed herself clearly – as she prided herself on doing, who knew her better than her? – all she could think was that she didn't feel that Sadie's want was as real as hers. How could it be when she slept so neatly and Ada watched her so desperately? Sadie was only fully there in moments and trying to stretch them out was pathetic and it was better for them both that Ada not humiliate herself further. Or maybe she had simply been thinking of something else, somewhere she needed to be later that day and this overlay was fiction. Ada found her own motives unusually obscure and she thought about asking Sadie what she thought but Sadie probably wasn't in the mood.

So instead, she asked, 'Are you moving out?' and Sadie said, 'Do you want me to?' and Ada said no and it was true. She had told Stuart she would talk to Sadie but in this moment, Stuart had nothing to do with either of them and she wished she could explain that to Sadie. She realised she didn't want him in her room, particularly, because it didn't feel like her own any more. But that would change, maybe fast if Sadie packed a bigger bag.

Sadie said, 'I might not be back tonight,' and Ada said, 'I have my gig tonight anyway so we couldn't have hung out,' and Sadie looked at her like this piece of information was so irrelevant. Sadie passed the bed and Ada reached out for her wrist, a mirror of her memory, and Sadie waited until she released it. So Ada had been right and there was no fight in either of them after all. She said, 'Have fun in Ealing, if that is a thing you can do in Ealing,' and Sadie was halfway out the door and said, 'Hope the gig goes well,' and then she was all the way out the door. Ada lay back on the bed, diagonal, and then she messaged Stuart and waited for the panic to subside.

Ada arrived at the pub at seven for sound check and her weekly burger. She climbed onto a bar stool and waved to Clem who nodded at her then turned to send an order for a veggie burger into the kitchen. Ada realised that if she was eating meat again, Clem would be the person she'd have to tell first and decided it wasn't worth disrupting their easy flow. A regular might not be a regular if their order changes. The veggie burger was OK, after all. Clem brought Ada a glass of house white and without saying hello said, 'I want to talk to you about something.'

Normally Ada would welcome the extra attention but an exhaustion was creeping over her bones, too early in the night, she needed to get on stage soon, so she reached into her well and said, 'Something good?' She remembered that Clem had snapped at her the last time she was there which felt like a different time, a different, sparklier Ada. She hoped Clem wouldn't snap again, unsure if their relationship could survive a meltdown at the bar.

Clem leaned over the bar and explained. Ada was right – 'I'm always right, Clem,' she replied, but without much vigour. The theatre space wasn't making enough money, it was empty five nights a week sometimes. Clem had spoken to the owners about it while Ada was in Florida and they agreed that they didn't want to convert it to just another bar but they didn't know what to do. Ada had a brief moment of resignation at yet another revenue stream shutting her out but then – 'So I told them I'd find someone to programme it,' Clem said and Ada said, 'Wait, do you mean me?' and Clem said, 'I don't know that many people who do what you do,' and then, 'and I figure you could use the work.'

Ada sensed then that Clem was protective of her, maybe worried about her, and she knew to use that to her advantage. They discussed what the role would be – programming, running the shows, whatever needed doing to get people to come watch stuff – and what the pay would be – minimum wage for three days a week of full-time work and a cut of the door. Clem said that she actually needed another person behind the bar but she could use that money to pay Ada 'but only if you think this will work.' Ada said, 'I've never done anything like this, I can't believe you'd offer me this,' and Clem said, 'I kind of thought you were asking for the job when you gave me shit about the space being empty.' Ada said, 'You credit me with a lot of … guile,' and Clem said, 'You're all guile. Anyway, you should take this job.'

The best opportunities always came to Ada when she wasn't looking for them and she was proud of this, proud of the way things turned up for her. Whenever things were dire something turned up but when she said that to Mel it didn't sound as whimsical as she'd hoped. In fact Mel had said, 'I think you're describing privilege,' and then, 'But hey, what-ever works,' and Ada had mostly kept the thought to herself since then.

Of course, the worst opportunities showed up in exactly the same way but Ada thought that was true for everyone. People didn't go looking for something bad to happen to them, mostly anyway, but they looked for something good. And she didn't have to. And here it was happening again. It was a skill, she was sure, she just didn't know how she'd acquired it.

Ada told Clem she thought it might work and Clem said she'd take it to the owners and see what they said. Ada said, 'I appreci-ate you going to bat for me,' and Clem said, 'You're always here on time and people seem to like you and you were bitching about that temp job you had for months so I figure you can do basic shit.' And Ada felt protected and looked around the dark sticky bar and considered that it might be home.

The bill that night was mostly new acts who brought along a tonne of their friends, kids with deliberately bad haircuts only a few years younger than Ada who got drunk and cheered loudly. There were also always some older acts who were there to try new material and Ada loved being the bridge between the new and afraid and the old and resigned. She threw in more crowd work than usual, starting a conversation between sets with two people in the front row who turned out to be on a first date, the woman more eager to talk than the man. It felt easy enough to keep the audience warm and she knew the newbies would appreciate her efforts.

There was a girl with a ukulele, as there was most nights, and she had dyed red hair and a voice like Zooey Deschanel while she was singing and a voice like Essex when she wasn't. Ada placed her at maybe twenty-two or twenty-three and she claimed to be nervous at the start of her set then showed no signs of those nerves after that, a trick Ada knew would only work while she was this young. Ada found her attractive but felt idle about it, figuring that striking the kind older woman role for a few weeks might eventually lead somewhere.

The night ended and Ada went down to the bar to drink with quiet Steven, realising as they chatted that he might be the simplest relationship she had. People who saw photos of him found him handsome but in person he directed his good looks so entirely inward as to almost disappear. So he and Ada had an easy friendship and he enjoyed catching up on the Sadie-and-Stuart saga every week after their gig.

She told him she and Sadie had fought, sort of, and he said, 'Oh love, I'm sure you'll make up,' and she didn't know how to explain that she wasn't sure if they were apart, even. Clem poured them drinks and then one of the older comics offered Ada a line and she did it, with no goal in mind, and they drank some more. She wondered if she'd be able to do this if she was actually working at the bar and later when she was walking back from the station she considered saying no to the job offer. But she'd need to discuss it with Mel first. Mel would know what to do.

When Ada let herself in, she heard voices in the kitchen and came in to see Mel and Will – it took her a moment to place him as the same contained man she'd met at the party – eating stuffed pasta with peas and cheese grated over the top. Ada said, 'Well, hello, you two!' and Will jumped up and hugged her and she realised he was less contained and pretty drunk. Mel said, 'Oh no! I thought you'd be out at your gig!' and Ada said, 'I was, it's like midnight,' and Mel said, 'Is it? Noooooooooo.'

She went back to her bowl, throwing three pieces of pasta in her mouth at once. Ada said, 'What have you been up to?' and Will explained in a rambling way that they had gone to the theatre. It was a 7 p.m. show and they hadn't eaten first and then it was nearly three hours long and they'd had drinks before and drinks during. 'And then we came back here but the Overground wasn't running and then Mel cooked!'

Ada said, 'Would we say this was cooking?' and Mel said, 'I ate this meal three nights a week before you moved in.' Will finished his last piece and said, 'There's mushroom in this pasta you know, and Mel added peas. That's two of our five a day!' And he and Mel started laughing and Ada said good night.

Her room was empty and Ada realised a part of her had been assuming it wouldn't be. Sadie had said she might be out tonight but they hadn't finished talking, had they? The bottle of bourbon and two glasses from the night before were there and Ada picked up the one that had been Sadie's. She poured some bourbon in, drank it and sat on the floor with the bottle. She was wearing a black corseted taffeta dress that laced up at the back and she allowed herself to imagine Sadie unlacing it for her then decided to stop. She undid the dress herself, she was practiced at it, and continued drinking with it unlaced and flopping forwards over her legs.

Ada had read about a phenomenon where people were so tired but they stayed up late anyway because it was the only time of the day where they had control of their lives. They weren't accountable to their boss or their partner or their kids or the bus timetable or meal planning or a neighbour who didn't like accepting their packages. There were hours between midnight and 2 a.m. when they were only accountable to themselves and so they stayed up even though they knew they'd be tired the next day.

Ada, in practice, had many hours in her day without

accountability but she felt recently that she had been stretching her energy thin. Her room was tidier than usual because Sadie was there and she kept her stuff neat and so Ada tried to as well. But Sadie was gone now and Ada stood up and walked to her hanging shirts and grabbed a sleeve. She considered pulling it off the hanger and throwing it on the floor or putting it on and rolling around in the bed. But it wouldn't fit her and anyway, they were actions done in anger.

Ada wasn't angry at Sadie. This feeling, like almost all her feelings about Sadie, was muted by necessity. Sometimes when they were naked together, Ada let the volume turn up, the rush of colours of the potential of what she could feel mixing and spreading through her body. But she couldn't sleep beside her and feel that way all the time. She wouldn't survive it. Ada wondered if Sadie was sleeping now or if she was taking pleasure in another person's body and if she would laugh with her too.

Thirty-eight

04/10/2017

Ada Highfield   08:01

I have left two cups of tea outside your room because THERE IS
A BOY IN THERE, OK I'm staying calm, very normal, very chill

Ada Highfield   08:02

I am going to stay in my room like a grown-up but you had
better be home for dinner tonight because I have QUESTIONS

Ada Highfield   08:41

OK I heard you leave, please confirm at your earliest conveni-
ence that I did not hallucinate Will in the kitchen last night

Ada Highfield   08:43

Wait I just saw the time, you two are going to be so late! And
BUSTED.

Ada Highfield   08:45

So is he your BOYFRIEND

Melanie Baker   10:11

Omg I'm going to murder you, we were on the bus together and he looked over at my phone as BOYFRIEND flashed on the screen

Melanie Baker   10:12

I'm in the loo at work and I might die here

Melanie Baker   10:13

Why did I think drinking during a 3 fucking hour play was a good idea

Ada Highfield   10:15

Why did you think going to a 3 hour play was a good idea???

Melanie Baker   10:16

Aren't you an actor or something

Ada Highfield   10:17

Stop avoiding the question!!! Is he your boyfriend

Melanie Baker   **10:18**

… yes he is

Ada Highfield   **10:20**

AMAZING!!!!!! I might cry. Wow I have a new daddy. Will he take me to the circus

Melanie Baker   **10:21**

I'm sure he will, he's a very good daddy

Ada Highfield   **10:22**

Excuse me you filth monger, are you making a sex joke to me about your BOYFRIEND right now

Melanie Baker   **10:23**

I am but in my defence I'm so hungover I might die

Melanie Baker   **10:24**

I have to go back to my desk, I was already late today and now I'm going to be the girl who died in the bathroom

Melanie Baker   **10:25**

Please cook something with carbs for dinner

Ada Highfield   **10:26**

And will daddy be joining us?

Melanie Baker   **10:27**

No, he absolutely needs to go home and change his shirt, it does not smell great

Ada Highfield   **10:28**

Hot

Melanie Baker   **10:30**

OK I really am going now, can you tell Sadie sorry we finished her dolmades, we ate them for breakfast on the bus

Ada Highfield   **10:33**

If I see her I'll tell her

Melanie Baker   **13:08**

Wait if you see her, what does that mean

Ada Highfield   **13:10**

I'll explain tonight

Thirty-nine

Sadie didn't come back and Mel was going to leave her. Ada's home life shrunk so rapidly from three to one that she couldn't take in each disaster in turn and instead absorbed them both as a coordinated mass abandonment. This wasn't dramatics, to Ada, but a real material loss and she didn't know what to do with it.

Mel had come home from work to a creamy, cheesy potato bake that Ada had worked on all afternoon. Peeling, slicing, grating, baking. She had also made a simple salad for the side, knowing Mel liked to feel like she was achieving balance even through a hangover, and the freezer was stocked with mini Magnums. She had planned the dinner as a celebration – of Mel's new relationship, of her new job – but found she couldn't get Mel in the mood.

They talked about Will, how they'd been circling each other for a year at work, eating lunch and sending emails with little jokes. But Will had been with his partner since university and Mel didn't allow herself to hope. Then just before she left for Edinburgh, Will told Mel he'd left his girlfriend and would like to see her when she was back. Ada gave herself a private moment of hurt over Mel keeping this from her and then asked for the rest of the story.

He had visited her in Edinburgh the final weekend – 'I had no idea, you sneaky bitch!' – and they'd been together ever since and because of the months of build-up it felt like they'd jumped forward in the relationship. Ada said she couldn't wait to get to know him better and Mel suddenly asked her about Sadie. Ada said she was with another woman and waved her hand dismissively and refused to be drawn out more. And then Mel told her she was moving to Bristol with Will.

It is not always the obvious people who will be cruel, Ada thought. People often puzzled over her closed friendship with Mel, seeing Ada as domineering (they said 'fun') and Mel as conservative (they said 'quiet'). If they were a couple, Ada would be the life-of-the-party hostess and Mel the hard-done-by scrapper, keeping them afloat. But Ada loved Mel in a way that she realised, this night, with this announcement, Mel couldn't possibly love her back.

Mel was moving to Bristol because Will was offered a trans-fer there and so yesterday Mel asked for one too. Will never planned to be in London long-term, 'and neither did I,' said Mel, though Ada clearly remembered her drinking a negroni and watching a drag show in a Dalston basement and saying, 'Why would anyone not want to live in London.' That hadn't been that long ago and something had changed and could it only be Will? Ada tried to articulate this in a generous way but it came out like, 'You love London, though. Does Will know that?' which was accusatory and petulant and Mel said, 'You can love somewhere and not want to live there,' and Ada wondered if Will hated her and thought he probably did.

Ada asked if she'd need to find a new flatmate and Mel said, 'If you want to stay? I guess? But—' and then there was a series of words and disclaimers that amounted to a suggestion that Mel's brother would raise the rent once his sister didn't occupy the flat. Ada said, 'Well, I'm like family,' and then they both went quiet. Ada said, 'So I guess I'm moving to Bristol then!' and Mel looked at her and there was a flash of something like revulsion on her face and Ada, who hadn't really been joking, said, 'Joking, joking.'

She explained that she'd been offered a job by Clem and Mel said, 'That's amazing!' She was too happy about it, guilt making her act as though this was the opportunity of a lifetime. Because she knew she was abandoning Ada, as much as she positioned it as benign. They had made promises to each other in so many ways and now they ate the potato bake together, digging their forks into the baking dish. Ada poured them both a glass of pinot gris and then suggested they see what was on television and Mel said, 'Like ... real TV? Probably Strictly?' and Ada said, 'Good point, Netflix.'

They moved to the living room and Mel said, 'Sorry to dump this on you while Sadie is away,' and Ada said, 'It's fine, Mel, you're allowed to move.' Then she stood up and said that actually she might need to do some research on acts for the theatre in case she had to present to the owners or something and Mel asked if she needed help. But Ada told her to nurse her hangover with some trash TV, took the bottle of wine upstairs, closed her door and got into bed with it.

Sadie didn't come back that night. Ada stayed in bed, half waiting for her and half feeling she'd never see her again. She was leaving for Brighton in the morning and in another life, she would be dancing to The Kooks while complaining there were no good bands from Brighton and Mel would try to convince her to pack boots in case it rained. She felt peculiarly teenage, like the child of divorce that she had never been and she tried to explain it to Stuart but he was out with friends and responding sporadically. She said, 'Don't get too drunk!

Train in the morning!' and then felt fucking pathetic and he didn't reply anyway because he was, almost certainly, getting too drunk. They shared that, she thought, her and Stuart, a need to be out, and she wondered if that's what she should do, but she couldn't, right then, even leave her bed.

Mel knocked on the door at ten to say good night and then she stood in the doorway for a little longer. Ada said, 'I'm going to Brighton tomorrow to see Stuart,' and Mel said, 'That's exciting! But do you need a train ticket?' and Ada said, 'No, I got it,' then, 'thank you,' but she didn't feel very grateful. She said, 'I'm looking forward to having real time with Stuart, it's been kind of hard to connect with him since I got back from Florida.' Mel said, 'Well, you don't really know him, maybe he gets like this. It's probably nothing to do with you,' and Ada thought that was supposed to be comfort but she wasn't sure.

Mel stood a little longer, it seemed she might stand there all night, and then she said, in the voice of someone who had rehearsed, 'I know it's going to be hard with me leaving. But I'm not doing this to you, I'm doing it for me.' And Ada said, 'That's cute, did you write that with Will?' then, 'Sorry, I'm just upset about Sadie,' because that was the safer confession to make. And Mel said, 'We'll be OK. I love you,' and Ada said, 'Love you,' and Mel went to bed and Ada was really, really angry.

When Mel's alarm went off in the morning Ada considered not making her tea and then felt like that would be some sort of irrevocable statement of intent, so she got out of bed and did it. But she rushed it so there was no chance of a hallway collision and she was back in her room with the door closed by the time Mel was moving around. She packed quietly, pairs of leggings and two colourful long-sleeved dresses that were only clean because they were too warm to take to Florida. When she got on the train later, she realised she was also already wearing leggings and a long-sleeved dress. This changing of her uniform was a clear sign that autumn had begun and she did not welcome it.

Ada hadn't booked a seat on this train and the only one available in her carriage was at a table of four. The other three seats were occupied by teenagers who Ada assumed were skipping school and she decided to sit on her backpack near the door instead. The light through the window was watery and vague and Ada felt romantically matched to it. She had messaged Stuart to say she was getting on the train and he'd responded with a thumbs up so she was already prepared to be annoyed at his hangover when he arrived. But she knew that wasn't the right energy for this trip so she tried to get it out now, alone on the floor of a rocking train.

When Ada had been younger, the popular mental health jargon had been that people needed to take responsibility for their own happiness. When she was home sick from school, she'd watch daytime TV, the American talk shows imported for whichever portion of the Australian audience was free at midday on a Wednesday. And there would be pop psychologists on, and experts in manifestation, and girl bosses before the term existed.

Instagram had repackaged this sentiment in pastels but it was the same. It told Ada now that she needed to protect her happiness but also that she wasn't responsible for the happiness of other people and she had rolled over in her mind how anyone could be happy if they were only protecting their own. She was an independent young woman, that's what older people always said to her. That she 'knew her own mind!' in an admiring tone, and her parents agreed with them. That

Ada, there's no stopping her once she sets her mind to something. She went after what she wanted, she didn't take no for an answer, she was so modern, god so modern. Ada closed her eyes and leaned against the wall and listened to the screech of the train's mechanics.

It was spitting when she got to Brighton. Ada found comfort in the screams of the seagulls that hit her as soon as she left the station and the air was grimy but carried a hint of freshness that she couldn't find in London. She walked to Rob's flat, ten minutes down the hill and as she did she could see the water in the distance, flat and slatey but still inviting. She and Stuart could go down there tomorrow and she'd put her feet in and she'd look right to the burnt-out pier and left to the pier that was still alive. She realised she wasn't thinking about Mel and felt happy but then realised she was thinking about Sadie, somehow, and blamed the sea.

Ada reached Rob's building and let herself into the flat with the key the neighbour had left in the letter box. The place overlooked one of the lanes, the colourful, counter-culture streets of Brighton that had long since been given over to cocktail bars and overpriced incense. He had a box-sized kitchen, partly blocked from the rest of the flat by a waist-height wall and a closet bathroom with no bath. But the main feature of the flat was his huge bed that butted against the chest he used for both storage and a table. It was clean and felt cozy, with the street noise below providing a cheerful background track, and Ada could almost believe that she was about to have a very romantic time.

Ada had told Stuart she had been to this flat once and she knew he'd drawn his own conclusions but in fact she and Rob had never had sex. She had been in Brighton last year for a gig and Rob was on the same bill. She had planned to get the last train home but had stayed drinking with the other acts and when she tried to leave Rob said, 'No! Don't run away! You can stay at my place!' Ada had considered Rob, ten years older with bad teeth and a sweet smile, and agreed.

When they got back to the flat, she had expected him to get another drink but instead he made her a chamomile tea and they sat cross-legged on either side of the chest, sipping them and talking about their careers. Rob had gently encouraged her to find a regular gig because 'it's a tough old road waiting for something to come up' and she had said that actually she was an actor, she only took these cabaret gigs for something to do. And Rob said he had hoped his comedy gigs would get him some acting jobs but apart from some bit parts in long-ago-cancelled sketch shows it had never really taken off.

'But you're a lovely girl, you've got something special about you,' he had said to Ada, and then he yawned and said, 'Best be getting to sleep if you're heading back in the morning.' And they had got to sleep, comfortably separate on the huge bed. The next morning Rob had walked her to the station, picking them up coffees on the way, and kissed her on the cheek goodbye. Ada had thought maybe she loved him for months after that but he never responded to her messages beyond an affectionate 'hope you're going well lady' and she gave him up.

Rob was doing well this year, she knew, on a tour of university towns supporting a much bigger comic, and she wondered if he was satisfied making nineteen-year-olds laugh at the age of thirty-eight. She hoped he was. She looked around his flat for a sign that someone else had been with him in here but there was only a wall calendar with show dates and some frozen vegetables to provide signs of life. His existence fit neatly into the bag he took on tour and maybe

the guitar propped up against his wall and that was so beautiful that Ada thought she might cry. But she pulled it together
and messaged Stuart instead. She said she couldn't wait to see
him and he said he'd got his train times confused, he wasn't
actually getting in until close to six.

This was almost more than Ada could bear. But she said OK,
why didn't she make something for dinner so they could stay
in tonight and Stuart sent a thumbs up again and she considered throwing her phone out the window onto the bumpy
cobbled street. She went shopping instead.

Ada walked until she found a fancy-looking wine shop and
bought some craft IPAs and a French pinot noir and a white
from Austria. The man in the shop asked her what she knew
about Austrian wines and she said, 'Only that I'm buying
one!' and so he answered questions she hadn't asked while
he packed her bottles. She carried the heavy, clinking bag over
her right shoulder, her back sweating underneath her backpack which she'd emptied to fill with groceries.

Ada had passed a Tesco on her way to the flat but she searched
on Google Maps for a Waitrose. She knew what Stuart would
have to say about these class signifiers and figured they could
fight about it later then fuck. She remembered Stuart saying
that he was a terrible vegetarian because he had no idea how
to cook tofu and she started to make a shopping list.

The shopping list had tofu and udon noodles and ginger
and garlic and fresh chillis. It had hoisin sauce and oyster sauce
but then she took the oyster sauce off because she was vegetarian and so was he. It had carrots and 'greens', she'd decide
which ones when she got there, and sesame oil and vegetable oil in case Rob didn't have any, she should have checked,
and sesame seeds as well. Soy sauce, of course, and maybe
some kind of sticky chilli thing too, she'd see what they had.

Eggplants, miso paste, she'd make that too. Paper towels to dry the tofu. She filled her basket with these things and then on a whim went to the frozen section and got vegetarian dumplings, the kind that Americans called pot stickers and she'd never understood why until she cooked them herself and then it was very obvious. She got chocolate too, a box of Lindt balls, which seemed special.

The walk back to Rob's was weighed down on all sides. She had moved the wine bottles to her backpack and both arms were carrying grocery bags. She'd got bags for life that she could leave here with a cute note for Rob to find. Something funny about baggage or maybe saying she'd give him five stars on Airbnb. It didn't matter exactly.

By the time she got back to the flat she was much too hot and so she stripped down to just her dress, throwing her leggings and underwear and damp bra onto the floor. She wasn't going back out tonight. She pushed at the window next to Rob's bed and it would only open a little but the sounds of people walking below screamed into the room. She figured this must be how Rob could afford to live so centrally and decided on balance it was worth the noise when you didn't want it for the noise when you did.

Ada looked at her phone, saw she had two hours until Stuart was due to arrive. She messaged him saying she was preparing a feast so he'd better be hungry then she realised he was probably on the train and remembered the patchy reception she'd had on the journey to Liverpool. She allowed herself to feel excited about seeing him, touching him, waking up with him. Feeding him and showering with him. Choosing something with him before they left, whatever they decided that was.

Ada told Stuart she was putting her phone aside to focus on cooking and sent him Rob's address again and instructions from the station, 'because I know boys famously can't read maps, that's the stereotype right?' She saw that he had seen it, got the little blue ticks, and began. She usually listened to podcasts while she cooked but she wanted to create a mood for herself, she wanted sensuality. She lined up the playlist she had created for masturbation that was called Buzzing and that she'd showed Sadie one night, not even pretending to be embarrassed. Sadie had said, 'I get it ... and there's good stuff on here!' but when she'd tried to play it, Ada had said, 'No no, not for you!' and Sadie had laughed and said, 'Fair enough, I respect the process.'

And Ada thought about that and then didn't think about it as she gave her brain over to cooking, Jill Scott's 'Gettin' In The Way' carrying her along, her body heating instinctively while she searched for knives and pans. Rob's kitchen was expensively supplied and Ada was shocked to discover that one whole under-bench cupboard was devoted to matching Le Creuset. It was blue-grey and she wondered when he had chosen it, how long he'd been collecting it. Perhaps he and an ex had bought the little espresso cups and then when she left he'd stuck with it, first out of nostalgia then defiance and then eventually because he just got used to it. Then she told herself maybe Rob liked to cook. What did she know?

Ada halved the eggplants, scored them in a criss-cross pattern, rubbed them with miso and sesame oil and spoonfuls from the jars of ginger and garlic she'd bought in case Rob didn't have sharp knives (he had a full set, Rob, you wonder). She put them aside and started drying out her tofu, squeezing it between sheets of kitchen roll and wondering if

Forty

05/10/2017

Sadie Ali 17:03

Hey, I'm on my way over, wanted to let you know in case you would rather I didn't?

Ada Highfield 17:06

Of course that's fine

Ada Highfield 17:07

I'm actually not there

Sadie Ali 17:08

Will you be back later? Should I stick around?

Ada Highfield 17:09

No, sorry, I'm away for a couple of days

Sadie Ali   17:10

Ah I didn't realise

Ada Highfield   17:11

Yeah so you can stay if you want

Ada Highfield   17:12

I mean you could stay if I was there too but I'm getting the feeling you don't want to do that?

Sadie Ali   17:13

I was going to ask you the same thing

Sadie Ali   17:14

I mean I assumed you wouldn't want me to

Sadie Ali   17:15

Ugh I hate texting

Sadie Ali   17:17

Can we talk when you're back? Are you in Liverpool?

Ada Highfield   17:21

Sorry cooking, not ignoring you

Ada Highfield 17:22

I'm in Brighton

Ada Highfield 17:23

But with the Liverpool guy

Ada Highfield 17:25

I'm guessing you've been staying with the Ealing woman?

Sadie Ali 17:27

Yeah

Sadie Ali 17:28

Do you think we'll ever use their names?

Ada Highfield 17:30

Nah this works

Sadie Ali 17:31

Yeah OK

Sadie Ali 17:33

Well I guess I'll come over and get some stuff

Sadie Ali   17:34

When are you coming back?

Sadie Ali   17:35

I want to see you before I go

Ada Highfield   17:38

Before you go? Like in 2 weeks?

Sadie Ali   17:39

Yeah

Ada Highfield   17:40

Why wouldn't you see me

Ada Highfield   17:41

I'm back on Saturday morning

Ada Highfield   17:42

So are you going to stay in Ealing until you go? It's OK if you are but I guess it would be good to know

Sadie Ali   17:43

No I don't want to crowd her

Sadie Ali 17:44

But I actually need to visit a friend from Perth

Sadie Ali 17:45

He lives in Newcastle and I'd been putting it off I guess but running out of time now

Sadie Ali 17:46

So I'm going there for a week on Sunday

Ada Highfield 17:51

OK I really have to finish cooking but if you're around Saturday night we can talk about it?

Sadie Ali 17:52

I can't do Saturday night

Ada Highfield 17:53

OK well have fun in Newcastle

Sadie Ali 17:55

What are you cooking?

Ada Highfield 18:03

That miso eggplant thing you taught me

Ada Highfield   18:04

And just some veggie udon noodles

Ada Highfield   18:05

Nothing exciting

Sadie Ali   18:14

That sounds delicious

Sadie Ali   20:34

Ada I just saw Mel and she told me she's moving to Bristol, are you OK?

Sadie Ali   20:36

I'm sorry Ada

Forty-one

Ada hadn't wanted to hurt Sadie by telling her who she was with. She had thought maybe a little hurt was due but she hadn't intended to cause it. There had been no rules between them, she always knew that, but there was still something like disappointment getting through to her from Sadie's messages. Or maybe that was her own disappointment reflected. She wondered if she would have ended things with Sadie like she had planned when she was in Florida if Sadie hadn't preempted her. She wondered if she would have done it all differently from the start if she'd known she didn't even have Sadie until October, that Sadie could in fact find another bed as easily as she'd found Ada's. She wondered what would have happened if she'd let Sadie stay in the living room that first night and if Sadie had ever thought there was a chance she might.

But she couldn't worry about Sadie any longer because she needed to cook this crumbled-up tofu in batches so she didn't crowd the wok that Rob surprisingly had sitting on top of his fridge. The oil was spitting at her and she hung a tea towel over her dress, draped like a bib. She was grateful that Stuart would have to text her to get in because she felt she was slipping from charmingly bedraggled into mess territory. She finished the frying and set the tofu aside, inhaling the smell of sesame filling the increasingly sweaty kitchen.

The alarm on her phone went off, breaking through her playlist. She'd set it for the time Stuart's train was due. She turned the heat down on the stove and ran to the bathroom, splashing water on her face and flapping her dress to get air underneath it. She grabbed her bra from the floor and put it back on without taking her dress off then looked in the mirror and pulled out her hair elastic so her hair fell down in kinky damp bunches. She considered it, tied it back up and went back to the kitchen.

She was slowly pan-frying the vegetables, keeping the heat low so that she could dump everything in there and have it fresh and perfect when Stuart arrived. She decided to cook the dumplings after they'd eaten the noodles and the eggplants, maybe have a second dinner round nine thirty or ten, maybe in Rob's bed (though better not leave grease stains). She took deep breaths then when that didn't work she got a grapefruit IPA out of the fridge, opened the can and drank a mouthful. Ten minutes passed and then fifteen and she waited for Stuart.

At the half-hour point, Ada turned the wok off entirely and watched the carrot strips and greens wilt down into an oily mound in the centre. She messaged Stuart asking if he was lost and when he didn't reply she messaged again telling him not to bother buying drinks, she had them covered. She carried her phone back to the stove and stood staring at it, then at the wok, then back at the phone as she finished her beer. She waited ten minutes and then messaged him again saying she was getting worried now, had something happened on the train?

Ada knew this next move was silly but she went to the *Guardian* website thinking a train crash would be news. For one moment she saw a headline that she thought was it and then her brain slowed down enough to recognise that it said something about nursing training, NHS shortages, everything concerning, but nothing concerning her. A shameful part of her realised there had been a brief spot of relief when she had thought Stuart was caught up in a catastrophe, because if he wasn't then the catastrophe was only hers.

Ada thought that this was why people used labels for their relationships, probably. Because what if Stuart did die and she had to account for herself in the circles of grief? His house-mates knew her and his brother had heard her name but where would she sit at the funeral and would she be invited to the wake and what would she say on Facebook with no photos of them together to share and very few mutual friends? And who would comfort her? Who knew them both and who recognised her feelings as real? Yeah, this was why people said 'boyfriend', and even more why they said 'husband', because then their grandmother understood and so did bank managers and so did her friends from high school who she hadn't spoken to in years but still posted happy birthday with a little kiss.

Ada realised she had started convincing herself that her lover was dead and felt light-headed and insane and so she messaged him saying, 'Are you dead? You're like an hour late.' He hadn't seen any of her recent messages, nothing since he would have got on the train. On the first of three trains, she reminded herself. One journey, two changes, not like her direct run. So then she started imagining what might have happened in London or in Hove, the kind of smaller crimes that wouldn't hit the *Guardian*, a mugging or a beating or a fall down an escalator.

Or maybe he had lost his phone, left it on one of the earlier trains and now he was walking through Brighton trying to remember the address. She willed him to remember her phone number then realised that was pointless, an impossible ask, and so she willed him to go to an internet cafe – did they still exist? – and log on, message her, and she could come and collect him. And if he'd lost his phone, maybe she could put her phone away for two days too and they could unplug and embrace their solitude.

Ada had turned off the oven but now she put it back on, low, so the eggplants would be warm when he arrived, which she felt sure, now she'd figured out the phone-losing thing, he would do. He should have been there an hour ago and then he should have been there two hours ago and he hadn't looked at any of her messages and she was looking, checking, every couple of minutes for the double blue tick. They'd been delivered and she googled 'messages delivered phone broken' and saw that if his phone was fully broken then no, the messages wouldn't get there, so she ruled that out of her speculation.

Ada poked at the cooled damp vegetable mush at the bottom of the wok and decided she needed to eat her serve, she'd had a beer and no food since breakfast and she couldn't be seeing things clearly. So she heated up the wok again and separated the carrots from the greens as best she could. She put the tofu back in, then the cooked noodles, and she stirred it all together, letting it heat through. She poured her sauce over, hoisin and soy and white pepper from Rob's spice rack and other things, she couldn't remember exactly what she'd mixed in there so many hours ago and then when everything was hot and sticky she served it into two bowls and put a paper towel over one.

She sat down on the floor of the kitchen and picked up a noodle between her fingers and squashed it into her mouth.

She did this a few more times before she was sated enough to find chopsticks and then she sat with her knees pulled up near her mouth, her bowl balancing as she picked up the noodles one by one and devoured them. She pulled out the eggplants, nearly black but, she knew, gooey inside. She tore at one with two forks, pulling it apart so it opened and to reveal the creamy middle and she ate until her stomach felt hard and hot.

Ada picked up her phone again and checked, saw no blue ticks, and felt a little sick. She got another beer from the fridge, a double IPA that she knew would make her feel the tired kind of drunk and opened it, took a sip then gagged over the sink. It was too much, too strong, and she needed some clarity.

She opened her Facebook app and went to Stuart's profile. She could message their mutual friends, maybe, there were eight though no one she knew well. All festival friends who didn't translate to the rest of the year. They would be confused to hear from her and she didn't think they could offer her the answers she needed and maybe no one could but how long could she wait here?

At the top of Stuart's profile was a photo of him and two of his housemates with an 'about last night' caption. She checked who'd posted it and, as suspected, it was Paul, who was still in the 'posting through it' stage of his break-up, documenting every night out in case his ex-boyfriend was looking. In the photo, Stuart was holding a flight of shots and Paul was kissing his cheek and Tom (Tom?) was either winking or about to pass out. It had been uploaded an hour ago and Ada wasn't friends with Paul but she thought maybe she could message him anyway, or call him somehow, could you call a Facebook profile?

Then Ada looked underneath the photo and saw that

Stuart had liked it and then, while she was looking at it, he commented. A sign of life. A kiss emoji, the one with the little heart in the side of the mouth.

And that didn't make sense because Stuart was dead, someone had tripped over and pushed him onto the train track, a tragedy that the pusher would never recover from. Or if he wasn't dead, he was asking strangers to borrow their phone because he'd been mugged between Hove and Brighton, the train was crowded so he couldn't say who did it but all he knew was his phone was in his pocket when he got on the train and gone when he got off. Or maybe he was at a laptop around the corner, a friend lived in town and he'd remembered their address and oh, thank god, they were in. Could he borrow their laptop? Someone was waiting for him and his phone had died and he's so stupid, he hadn't packed a charger. And maybe in this scenario he had opened Facebook and seen the photo of him and quickly liked and commented but any second now he would send her a message and so she waited.

Ada hadn't messaged Sadie in hours, and she hadn't messaged Mel at all. Normally Mel would have checked in with her, was she OK, what was it like to see him again but that was missing too. And Ada knew that if she used this, if she told Mel that she had been stood up, or that Stuart was dead and his murderer was using social media to make people think he was still alive, either way, whatever she told Mel, maybe it would make Mel feel so sorry for her that she would forgive Ada for whatever it was Ada had done. Whatever Ada had done that was so unforgivable that she renounced her rights to her despite everything.

But Ada wouldn't tell Mel and she couldn't tell Sadie. She had friends, so many friends, since the time she could talk, Ada had had more friends than could easily be invited to a birthday party but she didn't have anyone she wanted to share this with, this shame, this bloated, sickly loneliness. She thought about wallowing but decided there was something to try first, something that might ease her through the night. She picked up the sour, now too warm beer that she had opened earlier, checked the local time in Florida and FaceTimed Hank.

It rang almost to the point of giving up and then her handsome, large-handed almost brother-in-law answered her call.

'Ada!' he said with joy or surprise, probably both, she would accept both.

'Hi, Hank, I just … wanted to say hello to everyone,' she said, and he was locking his car and crossing the front lawn. He said he had just got back from work and she said, 'Oh of course, you're back in the office!' and he said yeah, it was awful, all he wanted was to be home with Gabby and Orion all day. He got to the front door and opened it and there was Gabby, standing and holding their baby, and she looked like she'd been crying and Ada wished she hadn't called.

Hank said, 'Gabby! Ada called!' and Gabby looked at the screen, seeming baffled by her little sister's intrusion into her day. Hank handed Gabby the phone and took Orion and said, 'Show her the baby!' So Gabby, who still hadn't said anything, held the phone close to Orion's rounding face and Ada said, 'Hi my little dude' and Orion blinked and grimaced and she felt grief at how he'd changed and how he would keep on changing.

Hank said, 'Does he need a new diaper?' and Gabby said, 'Yeah, but he just went when I heard you pulling up,' and Hank said, 'A likely story!' but cheerfully, like he said everything. He took Orion to another room. Gabby flopped on the couch and held the phone up to her face and spoke to Ada for the first time.

'Why did you call Hank?' she asked and before Ada could

answer — how *would* Ada answer? — she said, 'I would have picked up if you'd called me.' It was close, too close, to acknowledging things about them and Ada felt that the baby or the exhaustion had pulled down too many of Gabby's walls. They were unsafe now.

But Ada said, 'I thought you might be sleeping,' and Gabby laughed and it was a bad sound but she said, 'How are you?' Then she squinted past Ada and said, 'And where are you? That's not your room, right?' Ada said she was in Brighton and then said, 'I'm on a sort of … mini break with this guy I'm seeing,' and Gabby said that sounded nice and Ada agreed that it did. She asked about Orion's feeding and his sleeping and Gabby was specific about both and then she heard the baby crying from another room. Gabby said, 'I'm sorry, I have to get him,' and then, 'Call again,' and then she was gone and Ada was on her mini break alone.

Ada only knew the term mini break because of Bridget Jones and she had meant to use it sarcastically but it had come out of her mouth sounding aspirational. She finished her beer, returned to the kitchen and put the bowl of noodles in the fridge. They could be breakfast, she figured, no need to waste them. And maybe Stuart would be here in the morning and they could share them and he would explain.

He would explain that he had freaked out because he liked her too much and he was a stupid boy with stupid-boy commitment issues. Or he would explain that he was so hungover that he thought he'd be sick on the train and he couldn't tell her that because it made him seem so juvenile. Or he would explain that he had diarrhoea and there's simply no sexy way to tell the person you're fucking that and she would laugh and say the toilet is basically in the bedroom in this flat so it's a good thing he didn't chance it. But in the future, he could be honest with her, they were both just humans with bodies after all. No shame in the things that bodies do.

Ada pulled out a plate and laid the eggplants on it, taking one final bite of a now cold, squishy end and letting the miso flavour fill her mouth. She put the plate in the fridge too. What a feast they would make for lunch. The miso would be even richer after soaking in overnight. They could take it down to the beach, sit on the rocks and take turns tearing it apart with their forks and waving away disappointed seagulls looking for chips. A blustery picnic, huddled in their coats, full of forgiveness and forgetting.

She opened the bottle of white wine and took a tumbler from the cupboard, the kind of cloudy glass with a colourful rim favoured by beach houses the world over. It was because the glass resembled glass worn down by the tides, she guessed, but who were they fooling, this cup wasn't made from that glass. But it was pretty all the same. Ada poured the wine, drank and found it slightly bubbling, as though the fermentation was happening in front of her and maybe continuing in her guts. She sat on the floor, leaning against the chest and googled 'Austrian white wines' which was easier than listening to the man at the store.

Around midnight she ate some Lindt balls and decided there was no need to cook the dumplings tonight. There was still tomorrow.

Forty-two

06/10/2017

Ada Highfield   **00:06**

I am trying to be understanding here but you need to tell me where you are

Ada Highfield   **00:07**

Facebook tells me you're alive, thank you Mr Zuckerberg, but I need a little more than that

Ada Highfield   **00:09**

If you're mad at me I want to know so I can apologise or more likely explain why you shouldn't be mad at me

Ada Highfield   **00:11**

You missed a great dinner

Ada Highfield 00:21

If you are trying to make a fool of me or this is some kind of sadism, trust me when I say there are way more fun ways of exploring that whole dynamic

Ada Highfield 00:27

You have hurt my feelings though mate, I'll give you that

Ada Highfield 00:29

You have really hurt my fucking feelings

Ada Highfield 00:31

If you needed more time you should have said that but I am trying so hard to give you what you want

Ada Highfield 00:32

That's all I've ever done

Ada Highfield 00:33

Did you miss your train or were you never coming?

Ada Highfield 00:36

OK this is disgusting, I'm going to sleep

Forty-three

Ada woke up alone and early and she would have loved to have that moment when you wake up in an unexpected place and you don't know where you are or what happened. That moment would have been a relief. But she woke up with full knowledge that she was in the bed of a casual acquaintance who had once rejected her and she was completely alone. It was as though the realisation had lingered behind her eyes the entire time they were closed, waiting to pounce on her as soon as she opened them. She rolled over, looked at her phone, saw no messages and rolled back.

When she woke up again, rain was spitting against the window and she felt queasy and too hot. She pushed the duvet off her and went to the toilet, sitting on it naked and scrolling Twitter, checking Gabby's Instagram feed for pictures of Orion or a hint at how she was feeling. But the pictures were well lit and obscured everything and she liked them and clicked out.

Ada stayed naked through the morning, heating up the second plate of noodles in the microwave and eating them in bed while watching a YouTube make-up tutorial about contouring by a drag queen. Ada had never contoured, wasn't convinced she ever would, but she appreciated the transformation and needed noise and colour to keep her going. She wondered why Rob didn't have a TV but figured he watched everything on his laptop, like her, unless she was watching with Mel and maybe Mel would take the TV to Bristol with her? Or was it in the flat when she moved in? She supposed they'd have to have a conversation about that but it wasn't time yet.

Around eleven, Ada checked her messages to Stuart and saw that he had, officially, finally, seen them. Ada considered what this meant. Had he turned read receipts off yesterday before doing whatever it was he had done? And had he turned them back on now for an extra dig? Or had he really not opened her messages yesterday? Had he muted her or simply looked at the notifications rolling in and avoided tapping them? What kind of self-control, what kind of *psycho*, did you have to be to not even look at the messages someone was sending you when they were desperate for you?

Ada knew she'd never have the willpower. In fact on the few occasions she had definitely, absolutely not wanted to message someone, she'd given her phone to Mel until the urge passed because she knew she couldn't trust herself. One of those people had been Rob, Ada remembered now. She had showed their relatively one-sided conversation to Mel and Mel had gently said it seemed he wasn't looking for anything romantic with her. Ada conceded that she had no real reason to think he was and so for the next few weeks whenever she thought of him she would give her phone to Mel.

And eventually the need for contact left her and she hadn't messaged him in ages, actually, until she frantically asked if his flat was free so she could bang someone else in it. No wonder he hadn't wanted her. Who does that? Ada did, and that was OK, she told herself, that was fun and wild and she was young and cute but today wasn't the day for that kind of self-talk. Her reserves would refill but not yet.

The sky cleared a little so the air still looked watery but wasn't actually raining and Ada decided to go out. She had briefly considered getting the train home that day but what if Sadie was there or if Mel asked questions? And she couldn't really afford another ticket, if she was honest with herself, and apparently today that's what she was doing. So she showered and washed her hair with Rob's two-in-one to get the vague scent of grease out of it. She dressed and shook her head like a dog and rubbed it with a towel and couldn't quite get it dry so gave up and went out with it damp.

Ada passed a cafe and realised she hadn't had coffee and she figured things might feel a little better once she did. She bought a flat white and thought about when she first moved to London and only certain cafes sold flat whites and they were the ones run by Australians and Kiwis. And now this corner spot with overstuffed lounge chairs in Brighton sold them, and the caffeine hit her as she drank it and walked, and she did, actually, feel better. It was still despair and it was still devastation but at least her addiction had been fed and that's why you have addictions, right, so that some sensation is guaranteed.

Ada walked to the beach without thinking about it and saw it was mostly empty because it was wet, and it was a Friday and most people were at work or at school or had better things to do than visit a beach out of season. She lingered over drinking her coffee as it was pulling double duty keeping her warm and when she finished it, she threw out the cup and stepped down onto the rocky shore, pulling her denim jacket tight as her still-wet hair hit her face. She searched in her pocket for a hair elastic and tried to tie it back but she could only gather about half of it at a time and she gave up, letting it fly.

Ada walked towards the water, the rocks pushing through her pink Converse as though she were barefoot. A beach wasn't really a beach without sand, she had said to anyone who would listen when she first moved to the UK. If you can't take a bucket down there or turn your legs into a mermaid tail then what are we doing here, really? But after so long, she had acclimatised to the rocks, like she'd acclimatised to the cold, and the screaming underground, and the distance from her mum. Reluctantly but enough to survive and sometimes find joy.

Ada walked until she reached the water where there was a little sand peeking through. She sat and put her backpack behind her and looked over at the rusty burnt pier that was kept there as a monument or a haunting or some sort of English obsession with the past that she couldn't fathom. It looked dramatic and dead today with the grey clouds rolling behind it and she wondered, if she stayed long enough, if she would ever see it struck by lightning. Was it safe having all that metal standing in all that water and then, wait, is that how it burned? Ada considered googling it but decided not to know.

She got on her hands and knees and leaned forward, trying to touch the water without getting the rest of her wet. She held out her right hand and touched the tip into the salt and then the tide pushed in a little further and her arm was drenched up to the elbow. It felt fantastic and heavy, the denim of her jacket sodden and her skin frigid underneath. She pulled herself back and sat up on her haunches, just out of reach of the sea.

Ada shook her hand, the water flying off, then absentmind-edly put a finger in her mouth to chew on. She tasted salt, realised she was very close to just drinking sea water, and felt exhilarated by her almost madness. Did drinking sea water make people mad or was it a symptom though, she couldn't quite remember. She reached her other hand towards the water and dunked it in then rubbed it across her face. The coldness of it shocked her and as she sat there letting the wind dry it, her cheeks felt cracked by the salt. This was healing, she decided. This was time to heal and by the time she got back to London she'd be better.

There were rituals involving water and rebirth and other witchy things though Ada couldn't recall the specifics from her brief teenage Wiccan phase. But she knew enough to know that these rocks were grounding, even as her bum went numb, and this ocean was forgiving, even as it whipped and retreated. She had been rejected, vastly rejected, she saw that clearly now, and no amount of rationalisation would take it away. If Stuart called her today, all apologies, all promises, she would forgive him, she knew. But the balance would never reshift between them. She was sunk forever.

And she also knew that in years to come, when her life moved on, when her life was beautiful, she would still feel the sharpness of this rejection. Not every day but enough to colour her years. She would be in a supermarket, picking between two different pasta shapes, did her lover or her new flatmate or her baby prefer spirals or bowties? – and she would be winded by the memory of sitting alone in a flat in Brighton, waiting for a man who didn't respect her at all.

A rejection by someone you feel yourself above is a disorienting experience and, Ada acknowledged without shame, that was what was happening. She wondered if someone who held themselves in less esteem would feel heartbreak less acutely because they felt it was what they deserved. Ada didn't feel she deserved this. She felt she deserved the worship of Stuart's early attempts. Because he had no right to hold her at all and even less right to stop when it suited him. That kind of injustice could really ruin your nice day out by the seaside.

Ada picked up a time-smoothed rock and threw it into the ocean, not getting very far, her arms heavy with damp sleeves and the whip of the wind. She tried to imagine what a relationship with Stuart would have looked like in the longer term. Mel wouldn't have liked him, she was sure, but that barely mattered now that Mel's likes and dislikes were increasingly obscure to her. Her parents would be kind to him but privately find him sullen, a word too juvenile for a man his age. Ada would lay herself out for him and he would take her then abandon her then blame her for her abandonment. Or worse, they would simply become bored once the distance wasn't forcing the issue of romance. It would have been a sad downward spiral with tiny highs and banal lows and Ada felt furious that he hadn't let it play out as it was supposed to.

Love was a way of passing the time, Ada thought, as she threw another rock into the water. Did she have a lot of love to give or a lot of hours to fill and was there any difference? A seagull landed nearby, its feathers standing up and out, styled by the weather. It looked at her and she raised her hands to show she had no food then wondered what made her think a seagull would understand her. But it did, evidently, because it flew straight up and was thrown off course by a gust immediately.

Ada's feet were hurting with the cold and as she stood up she felt her bones grind back into place, stiff and over-salted. She blew a kiss up to the seagull, still attempting to steady itself in the sky, and then looked around to see if anyone on the beach had seen her. But it was empty, still, and she felt the rare thrill of being alone in a public place. She went back to the flat, her progress squishy and slow.

Once inside, Ada realised how icy she had become and pulled off her damp clothes, lying her jacket across the radiator by the bed. It was cold to the touch but the room had been toasty when she woke up so she hoped whatever mysterious mechanism turned it on would activate soon. She went into the bathroom and turned the shower on as hot as it would go without burning her skin then stood under it, letting herself thaw. With some effort she started to cry, figuring it was a good time to get that out of the way because she knew it was coming.

Ada heated and ate some of the leftover eggplant in her towel and considered what to do with her evening. She knew other people in Brighton but none of them seemed right for either a consolation conversation or a distraction kiss, and anyway, the rawness of solitude was sitting right with her. But she knew she couldn't handle the flat all night alone.

She made it to six, listening to podcasts about rewilding Somerset and an algorithm that predicted people's purchases with alarming accuracy and an interview with an author she had never read talking about the death of his wife. She put on the final dress she'd packed and took a bright orange waterproof out of Rob's only wardrobe as her jacket was still soaking on the ice-cold radiator. The waterproof hung to mid-thigh and the sleeves covered her hands and Ada wondered who these women who looked good in 'boyfriend jeans' were. Sadie, probably, ironically. She combed and braided her hair, still damp from salt spray and two showers, and looked younger than she felt. When she let out the braid the next day, her hair would be wild, and she found that was a nice thing to look forward to.

Ada left the flat and decided to go into the first place she could smell from the street which was a game she liked to play when she travelled. When Mel had flown them to Madrid for three days for Ada's birthday, they had ended up eating churros for dinner on the first night because the smell of dough overpowered the more appropriate establishments on that street. When they'd got back to their Airbnb Mel had brought out a block of expensive parmesan she'd bought earlier and they'd eaten slices of it, desperate for something savoury.

Ada smelled garlic at the end of a lane and walked towards it. It was dark, the sun running away earlier already, the grey thick cloud obscuring any lingering hits. Ada found a bright corner Italian restaurant, the kind with a board outside with actual chalk writing. All the visible tables were filled with families eating over checkered tablecloths. Ada went inside.

The waiter didn't react when she said she was eating alone and she wasn't sure if she was disappointed or relieved. Ada liked eating alone in restaurants and drinking alone in bars but often the person greeting her was either concerned – a young woman alone! – or overly conciliatory – a young woman alone, how normal but also chic! This waiter simply directed her to a round table set for two near the back and took the other setting away without comment.

Ada ordered calamari to start and a glass of house red and they both arrived quickly with a basket of warm, pre-sliced baguette and a mound of salty butter. She spread the butter thickly on a slice and popped it in her mouth whole, the pooling butter running onto her chin. She followed it up with crisp calamari, dipped in aioli, the various shades of creamy beige filling her with comfort and joy. When the waiter came back, she said she'd have a pizza for her main, the mushroom and artichoke, but as he wrote it down she changed her mind and asked for the four cheese instead. He smiled like she'd made an exceptional choice and when she asked for another glass of wine he smiled again.

The meal took her close to two hours which was a long time for even a seasoned solo eater. The restaurant didn't rush her, letting her finish the whole serve of calamari and most of the bread before bringing her the pizza. She was already approaching full but she ate each piece slowly, sprinkling it with chilli flakes and oregano and chasing each mouthful with wine and water. She thought about sending a photo of the empty pizza tray to Ben, but she realised he might offer to come to Brighton on the next train because that's the kind of thing he liked to do, so she kept the sight for herself. When she was done, the waiter asked if she'd like to see the dessert menu and she said yes, of course, and picked the tiramisu.

Ada hadn't liked tiramisu as a child but Gabby had often chosen it at restaurants, claiming that it was the only way Ada wouldn't try to eat off her plate. But as Ada bit into it now, she thought Gabby should have been grateful to her for forcing these flavours on her young. Her usually stretchy leggings were digging into her belly button but every mouthful soothed her with cream and then tingled her with coffee and soothed her again with the dark heavy flavour of liquor and nothing would keep her from finishing.

When her plate was cleared, she asked for the bill, her insides glorious and gorged, and it arrived with a small glass of something dark, 'on the house'. The waiter told her it was amaro made in the village the owner came from in Italy and Ada wondered if that was bullshit. She sipped it and it was like a liquid garden, a pleasant shock. She said it was delicious and he said, 'It aids digestion,' and smiled pleasantly and she said, 'Well, I'll need it after all that cheese!'

Only after she had paid with her credit card and thanked every person who worked there on the way out and pulled on Rob's waterproof did she consider how weird it was to joke about poo with a stranger. But 'aiding digestion' was a useful euphemism and the amaro did seem to be doing its work, as she felt oddly fresh and unwilling to go home yet. She turned one corner and then another and found a dark, loud bar and went inside.

Forty-four

06/10/2017

Melanie Baker **Melanie Baker** 21:13

Just checking in, hope you're having a sexy time with Stuart!

Melanie Baker 21:16

Anyway, what time are you home tomorrow? Should we do dinner? I can cook although I really doubt you'll want that

Melanie Baker 21:29

Don't worry about responding if you're busy (I hope you are wink wink)

Melanie Baker 21:30

I'll see you when you get home

Forty-five

The bar was divey and mostly full of students. The wall was covered in old gig posters so Ada looked for a stage but couldn't see one. Maybe they didn't have gigs here any more and all the locals would be very sad about that, no one likes to lose a music venue, including people too old to go to them any more. At least no one said they liked losing a music venue, but music venues kept disappearing and the things that popped up in their places were always busy. So what, Ada wondered, was the truth.

She stood in the crowd for the bar, being bustled around by girls younger and drunker than her and pressed on either side by two young men laughing and talking over her head. This was a place Ada felt safe. In a wedge of people with their own motivations which may but likely would not intersect with hers before they all went home to their beds or someone else's and tomorrow to the lives that weren't quite satisfying until they went out again.

Ada's high school had given them all the usual lectures on drugs and sex and had also invited a police officer to talk to them about drink spiking and upskirting and all the reasons it was better, in all, to stay at home. And if you did have to go out you should never be separated from your girlfriends – the police officer was clearly using the term platonically – because around every corner in every bar lurked the drink or the drug or the man who would kill you.

But Ada felt that what that education, such as it was, missed, was everything. Everything about the beauty and the community that came with being out in a place where you didn't know how long you'd be there and no one could see your face clearly. Taking a pill from a stranger and then spending half an hour sitting on a toilet, clenching and unclenching your fists and your jaw until you were level enough to rejoin the crowd and when you did everyone was so happy to see you, even the people you didn't know. Holding the hand of another stranger as they recounted the time their grandmother died and then came to them in a dream but she was a dog and you are only a little bit sure that's what they're saying because the music is so loud. Everyone becomes lip readers or gets to know you through touch and every second of caught eye contact is a high.

There was a dance floor at this pub but Ada could see that it wouldn't be there if you arrived in the afternoon. The tables had been pushed together enough to leave a space for moving and laughing but nothing felt permanent. Ada ordered a vodka and cranberry juice, make it a double, and took it to the dance floor with a long straw. She sipped and moved to Drake and Robyn, singing along with a girl she would never see again who had been unsuccessful in getting her friends to join them.

When her drink was done and the girl rejoined her table, Ada went into the bathroom. The cubicles were bathed in blue light which her mother had told her years ago was to stop people finding a vein and Ada hadn't known what she meant but eventually figured it out, some time around the

policeman's visit to her school. But Ada loved the accidental aesthetic of the blue-light bathrooms, which had come to
feel like a spiky kind of home. She sat on the toilet and saw
a mirror directly across from her above the narrow sink. She
watched herself peeing and grinned, looking like an alien,
like something terrifying and loveable.

When Ada came out of the toilet, she ordered another
double vodka cranberry and drank it leaning against the wall,
watching the crowd. She felt she'd taken what she needed
from them for the night so pulled Rob's jacket out from under
the chair where she'd stashed it and walked outside into the
cold air. She took the long way home so she could walk along
the waterfront, passing cozy couples and stoned teenagers
and a few harried-looking parents with sleeping babies under
covered prams.

Walking home drunk was one of Ada's great pleasures in
life. After days like this, when the road was slick with fresh
rain and the lights were golden yellow, she felt like a creature of the night, flying towards her destination with her feet
dragging on the ground like the hot, crazy one from *The Craft*
(she heard Hank in her head: 'I'm a Neve man myself'). She
realised she'd overshot her turn-off and had to go back but
she didn't mind. She walked and stretched her arms above her,
reaching for the ceiling that always felt just above her head in
England. But it wasn't there and she nodded goodbye to the
black ocean and turned left up to Rob's street.

Ada got in, creeping up the stairs quietly so she didn't disturb
any of Rob's neighbours and reflecting that if she hadn't been
alone she might not have thought to do that. Maybe she was
nicer alone, when the only impulse she followed was her own,
or maybe that was an excuse. She came into the flat, stripped
off all her clothes and checked Rob's jacket for marks before

carefully rehanging it. She checked her phone, saw messages from Mel and some from Ben and then as she was looking, she got one from Rob asking how she was getting on. She replied to him, full of gratitude, and he said he was glad he could help and would she pop the key under the neighbour's door when she left.

Ada sniffed her dresses and chose the least soiled one, the one she'd been wearing in the morning, which was still damp but didn't smell of grease or sweat or booze. She put it aside and packed everything else into her bag, not bothering with folding. She opened the final beer in the fridge and drank it as she wiped down every surface, surfaces she'd wiped earlier but she wiped them again. She tipped the last bits of eggplant into the bin, there were only scraps left, then tied up the bag and took it to the door so she'd remember to take it out in the morning. She left the bottle of red on the bench and grabbed an unopened letter from the pile near the door and a pen from her bag.

She wrote on the envelope, 'Thanks for letting me crash, you're a hero and a gentleman. There are dumplings in the freezer, veggie I'm afraid but a fancy-looking brand so enjoy! Also your kitchen is so kitted out! Secret master chef Rob? Let's talk cooking sometime. Thanks again, I can't thank you enough really. Lots of love, Ada.' She leaned the envelope against the bottle and finished her beer. She slept heavily that night and woke up still full, rubbing her stomach as she stretched herself alive. And then she had to go back.

The first week back in London with no Stuart and no Sadie and a shadow of Mel was made easier by Clem's demands. Evidently this deal with the owners was even less done than Ada had thought. After the Tuesday night gig, Clem had sat her down and asked her for figures – how much could they charge and how much did the acts need and this wouldn't cost them anything in new equipment, would it? These amps were still fine? And Ada said, 'Clem, I don't know anything about amps, Steven handles all that,' and Steven was there and said, 'The equipment is all fine. I'd be happy to do tech for nights I'm not performing,' and Ada was grateful to her quiet friend. Clem asked Ada to send a list of potential shows by the end of the week and Ada asked if that meant she had the job and Clem said no, this was the job to get the job and Ada sniffed and said, 'I demand to see my union!' And she realised she might need this thing which she did not want because Mel was leaving her and Steven could only look after her so much.

Her period started when she got home that night and as she lay pressed over her heat pack she heard Mel and Will's voices in the next room. She wanted help, she wanted to be held, but the pain overwhelmed her self-pity and so there wasn't room for crying. She was up and down all night, turning on the shower at 4 a.m. and running the hot water over her back until she couldn't stand up any more. She went back to bed wrapped in her towel and when Mel's alarm went off in the morning she texted 'sorry, period' and Mel made her own tea and sent her a kiss in return.

Mel was out the next few nights and on the weekend, Ada went to birthday drinks for the director of Ben's show who she had never met but Ben assured her was a great contact to have. She wasn't sure about that but she was sure that she couldn't stay at home another night, sending Facebook messages to comedians and musicians asking for their appearance fees. She had sent a speculative programme and budget to Clem and then texted her because Clem seemed the kind to not check her email and Clem had just replied, 'Thanks.'

Ada knew it was coming up to the time, or probably past

the time, that she should contact her temp agency or message friends with bar jobs to see if they needed an extra hand. But she held on to this offer from Clem, this *near* offer maybe, though she already feared she would grow bored with it. She loved receiving messages asking her to perform but it turned out she enjoyed sending them a lot less. But it was close enough to what she wanted and if she was going to stay in this flat close enough was necessary.

Ada was getting ready to go out on Saturday night when Mel messaged to say she'd be home later and did Ada want to order in? Ada was pleased to be able to say no, sorry, she had a party to go to, and then she asked Mel if she wanted to come with her, knowing Mel would say no because Ben and that whole acting crowd made Mel feel inadequate. Ada always told her she was more creative than any of them, any idiot could be an actor, look at her, and Mel would say, 'Oh, I don't care about that, they're just all so self-obsessed, it's boring.' She was right but Ada fit seamlessly with them and Mel didn't seem to mind her self-obsession, until recently.

Ada looked around her room. She had rehung her dresses so the coat hangers that had been Sadie's were reclaimed. Sadie had clearly taken all her clothes to Newcastle and Ada knew that would make things cleaner but she craved more mess from Sadie. They had sent a couple of messages back and forth, Sadie asking Ada if she would be looking for a flatmate because she had a friend who might be looking, Ada saying she wasn't sure then asking about Sadie's trip. Sadie sent some selfies with her friend, saying they were having a great time reconnecting and then she followed up saying she loved his boyfriend and Ada wondered if she was trying to tell Ada that this wasn't a romantic trip. Which Ada had already assumed. She didn't ask about the woman in

Ealing and Sadie didn't ask about the man in Liverpool and they were very, very polite to each other. It was dull, in the aching sense of the word.

Ada didn't know if she wanted a new flatmate or if she needed to get out of this flat that might not feel like home any more. She could handle a new place that didn't feel like home, she thought, but to lose intimacy with a home you had loved was too acute. And going into winter she needed things to be either soft or thrilling. Nostalgia and loneliness wouldn't get her to April any faster.

Ada met Ben for Turkish food before the birthday drinks, sharing the mixed mezze platter like they'd done so often over the summer they met, doing the theatre workshop together. Ben told her that the show was going to be good, he thought, although sometimes he watched scenes he wasn't in and worried that actually it was going to be very, very bad, and Ada assured him that she would lie and say she loved it either way. He thanked her then leaned in close and told her he'd started sleeping with one of the other cast members, the lead actually, he was playing Nora. They were trying to keep it under wraps until after opening night and Ada said, 'Showmance or romance, do you think?' Then she listened and ate and loved Ben and loved him more when he insisted on paying.

The birthday drinks were in a pub by the canal and the front section was full of men in straight-legged jeans watching the rugby. Ada asked Ben if this was definitely the right place and he said, 'What, a gay man can't enjoy a rugby pub?' and Ada said, 'Yes, sorry, so homophobic of me, you love rugby.' And Ben took her through to a private back room with its own bar and heavy-hung lanterns and a lineup of pre-made negronis. She said, 'This is more like it,' and Ben said, 'I do like rugby though, you know,' and they grabbed glasses and sipped and scanned the room.

Ben pointed out his director, a tall lanky man wearing only a waistcoat on his top who Ada knew must have more money than his aesthetic suggested. He waved to them then went back to his conversation and though Ada stayed three hours she never actually said hello to him. She was caught up talking to friends and people she vaguely recognised from festivals. Ben dizzily introduced her to his new lover who said, 'Ah, Ada, the Holly to Ben's Capote,' and Ada didn't know what he meant and knew Ben didn't either though he laughed and laughed. She only got to the director as she was leaving, to say thank you for inviting her. He kissed her cheek and said, 'Of course!' so she left him believing they had met before, and anyway, maybe they had.

Ben walked Ada out the front of the pub to hug her goodbye. He was sticking around to see if he and Nora could sneak away later and Ada asked him if he found all the secrecy hot and he said, 'Of course!' Then she asked him if he'd like to take Mel's room, because she knew he was still living with his parents and because Ben was fun and the negronis had been free all night. And Ben said, 'Oh my god maybe! We would be such a party house!' and she regretted asking him straight away.

When Ada got home, she tried to imagine walking in the door to see Ben and found she couldn't project her response. She loved Ben but did she have the energy to be the Ada that Ben loved in her own home? Ben was a great cook, she knew, and she didn't think she was ready to share the kitchen, though she'd shared it with Sadie. She remembered when she was little and terrified of Gabby, she would think that at least Gabby was a sister because she couldn't imagine having to live with a boy. But her views on boys had changed, she supposed.

'Ada?' Mel called from the living room and Ada went in to see her watching one of the thousands of British panel

shows hosted by pale male comedians and featuring the same
blonde woman as a guest as far as Ada could tell. She needed
to learn more about the comedy scene if she was going to take
the Clem job, probably. People like to go out to watch comedy.

Mel muted the TV and Ada sat next to her on the couch.
She said, 'I asked Ben if he might want to take your room and
he seemed keen,' and Mel said, 'Oh he'd be a fun housemate!'
and Ada said, 'That's cute but don't pretend you like him.' Mel
said, 'Sure, but you like him, and I can tell my brother he's nice
and responsible,' and Ada said, 'Why would you lie to your
brother?' Then she told Mel she'd been drinking negronis all
night and should probably go to bed but Mel said no, let's
have a drink, let's have dessert, wait here.

And then she brought in a mini Magnum for each of
them – mint for Ada, white chocolate for Mel – and two
glasses of Frangelico. She explained that she wanted to use up
some of the old bottles of booze on the high shelves before
she moved and Ada said, 'Sure, I love a project.' Then Mel
asked how things were going with Stuart and Ada had to tell
her that he never came to Brighton and Mel was so angry that
she waved her Magnum and a little piece at the top cracked
and landed on her lap.

It felt good to let Mel take on anger because Ada had felt
sad, a background hum of sadness, all week, and she didn't
have the energy to lay anger on top of that. Even though she
knew it was deserved. She tried to tell the story of the noodles
like it was funny but then Mel held her hand and she exhaled.

'It was humiliating,' she said, and Mel nodded, she didn't
try to pretend that cooking for a no-show lover in a studio
apartment on a cold day wasn't humiliating.

Mel said, 'I know how much you liked him—' and Ada
said, 'Yeah but what did I like about him? He was so juvenile!

And obviously there was no future there, right, like what was I going to do, move into his hovel? I just … it should have been me who got to choose what we were.' And Mel nodded and that was kind.

'Maybe I need to just … not date or have sex or … pursue something for a while. Hopefully I get this job with Clem and then I'll be busy,' and Mel shook her head and said, 'No, if you gave up I couldn't bear it.' Her voice was heavy and she said, 'We can't all be afraid all the time,' and Ada said, 'You're not afraid,' and Mel said, 'I am,' and that was all.

Ada said, 'But doesn't Will make you … not scared,' and Mel shifted away from her and said, 'I don't love the way you talk about him,' and that was it, the harshest thing Mel had ever said to her and she was saying it for Will. And Ada said, 'Well I barely know the guy, you didn't even tell me you were dating.' Mel laughed and it was hard and she said, 'When would I tell you about that? When you were messaging your boyfriend or when you were moving your girlfriend into our flat without even asking me?'

Ada didn't remember it like that. 'You're like … Team Sadie though,' she said and regretted the terminology when Mel said, 'I'm not Team anyone, Ada, I'm not a fucking spectator to your life. Or I don't want to be.' Ada's instinct was to shrink but she fought it enough to say, 'I asked about Will and you never wanted to talk about it,' and Mel interrupted to say, 'What do you mean never? You asked like once, in passing, you weren't paying attention,' which was unfair, Ada felt surely this was unfair. 'That's like … a technicality. I tell you things without you asking all the time,' and Mel said, 'Your way isn't everyone's way.' And it was unfair, it all felt so unfair.

Ada aimed for lightness and said, 'Maybe we have different love languages,' and Mel said, 'Not this bullshit again,' but she smiled because one night in winter they had drunk two bottles of bad merlot and done an online quiz about love languages and the next day Mel had thrown up and Ada had said, 'Your love language is absolutely bursting out of you,' while rubbing her back. It wasn't even that funny but it was working, a little. Ada said, 'I know you don't owe me an explanation,' and Mel said, 'I don't know what we owe each other,' and then she said, 'I'm sorry I'm leaving. I want to live with Will, I'm excited to. But this has been the most home that home has ever felt. I don't know. We've been happy.'

Ada had thought that Mel would level her but Mel loved her instead. And she laid her head on Mel's lap and Mel stroked her hair and it almost didn't matter that Mel spent the next four nights at Will's place and Ada spent them alone.

Forty-six

Sadie Ali   12:13

Hey! I'm back from Newcastle and I'm going in a couple of days and it'd be good to see you before then

Sadie Ali   12:14

I'm staying on a mate's couch in Walthamstow so I'm close-ish if you want to meet for coffee or something

Sadie Ali   12:15

But also no worries if you'd rather not, I'm sure you're busy

Ada Highfield   12:17

Why are you staying on a mate's couch?

Ada Highfield   12:18

What happened to Ealing?

Sadie Ali   **12:20**

As far as I know nothing happened to Ealing, or in Ealing ha ha
little London humour for you there

Sadie Ali   **12:21**

But I'm not seeing that woman any more, since before I went
to Newcastle

Ada Highfield   **12:22**

Great Ealing joke, you're basically a Londoner now

Ada Highfield   **12:23**

Why didn't you come back here?

Ada Highfield   **12:24**

Mel is gone most nights anyway, you could have had a bed to
yourself if that's what you wanted

Sadie Ali   **12:26**

That's really nice, I didn't know if you'd be around and it
seemed kind of weird to ask

Sadie Ali   **12:27**

This is an OK couch though, I promise

Ada Highfield   12:29

So you fly out Friday? Only two more nights

Sadie Ali   12:30

Yeah tomorrow is my last full day

Ada Highfield   12:31

I'm out all day today, brainstorming this new potential theatre-job thing with Clem at the bar where I do my Tuesday gig

Ada Highfield   12:32

But do you want to come round tonight? I'll cook. I think Mel will be at Will's unfortunately, I know she'd want to say goodbye

Sadie Ali   12:33

That would be really nice if that's OK

Ada Highfield   12:34

Stop saying 'if that's OK' when it's something I've suggested, I wouldn't suggest it if it wasn't OK

Sadie Ali   12:35

Whoops sorry

Sadie Ali   **12:35**

I actually have a work thing I want to talk to you about anyway

Ada Highfield   **12:36**

Woah mysterious

Ada Highfield   **12:37**

Come round at 7:30? I'll be back by then

Ada Highfield   **12:38**

Actually come round whenever you want, you still have a key

•••

From: Gabby Highfield
To: Hank Mathers, bcc: me

Hello Aussie family and friends!

Sorry for the mass email but I know people aren't on Facebook as much any more so the glory days of the status update are over. Hank and Orion and I wanted to let all our most loved people know that we have exciting news – we're moving back to Sydney! My wonderful old company Banquette have agreed to take me back (hello Banquette fam on this email! Your girl is back!) so I'll be returning to work a little earlier than expected (when Orion is six months old). And Hank is going to be a full-time dad while we wait for his partner visa to come through. We can't wait to see everyone and to introduce our little guy to you all (if Nana and Grandad let anyone else see him, that is). We haven't booked flights yet but we'll definitely be home for Christmas, in the words of Tim Minchin, drinking white wine in the sun!

Lots of love and excitement,

Gabby (and Hank and Orion)

Forty-seven

Ada ended her day with Clem feeling only slightly closer to having a job. She had brought all her most temp-y skills to the task, presenting spreadsheets that she'd had to email Mel to print out at work, and saying 'projected income' enough that it felt like a real phrase. And Sadie was coming to dinner and Gabby was moving home but Ada stayed focused on Clem and this job which she needed with increasing desperation. She'd never been to the bar in the day before and it looked bored, all empty and with every light on, the grimy magic clearly an illusion. When she left at six, it was filling up with after-work drinkers and when she stepped outside, brown leaves were gathering in the wet Camden gutters and there was the grimy magic after all.

Sadie arrived exactly at seven thirty and let herself in while Ada was shaping balls of dough. Sadie came into the kitchen and said, 'What smells so good?' and Ada indicated to the oven with her foot and said, 'Butternut pumpkin. I'm roasting it for a cobbler.' Sadie said, 'Wow, I don't know what a cobbler is but I'm excited to find out,' and Ada said, 'It's a very autumnal dish, I saw it in the *Guardian*, daaaaahling.' She turned back to the balls of dough and Sadie hesitated, Ada felt the whole room hesitate, and then Sadie walked to her and hugged her from behind, squeezing her tightly and then stepping back and climbing up to her familiar place on the bench. She grabbed herself a glass and poured from the open bottle of Malbec next to Ada.

Ada assembled the cobbler and told Sadie about her almost job and how she almost wanted it. Roasted squash, red onion, cream, greens, tinned tomatoes, the little balls of dough on top. It went into the oven and she turned to Sadie who said, 'It doesn't really sound like the kind of thing you want to be doing,' and Ada said, 'I know, but I'm not sure if you heard, my rent is going up.' And Sadie said, 'That's kind of fucked of Mel to leave you in the lurch like that,' and Ada said, 'Maybe.' But she didn't want to talk about Mel. Loyalty or something like it.

Instead she asked, 'What happened with Ealing woman then?' and Sadie said, 'What happened with Liverpool man?' This was unusually coy for her but she held Ada's eye and Ada said, 'He ghosted me but importantly, only after I had got to Brighton.' Sadie said, 'What?' and Ada said, 'He never showed up,' then, 'I really hope your story is equally embarrassing.' And Sadie said, 'Oh, it is. The Ealing woman had, I dunno, gay-centrist vibes and I was like, hmm, OK, and then she said something dodgy about trans kids and that was when I booked the Newcastle trip.' Ada said, 'So we both picked winners then,' and Sadie said, 'I guess we did.'

Ada opened the fridge and looked inside, forgetting immediately what she needed. She kept staring though and said, 'Did she hurt your feelings? Liverpool man hurt my feelings.' She pulled out butter then put it back, she wasn't serving the meal with bread, and over her shoulder Sadie said, 'Not really, it never felt built to last. I'm sorry about the guy though.' Ada closed the fridge, she didn't need anything, and sat on the floor leaning on it. 'The thing is, like really, I think I loved him? But I also think I … invented him.' Sadie didn't say anything but passed Ada her glass. 'I think he wanted me so much and I wanted the person who wanted me to be like … something other than what he was. So I invented him. And we were never together, it was mostly messages and calls and then one drunk night and I fell in love with all the spaces that were left to colour in, you know? So when I threw myself at him there was actually nothing there to, like, catch me. No one. In the end he was just a story.' Sadie said, 'That's … I mean, I think in some ways you're very self-aware but also that seems like bullshit. He was a whole person, he wasn't a character, you just never saw past his outline,' and Ada said, 'Well, is that my fault though? Familiarity breeds contempt right? He was all romance but then when I returned it to him he was like … reactionary.' Silence and then, from Sadie, 'Men, right?' and they laughed, both of them, and it was all familiarity.

The night was easy and long. Sadie set the table, just for the two of them, and Ada realised they had never done that, they had always been three. She said so to Sadie who said, 'I don't know if Mel is more our child or our shared parent,' and Ada said, 'Come on, you and Mel are the parents together.' And Sadie thought about it and said that all things considered that was probably the most creepy option.

They sat down to eat and the balls of dough had gone shiny and brown from their egg wash. It smelled of cold nights and Ada knew she wouldn't make this dish in the summer. Sadie said, 'Wow, she's a looker,' and Ada said that before she served she needed to make a perfect mouthful for Sadie. She dug a fork through one of the balls of dough and pulled up a corner of it and underneath some golden squash and caramelised red onion and finally bits of creamy greens hanging to the bottom. She blew on it and Sadie opened her mouth and Ada fed her and Sadie kept her eyes open as she chewed. She said, 'Incredible,' and then Ada served them both and they kept talking, they couldn't say enough tonight.

Ada asked Sadie what the work thing she'd mentioned was and Sadie said, 'Well yeah, I kind of wanted to have this conversation in like a formal setting so you'd know I'm serious about it,' but she began anyway. She told Ada that a theatre company she worked with in Perth had received a grant to develop four plays over the course of the year, drawing on stories from their local community. That was the only guidelines they had to stick to, it was such a broad brief that they'd never thought they'd get funding, but they had and it was happening and they wanted Sadie to be part of the development team. Ada said, 'That sounds amazing. If the question is should you do it, then I reckon definitely yes,' and Sadie said, 'Oh right, no I am, I already said yes.'

She explained that they had her and another director on board, and two dramaturgs, but they needed to round out their group of actors. 'Would you want to do that?' Sadie asked and Ada said, 'Hypothetically or for real?' and Sadie said, 'For real. Like do you want this job?' Ada said, 'I don't think … you can just offer me that,' and Sadie said she could, she had the jurisdiction and anyway she'd sent Ada's showreel to her collaborators and they all thought she was great. She'd sent it last week, actually, and Ada wondered why she had talked to so many other people about this before Ada herself. It was like she'd settled it without her and maybe that was protective or maybe it was rude.

Ada said, 'But I haven't auditioned,' and Sadie said, 'It's a long development process. Like fifty per cent of it is how well do people get along. And you get along with everyone!

Every person you work with asks you back to work with them again. That's a huge thing for an actor,' and Ada said, 'It might be because I'm cheap,' but Sadie ignored her. She was asking Ada something real and big and Ada said, 'And it would mean living in Perth?' and Sadie said, 'Don't say it like that, Perth is good.' She explained that the head of the theatre company had three children and kept family-friendly hours which meant they'd be full-time but done by three most days, 'and then you're free to do whatever.'

Ada said, 'Why are you offering me this?' and Sadie said, 'What do you mean, why? You're an actor and this is an acting job,' and Ada said, 'But why are you offering me this.' and Sadie started to talk again about the good character references from other directors and Ada dropped it. If this offer was an act of desire it would not be acknowledged. And if it wasn't an act of desire she couldn't be sure that she wanted it.

Ada told Sadie then that Gabby was moving home, to Sydney, and Perth was in the same country as Sydney and what if that wasn't a good idea. They had barely made it through the Florida trip without a fight. 'I don't want my life to be like… about Gabby again.'

'But you wouldn't be. Perth to Sydney is a four-hour flight. You can get to Cairo in four hours. Run into many friends from Cairo?'

Ada said, 'How do you know how far Cairo is from London,' and Sadie said that whenever she told British people she was Australian, they'd ask her about Sydney, so she had come up with a system of explaining the distance.

'I didn't think I'd have to explain it to you though.'

Ada sensed some frustration in Sadie and said, 'Are you annoyed I didn't say yes straight away? I live in London, it's a huge question.' And Sadie said, 'Yeah but at this point, why do you live in London?' And Ada said could she think about it and Sadie said, 'Of course, sorry, I don't want to rush you, it doesn't even start until January, there's time.' And then she said, 'The pay is pretty good,' and then, 'OK I'll stop talking about it now.'

They drank more wine and then Sadie cut up an apple and some cheddar and they ate slices and talked. Around eleven, they decided to finish Mel's Frangelico and Ada sent a selfie of them with it, saying, 'Sorry!' and Mel wrote back right away, 'You're welcome to it! Give Sadie a hug from me. I'll miss her!' She showed Sadie the message and Sadie said, 'I'll miss her too, even if I'm annoyed at her up and moving to Bristol without warning you.' Ada said, 'But I should up and move to Perth?' and Sadie said, 'I thought we weren't discussing that any more tonight.'

They didn't discuss Sadie staying over either and she hadn't brought a change of clothes but at midnight they went up to Ada's room together. Ada held up her arms and Sadie pulled off her green jersey baby-doll dress, which had been too cheap and was already stretched out at the waist. Then Sadie stood very still and Ada unbuttoned her shirt, took it off and folded it on the window seat.

Ada stepped out of her leggings and then her underwear and Sadie stepped out of her jeans and they both removed their bras. They smiled at each other and then they went to bed. For a few minutes it was only holding and then Sadie rolled Ada over and gently pulled her up onto her hands and knees. She stood behind her and tapped her lightly and then a little harder. Ada said only, 'Yes … please,' and Sadie said, 'OK.' She pulled Ada's hair and Ada said 'yes' one more time.

The next morning the sun was out and when Ada woke up, Sadie was already looking at her and smiling. She said, 'It hasn't been this sunny in weeks it feels like, or maybe that was just Newcastle,' and Ada said, 'No it's like that everywhere, it's October.' Sadie went to make them coffee and Ada looked at her weather app.

When Sadie came back up, Ada was dressed in a polka-dot, one-piece swimming costume that she'd bought at a charity shop and had mostly lost its elastic. She held out her Speedo for Sadie and said, 'You can wear this one. We're going swimming.' Sadie looked out the window and pointed out that it didn't look *that* warm and Ada said this was the last warm day of the year, she could sense it, and they were going to the ponds. Sadie said, 'The ... ponds?' and Ada said, 'Don't knock it, it's surprisingly nice,' and then, 'I mean, it's OK, we're in the middle of London, what do you expect.'

And Sadie put on her Speedo and then chose one of Ada's more shapeless dresses and pulled it over the top. They both put on leggings and Sadie looked like a stranger in all of her clothes. Ada packed them a bag with towels and underwear − Sadie could wear some of hers and hope they didn't slip down − and water bottles and big jumpers for when they got out. They picked up pastries down the street and it was only 15 degrees out and at home this wouldn't be a day for swimming but here Ada knew that it was.

They took a bus and then an Overground and on the Overground, Ada leaned her head on Sadie's shoulder and breathed in her own smell because she was all over Sadie. They got to Hampstead Heath but it was the wrong side and Ada's phone had trouble finding them. She explained that she'd been to the ponds a thousand times but always with someone else navigating and Sadie said, 'It's OK, we can just walk until we find it.' They passed the mixed-gender ponds but decided to keep going until they found the women-only ones because Ada promised it was worth it. Ada told Sadie that the first time she'd been there, a woman in her seventies was sitting up, topless, reading Virginia Woolf. 'I swear it's like she was planted there, like an ad for the place,' and Sadie said, 'What a boss, I hope she's there today.' Then she said, 'Wait, this isn't where Virginia Woolf killed herself, right,' and Ada said she was pretty sure that was a river, not a pond.

They finally found the private little gate that marked the entrance and opened it, heading towards the water. Ada pointed to the lawn where she liked to lie in the summer, 'but we might be too cold for that today,' and Sadie said, 'Oh, you mean because it's like ten degrees?' and Ada said, 'It's at least sixteen! Balmy!' Sadie then said, 'You know Perth is pretty warm all the way through winter,' and Ada said, 'What an odd thing to share apropos of nothing,' and Sadie said, 'It's just a friendly little fact.'

There were in fact a couple of women reading on the lawn in the pale sunny patches. Ada felt a kinship with these older ladies who took the time, in the middle of a weekday, to find a warm quiet spot to read in the middle of the city. These spots were hidden, in London, and she wanted to find them all. A winter scavenger hunt, then come spring she could go to a different one every day, drink in vitamin D from different directions.

Ada and Sadie passed the faded dressing room and went to the edge of the wooden dock, looking down into the still water at the reflection of the spindly bald trees overhead. A woman in her fifties in a tracksuit and a lifeguard hat came to chat to them.

'I don't recognise you, have you swum here before?'

'I have,' Ada said. 'Heaps. Like a lot of times,' and the lifeguard looked at Sadie. She said, 'I haven't but I'm a strong swimmer,' and the lifeguard said, 'It's very cold in there, you two ready for that? We don't recommend summer only swimmers pop in once the weather turns, you need to acclimatise to it over time.' Ada said, 'We'll be fine, I promise,' and the lifeguard sighed and said, 'Well, give me a yell if you're not,' in a way that suggested she'd rather let them drown but, well, she was wearing the hat.

She walked back to her chair and her newspaper and Sadie whispered to Ada, 'How cold are we talking?' and Ada said, 'Oh she's just trying to scare us, don't worry.' They stepped away from the water and took off their shoes, their leggings and then, egging each other on quietly so the lifeguard wouldn't hear, their dresses. Ada said, 'Shit, the breeze is up,' and Sadie said, 'Kind of worried that we haven't even swum yet and I already feel like I'm going to die.' But Ada took her hand and they went to the edge again.

They debated the merits of using the ladder or jumping right in and Ada said, 'I think we should jump in anyway, maybe it'll scare away any eels lurking nearby.' And Sadie said, 'I'm going to choose to believe you're joking about eels,' and Ada said, 'Whatever you need to think to get in the water.' She turned and looked at the lifeguard who had put down her paper to watch them, and the skepticism in her face made Ada turn and jump without warning Sadie.

The water was colder by many degrees than the already chilled air and Ada sank underneath it with her eyes closed. She forced herself to stay under for a second longer and felt like her skin was trying to burn its way off her body. She had a sensation like being tickled but all over and then she broke the surface and kicked and paddled around in a circle until the water felt normal, almost. Like she could survive it if she didn't stay still.

Sadie was still watching her from the dock and said, 'Your face is bright red already!' She started to climb down the ladder and dipped one toe in then said, 'Oh god, oh no,' and Ada said, 'Shhhh, the scary lifeguard will hear you.' Ada swam to the ladder and held her arms out and said, 'Come on,' and she had just meant for Sadie to jump in but instead Sadie pitched herself forward, into Ada's arms. Ada half caught her, half sunk, and Sadie yelped with the cold.

Sadie said, through chattering teeth, 'Wow, all this and eels, what a treat,' and Ada smiled at her but her jaw was trembling too. She suggested laps and they swam a few metres to and fro and they were both laughing, the sound shaky and sparse through their panting mouths. Sadie said they should probably get out, the mean lifeguard had been right, they were summer swimmers after all. Ada swam a few metres away then called out, 'Why do you want me to come to Perth?' and Sadie said, 'For the job,' and Ada said, 'What if I came to Perth for you?' and Sadie said, 'Most people would say a job is a good enough thing to move for,' and Ada ducked under the water and swam towards Sadie, opening her eyes in the murkiness and then poking Sadie in the belly when she reached her. She heard the muffled shriek above her head and surfaced and Sadie was laughing and swimming away.

Sadie tried to get back to the ladder but Ada grabbed on to her and wrapped herself around her. Her arms went around Sadie's back but she kept her legs free, kicking, keeping them afloat. The sun was fading into the afternoon and Sadie was shuddering but Ada held on.

Acknowledgements

I began writing Go Lightly when a quick trip to visit my parents was indefinitely extended due to the first lockdown. I'd like to acknowledge the Bidjigal, Birrabirragal, Gadigal and Awabakal people upon whose lands I was sheltered through the pandemic and the writing of part of this book. Always was, always will be Aboriginal land.

The first and last and eternal person I need to thank is my literary agent Imogen Pelham. Without her, Go Lightly would not even slightly exist. She suggested I write a book, then reminded me over literal years of me ignoring her prompting, then read multiple drafts, gave detailed notes and sold the bloody thing, all while being extremely patient with my billion questions and spiralling emotional state. Every writer should be as lucky as I am to have a cool, elegant genius holding their hand through the process but I suspect very few are. Imogen is singular and I adore her and her faith and diligence is the only reason this career is viable for me.

On the topic of geniuses, the team at Bloomsbury UK are a ridiculously well-oiled machine operating in one of the prettiest offices I've ever seen. To my editor Emma . . . god where to even begin. You believed in Ada and me and championed us both and gave the most incisive editorial notes. I forget sometimes that you're a super successful powerhouse because you're also so kind. Every member of your team has been a dream to work with and I'm thrilled we found each other. Over the other side of the world, Hermione and everyone at Bloomsbury Australia have been brilliant and between the two teams I feel utterly cared for.

Across another pond, my absolutely unreal American agent Meredith and her super assistant Ethan are total bosses who have guided me through not only the creative side of American publishing but the seemingly endless tax paperwork. I'm so grateful for their patient counsel! To the team at HarperCollins, especially Mary and Edie, thank you for taking a chance on some random Australian when there are, frankly, a lot of Americans to choose from instead. I especially appreciate you taking on a book which is kind of rude about Florida! Sorry to Florida but not sorry to Flo Rida.

Now on to the friend bit which I will try not to drag out but like . . . my friends are amazing. Community! What a concept! Thank you to Christopher who agreed to READ MY UNPUBLISHED NOVEL (lmao imagine asking someone to do that) and give notes. You had no idea what you signed up for all those years ago when you cast me in that university production of *Closer*. Shouts to Kit Lovelace for creating Romantic Misadventure, a safe, joyful night where writers could hone our craft and tell jokes about our vulvas and find community. There is a direct line from that dingy bar to this book. Monica, very cool of you to publish a book a year before me so you can be available for me to text 'is this normal???' to like twice a week. And—

OK for the sake of space I'd like to thank everyone in the following group chats: Journalists Buying Drugs, North & South (hemisphere), Hair Rainbow, Days Of Thunder, Leroy Pizza Pals, Babies (and Ally), Yoghurt Pasta, Super Secret DISCs Club, DevotAd Chat To Divina, Crossing Continents, Four Little

Hoos, Communards, Godfather Gang and Legend Patrol. Also my LA fam who I mostly gossip with over Instagram DMs. I'm not sure how I had time to write a book when I'm constantly in communication with all of you but I love you? Phones are evil but without mine I'd die?

To my parents . . . you're really good at being parents! I have never once felt that pursuing a series of unstable professions was unwise because you have always believed in me and had a bed for me to sleep in when I ran out of money/broke up with someone/was grounded in Sydney due to the novel coronavirus. You also defy the maxim that people become more conservative as they age because you are both still utter lefty ratbags. Iconic!

To my brothers, their families and my partner's family – you have covered me with love and support and never asked me to be anything that I'm not. You rule. Bubble and Bumpers, I love you beyond measure. Every day with you is like winning the Piston Cup.

Finally and most abjectly, to my love, Tobi. You have given me more than I knew I could expect from a partner. I'm like one of those old sexist dude novelists whose wives did everything for them but I'm a woman so it's praxis, actually. You are funny and creative and endlessly gentle and you've always taken on all my problems (and my credit card debt ha ha?) as your own. To love and be loved by you is pure freedom and in that freedom I've found my greatest creative fulfilment. Each page of this book was made possible through your care and the perfect cups of coffee you make me every morning. Thank you. I love you.